Huntsville Supernatural

Volumes 1-3

By David C. Young

Huntsville Supernatural Volumes 1-3

David C. Young

ISBN-10 0-9882676-5-9

ISBN-13 978-0-9882676-5-7

Published by Young Press

This anthology contains books 1-3 in the Huntsville Supernatural series

Supernatural Secrets

Supernatural Feelings

Supernatural Apocalypse

Disclaimer

Nearly all of the characters in these stories are fictional. The Alice Stafford character was named after my brother's girlfriend as one of our family's unbirthday presents. The Jim Young character was named after my brother as one of our family's unbirthday presents. The reference to Benerson Little refers to a friend, author, and fencing master. The novel by Benerson Little alluded to in this book was not yet in print when the second book was originally published. That book, titled Fortune's Whelp, has now been published.

This story takes place in Huntsville, Alabama. Some of the locations, pop culture references, and name brands mentioned are real. Others are not. Details have been altered to fit the fictional plot. The representation of these items reflects neither the author's commentary on them, nor any type of endorsement by the publisher, author, or organizations concerned.

Acknowledgements

Like any writer, I have been influenced by my friends, family, teachers, and the works of great writers. Somewhere in that intellectual soup I hope to have found a style and voice that gives an interesting story.

My thanks go to Emily Carpenter for the suggestions and encouragement. Thank you, also, to Ariel Young for the editorial comments on this genre, that is to say once we figure out what genre it is.

Huntsville Supernatural Volumes 1-3

Book 1
Supernatural Secrets

Chapter 1

Somewhere in my pockets a phone was ringing. I fumbled it out before the third ring. It was a video call from one of our local residents, Greg Turner.

He said, "Hi, my wife and I were just thinking about calling you."

Using video calls and identifying who is with you is common practice amongst supernaturals. It is a way of finding out if it is safe to have conversations without unaware humans listening in. The fact that Greg jumped straight to this line of obligatory chitchat indicated an urgency in what he had to say.

"I was relaxing alone before getting moving on my days business. What's up?" I replied.

Greg said, "I sense a disturbance in the force."

Anywhere other than Huntsville, a Star Wars reference from a burly werewolf would seem out of place. I took a moment to note a bit of worry on his face. Whenever I look at Greg, I look past the brown contacts and picture the true yellow color of his eyes under his shock of curly brown hair. I made a quick decision to keep things light hearted, in hopes of keeping from blowing something small out of proportion.

"Was the meat lover's pizza special canceled?" I asked.

He ignored my crack and went on, "A human woman has been asking questions that directly lead toward the supernatural influence in our work."

The fact that he called her "human" with no adjective implies that he is guessing she is one of the billions of humans that are unaware of mankind's closest relatives on the evolutionary tree. If she had been a werewolf, his superior sense of smell would have caught her pheromones.

"What does she look like?" I asked.

"Long black hair, about average height, showing off curves and cleavage in a black and red dress. She said her name was Lucy Moore. My wife would punch me, if I told you how pretty she is," he replied.

From off camera, Nellie's fist appeared to punch him in the shoulder with a mostly playful amount of force. A playful punch form a werewolf would leave a green and purple bruise on a human, but Greg seemed not to notice it.

"Is it OK if I come by this morning to talk with you about a story idea I have?" I asked.

"Anytime," he replied.

Mentioning a story establishes a reason for my visit, under my cover as a writer for ScienceBlog, a popular science news service. At one time, I had done a bit of freelance newspaper reporting. As I got an advanced degree in science, I kept my easily understood writing style. That didn't go over very well with the scientific journals, which typically have articles written in a very esoteric, technically detailed style. That style of writing is precise, but so replete with domain specific terminology and references to previous studies that some articles are only easily read by a couple dozen people in the whole world who are doing closely related work. My newspaper reporter's understandable writing style makes it difficult for me to publish in the professional journals, but it is appreciated by science news forums.

I finished a few little things around the house, and headed out. I pretty much constantly kept the tools of my trade in my pockets and battered briefcase, so there was nothing in particular to pack. Between a smart phone and a tablet computer, and a wireless keyboard in my brief case, I carry a mobile office with the exception of high security computer connections that must be handled from my office, on the rare occasions that I should make an appearance there.

I wore dark blue dress pants and a light blue polo shirt with no logo, the epitome of business casualness. The car I drive is a silver mid-size sedan, chosen to be as common and nondescript as possible.

I'm slightly above average height but not enough so to be considered tall. I slouch a bit to make my height even less noticeable. My hair is an unremarkable brown with a typical short haircut. My glasses have frames that are understated and straddle the line between the current and previous fashions. Glasses are more common than not in a city with the highest per capita percentage of Ph.D.s in the country. My look and mannerisms are crafted to be as unmemorable as possible when dealing with humans outside of supernatural circles.

As I drove, I calmed and focused myself so that I would be alert but not overreacting. That is a good mindset to be in when dealing with anyone who is a bit stressed, and particularly so when dealing with people who are not human. Many of them could casually injure me without meaning to, an event made more likely by the fact that they considered me to be part of the supernatural world and would thus let down the guard of caution they maintained around unenlightened humans. I'm a normal human with perhaps slightly above average intelligence. Having a Ph.D. in physics gives me credentials to go talk face to face with scientists, both human and otherwise. My past research, no longer in progress, crossed the borders of physics, mathematics and computer science, which allows me to be part of multiple communities without any of them expecting me to be perfectly up to date on their field. This puts me in position to ask detailed questions and get the real answers at an appropriate level of detail. I have expended years of disciplined effort making my mind and body the most they can be, if in a slightly unconventional manner.

At first glance, Huntsville Alabama looks like any other small city. It has shopping malls with national chain stores, restaurants, and schools. Huntsville seems to have an over abundance of churches, as evidenced by the fact the some of them have taken to placing ads on local TV to attract new parishioners. At second glance, Huntsville is a bit different. The collection of rockets, a space shuttle and other exhibits makes the Space and Rocket Center a prime attraction. Huntsville is dubbed "Rocket City" and rockets show up in unlikely places; the elementary school library, a Deep South barbecue restaurant, at the edge of a golf course. Every now and then you see a hand built experimental car driving down the road, or one with odd

4

instrumentation mounted on the roof. With both NASA and the US Army having research and development operations in Huntsville, you can't swing a dead cat in Huntsville without hitting a rocket scientist. Many of the local residents consider Huntsville to be the closest thing, in real life, to the science fiction channel show Eureka.

I prepared my cover story as I neared DTS (Destructive Testing Solutions), where Greg and Nellie work. The current trend in business management is to eschew the old command and control practices in favor of a more collaborative management structure. Part of this format is to encourage grassroots public relations in which the press can talk casually with front line researchers without management and PR departments getting in the way. This format is a benefit to me, since the last thing I needed was someone from the public relations department quoting verbiage they had memorized from the company's press releases.

Most of the corporations in the Cummings Research Park build buildings that are modern, timeless, and a bit distinct, but not too much. The result is that the look of the buildings is as generic as that of government buildings, college campuses or track housing. DTS was no exception. The brick and concrete building has clean lines, a two-storey archway above the front entry and glass doors leading to a fake mahogany reception desk in the lobby.

The receptionist was a twenty-something woman with pale skin and dark hair. She was in a black dress, wearing deep red lipstick, and royal blue eye shadow. A wide black lace choker concealed a generous percentage of her neck.

I slouched a bit, peered owl-like through my glasses and said, "Dr. Brown to see doctors Turner," in a voice that was just slightly on the quiet side.

My name is actually Mike Mycroft Brown. If I introduce myself that way, most people get the mistaken impression that I'm telling them that I go by Mike which is short for Mycroft. That is exactly what my parents intended, but my father was a bit groggy filling in birth certificate paperwork at 3:00 a.m. in a maternity ward and filled in Mike as the first name and Mycroft as the middle name, completely forgetting the 1960s Hippy inspired middle name they had planned.

The receptionist asked me to wait a minute and offered me a nearby seat in the lobby. I doubt the tone and inflections of her voice would have been any different if I had introduced myself as a urinal cake salesman, or the crown prince of Arabia. The lobby had marble tile, deep green wallpaper, and a large flat screen displaying interesting facts which no doubt added up to tell about the greatness of their company. I took a look at the magazines on the end table. All of them had been purchased the same month about two years ago. Apparently, they didn't expect people to spend much time waiting in the lobby, and didn't want those that did to enjoy the experience.

A few minutes later, Greg arrived to escort me back to the labs where he and Nellie work with several human researchers. Outside the lobby, the building had walls painted tan and gray, flat Berber carpeting, and no other decoration. I was willing to bet there was an executive suite somewhere, which could be easily recognized by the elegant wood grain paneling.

Greg and Nellie's destructive testing lab displayed a disparate array of devices. Half were massive machines design to crush, bend, twist and puncture very strong objects. The other half were precision measuring instruments that seemed woefully frail in comparison. Adjacent was a room with thick concrete walls and four inch thick bulletproof glass. There were other outdoor testing areas out in rural parts of the county and on Redstone Arsenal where they can destroy things with much larger explosions.

Werewolves are intelligent, strong, and work great in groups due to their pack mentality. Their sense of smell is far beyond that of a human. Most werewolves enjoy hunting, but unlike the movies, prefer the latest state of the art weapons. Taking jobs in weapons development, or anyplace things get destroyed fits well with their personality. Most of the time no one else in the organization is aware that supernaturals exist, let alone that they are employed on staff.

Usually the arrangement is beneficial to all concerned. When it isn't, my real job gets more difficult.

Nellie greeted me and engaged in some small talk about mutual acquaintances. This was a subtle reminder that Greg is not in charge even if she chooses to let him do the talking. Female werewolves must work harder than the men to go unnoticed in human society. In addition to colored contact lenses, they usually employ makeup, padded bras and long sleeves. This keeps them looking decidedly female while hiding the fact that they could easily break the arm of most Olympic athletes. Werewolves don't transform into animals or monsters that show off the latest Hollywood makeup techniques. They are people that are a step better evolved to be strong, intelligent hunters than their more populous cousins of the Homo sapiens persuasion.

Greg told me about the visit from a woman identifying herself as Lucy Moore. She was asking about certain destructive tests on important pieces of work. These tests had gotten information about how composite materials fail on the molecular level, which should be beyond the capabilities of human technology. There is no way to tell how she picked up on these subtle anomalies, which are kept buried in internal technical reports. The more important question is whether she is working alone or getting intelligence from someone else, human or otherwise? If I were certain she was human, I would assume she had to be getting intelligence from someone else. However, I hadn't yet ruled out computer hacking, or being a walking lie detector to make it easier to get information out of people.

There is nothing magical about supernatural beings or their tools. However, the supernatural world's understanding of science and technology is a number of years ahead of the science known to the human community in a number of fields. There aren't as many supernaturals, but a single supernatural scientist who lives hundreds of years can make incredible advances in their lifetime. These areas of supernatural held knowledge are known as obscience or obtech, meaning science or technology that is concealed from the population at large. The human world does the same thing by hiding knowledge from competitors as trade secrets or classified materials. The human

7

world is a tangled web of who knows about what. Dealing with the supernatural community just makes it three times worse.

Supernaturals are long-term thinkers and usually have a plan. They almost always have a plan where the human world is concerned, since there was a greater risk of exposure and rules to obey. Greg and Nellie, like many of the vampires, empaths and others I work with, are integrated into the human research establishment in order to manage a gradual release of that technology to the human world, prevent catastrophes, and sometimes slow down the human's acquisition of science that they aren't yet ready to handle. The things that Lucy identified are a case where it is in the best interest of all to help a NASA project along, but the supernaturals are trying to avoid releasing a few advanced testing techniques to the human community at large. It was deemed the lowest risk of exposure to use those techniques as trade secrets of a corporation that provides testing services to NASA.

I asked a number of people in the lab about Lucy Moore's facial features. That gave little useful information, a fact that correlated well with the fact that all of them could be very precise about how much cleavage she was displaying, and how far up her leg the slit in her dress was cut. Estimates of her height and weight were varied. Opinions were split on whether her eyes were brown or blue.

Greg asked if this inquiry might be a play by conservative supernaturals, who had only grudgingly agreed that their project should be undertaken. I replied that it was just one of a half dozen possibilities.

The supernatural community uses the terms "liberal" and "conservative", and "moderate" in about the same way that the human community does. Conservatives are motivated by a fear of change, and longing for society to be the (possibly imagined) idyllic way it had been in the past, perhaps 50 to 500 years ago depending upon the individual. Conservatives tend to view the human community as a resource to be managed for the benefit of the supernatural community. Liberals embrace the world's diversity of experiences and cultures. Liberals want a society of personal freedoms and expression, unlike the conservative's desire for a well-ordered society. Liberals tend to view the relationship between the human and supernatural as a mutually beneficial symbiotic relationship. In the grand scheme of things, the difference between the two is small, but important to those vested in a given issue. Moderates tend to avoid conflict and look for a compromise middle ground, or side with the one that seems closest to it.

My job is to keep everyone working peacefully together. It is not a job description that would be envied by anyone that had gained a bit of wisdom in the world.

Chapter 2

I needed to think about what Greg had said while it was still fresh in my mind, so I headed to a nearby upscale sandwich shop. The shop was fairly large, but had walls that segmented it into four smaller seating areas, thus giving it a more intimate feeling. The food and drink were good, if a bit over priced. Most importantly, customers were allowed to sit there alone with their thoughts. I got coffee and a roll and sat down in the corner with a notepad computer.

There were only a few other customers at this time of day. A heavyset man was going through a black briefcase and wearing a Navy blue suit that screamed "salesman". A mousy young woman with brown hair was wearing a brown skirt and reading a large, hardback book. She was making notes in a spiral bound notebook. A middle aged woman was overdressed for the daytime in a tight fitting, blue silk dress. She was paying more attention to the time than her drink.

I opened an app for organizing information and begun jotting down facts with so many abbreviations and acronyms that it would be as useful as ancient Egyptian hieroglyphics to anyone that got a look at it. The world has become so data rich that you have to assume that almost any location is video taped, any network activity is watched, and the software on your own computer is watching what you are doing. One way to keep things private is to put them in an illegible form. I was equally adept at illegible handwriting, but I would be able to read it again later if I used the tablet computer. I couldn't always say the same for my handwriting.

I don't take notes when I'm interviewing people unless it's an intentional ploy to unnerve them. Visualizing a quick mental picture of one of my undergraduate lecture halls as I start a meeting puts my mind in record mode. My other, sometimes more valuable, asset is mindfulness. Mindfulness is the Buddhist term for having an exceptional awareness of the world around you, which is a similar mental state to what athletes call "the zone". I visualize mindfulness as a calm, soft voice at the back left of my consciousness. It gives me extra information about things I'm seeing, hearing, my body, my feelings, subconscious analysis... anything outside of the primary focus of my conscious mind. Mindfulness is also characterized by living in the moment and not being distracted by thoughts of the past, future, relationships, etc.

While I was talking with the staff of the destructive testing lab, that voice in my head noted that Greg hadn't polished his shoes lately, that I still have a twinge in my right knee from the last martial arts night, that there were Oreo cookie crumbs near the high speed camera analysis computer, and that the lack of information about Ms Moore's looks might be an important piece of information. I considered this last conjecture. Empaths can have what they call "strong thoughts". This means thinking the same thought on thousands of parallel neural paths simultaneously, thus emitting weak electromagnetic waves on the same frequency as brain waves. These are just strong enough to suggest to other people's brains that they focus on something that has already come to their attention. A vampire can emit human pheromones that are equally distracting. A human can use fewer facial expressions and more body language to accomplish the same thing, if in a more clumsy way, given some training and practice.

The overdressed woman left with a group of similarly dressed acquaintances. Given how uncomfortable she seemed, I wasn't inclined to classify them as friends. A college guy with EMO clothing and a bike helmet sat down to ingest concentrated caffeine and focus on a very large textbook. The mindfulness voice in my head noted these items without distracting my primary train of thought.

I considered some of the other possibilities. By definition members of two groups of animals are different species if they cannot interbreed. It's a well-defined distinction, but nature is seldom so neatly binned into categories. Nature is full of exceptions to the rule, such as the mule which is a cross breed of a horse and a donkey but incapable of having offspring. If there are millions of squirrels on a continent, they will probably differentiate into separate species such as grey, red, and flying squirrels. Species with no close relatives, such as the platypus are extremely rare, and usually very small populations. With billions of humans world wide, it would be surprising if there weren't other human-like species. The answer is, of course, that there are other human-like species such as werewolves, vampires, and empaths. There is nothing magical about these species, but their existence and points of improvement over humans makes them alien, scary and threatening to many humans. When possible, these other species try to blend in? with the human population because humans can be both xenophobic and incredibly brutal. Although a vampire or werewolf has little to fear from a human in a fist fight, humans by far outnumber their closest cousins.

In addition to the other species, there are genetic anomalies within the human population. Many of these are manifested as various diseases, while a few manifest as dwarves, giants, and incredibly flexible contortionists. Less obvious are the mutations that create savants and exceptional geniuses, the latter of which are both incredibly talented and very susceptible to various psychiatric disorders. Even average humans can learn seemingly superhuman skills. For example, anyone can learn to memorize large, detailed piles of information. Advanced memorization skills, such as the memory palace technique, were widely known in past centuries when a large percentage of the population was illiterate. Today advanced memorization techniques are often left out of the school curriculum in favor of reading and writing.

All of these various species and mutations create a nearly infinite variety of preconceived notions, prejudices, and political leanings. Even amongst people that are aware of supernaturals, there are personal opinions ranging from fear, to acceptance, to envy. The trick is to determine where Ms Lucy Moore fits into the supernatural landscape and what she is attempting to accomplish.

I began packing up my things and a second later the mousy girl put down her book. We headed for the trash can to drop off our paper cups at the same time. I dropped my cup in the trash and held the trash bin open for her to drop hers in. As she did, she looked up into my eyes and lost her balance, falling into my arms.

"Are you OK?" I asked as I gently pushed her upright.

"Yes, just clumsy," she said.

"Best to stay clear of large vats of toxic waste for a while, just in case. You wouldn't want to start slinging webs and climbing walls," I joked.

I got the Spider-Man reference wrong, but she laughed anyway. I noted that her nose wrinkled when she laughed. She was pretty, when she stopped looking at the floor and smiled.

"Hi, I'm Mike Brown," I said with my best warm, kind smile and voice.

"Lisa McDuff," she said while gently shaking my hand.

She didn't look like a McDuff, but the European heritages are nearly impossible to distinguish in the US. If anything, her genetic makeup looked vaguely Latin American. She was below average height. She had long, brown hair. She wore small glasses, and muted earth tone color clothes. She was wearing white socks and tennis shoes.

"That's quite a book you are reading," I said.

"I've always felt I should read a thousand-page Russian novel, but I need to take notes to keep from losing track of it. None the less, I'm determined no matter how boring it is," she said.

"I would rather have a disciplined co-worker of average intelligence than an undisciplined genius," I said.

"It's good I get points for trying," she said.

"You get points for succeeding, but perhaps a bit of respect for trying," I said.

"You sure make a girl work for it, don't you," she responded.

I laughed and told her I needed to get back to work. I didn't try to get a phone number. I wasn't trying to scare up a date, although it had been a while. Also, being too forward would scare off an introvert. Only after we parted did I kick myself because I had no way to contact her or find her again.

Chapter 3

I headed over to the local United Nations building. The UN doesn't have offices in most cities. However, there were enough UN interests between NASA and the U.S. Army to warrant it in Huntsville, Alabama. It is a red brick building that is small, and nondescript by government standards. The UN shares the building with a small local CIA office, and a national weather service office.

My true job is working for the UN. Specifically, I work for the Department of Collaborative Scientific Activities. Everyone drops the last letter of the acronym to call it DOCS, an appropriate moniker for a department that officially works with scientific researchers. What the department name doesn't indicate is that this is the department responsible for policing and protecting the supernatural community. It also employs a number of them as researchers in the development of technologies considered key to bringing long term benefits to the word population, both human and supernatural. Sometimes our job is to keep the existence of supernaturals secret from the general public.

The supernatural community doesn't have a global governing body, although supernaturals will vote on the position they want their representatives to make known to governments. The community will also vote on releasing scientific advancements to the human community, or otherwise aiding the human community in technical fields. The United Nations acts as a mediating organization, with perhaps even less true political authority than it holds over governments in the human world. In a policing capacity, the UN has more authority over supernaturals than the local police, primarily due to the lack of any other policing body attempting to claim authority. However, the UN recognizes that this is a *de facto* authority with no official legal grounds. UN operatives, at least the few that are in the know, are trained to tread lightly and respect local supernatural community conventions, in order to avoid creating a battle over the legal grounds of their authority.

The way to protect the supernatural community is to make humans believe that it does not exist, which will cause them to rationalize away little slips that give evidence of the abilities of those individuals. The leaders of DOCS are wise enough to realize that the worst way to make people believe that something doesn't exist is for the government to try to suppress or deny information. Case in point is how suppressing information backfired so completely when conservative Christian groups tried to suppress the Harry Potter books because they dealt with magic. A number of other books have catapulted to best seller status after being condemned by the Vatican. DOCS takes the opposite approach of encouraging the publication and popularity of a plethora of books and movies on vampires, werewolves and other supernatural beings. The more magical and fantastic the better, so that people will recognize those sources as clearly being fiction. Even the term "supernatural" is a misnomer for beings that are a perfectly logical result of evolution. Vampires don't melt or sparkle in sunlight, just as the effects of garlic, holy water, and crosses are pure fiction. A stake or silver bullet through the heart will kill a vampire, or werewolf, or jack rabbit, or anything else with a heart beat.

I entered the small UN building, and found the correct desk in the office on the first try. It goes to show how often I go into the office when I have to think about which desk is mine. I spent the rest of the day going through UN databases, and other sources we can access directly. I searched for information on Lucy Moore or someone matching her description. I got nothing on this first pass. I then widened the search by requesting similar searches for loosely defined descriptions of people and activities from other departments and agencies.

Having had a full if unproductive day, I headed back home. I have a small stone house. The house is a simple floor plan with a porch out front, living room, kitchen, two bedrooms and one bath. It is on a forty-acre track of wooded land east of Huntsville. Some of the previous owners had tried to farm the land with various crops, but multiple farming attempts seem to have failed. I did get some peach trees and blueberry bushes and a barn out of those previous attempts. Who ever built the house must not have liked neighbors. The house sits in the middle of the plot of land, rather than near a road like most farmhouses.

The next day, I headed out to see if there was anything going on in local supernatural politics. I wanted to find out if there was anything that might give someone a motive to go poking around asking uncomfortable questions about supernatural activities. It was a cool morning, but expected to get warm. I put on shorts and a T-shirt with the Schrödinger equation on it, covered by a blue sweat suit.

Huntsville's Buddhist meditation center is on top of a mountain where the afternoon temperatures are usually five degrees cooler than in the valley. The drive up the winding road to the mountaintop was a pleasant prelude to a meditation session. A well-experienced meditator could find their focus in the most chaotic of surroundings, but beginners often need a quiet, comfortable space, preferably away from the distractions of home, work and daily life.

I parked the sedan and walked past the Japanese rock gardens to the meditation area. There are platforms, gazebos, benches, screened gazebos, and small cabins that can be rented. The whole setting is beautiful, but the traditional Japanese rock garden is a contrast from the southern country style buildings, which looked like something you would see in a country music video.

I found the monk I was looking for sitting in a gazebo. He wore saffron robes and kept his head shaved. He went by the name Butsujo Sing, although he was not of Eastern descent. Those who knew him well, knew that he had been born in rural Alabama and given the name Bubba Joe Jackson. With the exception of his morning meditation, he spent most of his time out and around the community visiting with Buddhists, liberal supernaturals and others.

I sat down on a nearby bench to wait for him to finish. While I waited, I entered a shallow meditation keeping focus on everything around me. Buddhist meditation and mindfulness practices aren't the only way for a normal human to gain exceptional abilities, but they seem to be the most effective, judging from the fact that most of the humans that move in supernatural circles are Buddhists. Most supernaturals use meditation techniques, especially those with long life spans. Amongst the numerous benefits of meditation is keeping the mental faculties sharp and thus diminishing or delaying the effects of dementia and Alzheimer's disease in old age. A minuscule percentage of Christians engage in reflective prayer, which is very similar to meditation, as is self hypnosis.

My meditation was a mindfulness exercise to observe the world around me. I heard various sounds of birds, insects, my own shallow breathing, and Butsujo's nearly non-existent breathing. I saw wild flowers in various stages of bloom, a fern with one broken frond, a tiny tree frog, a dragonfly, and a beetle with an electric green carapace. I heard Butsujo take in a sudden deep breath, an unconscious bodily reaction to regulate the amount of oxygen in the blood. A few minutes later, he started to move, stood up with a little stretching, and brushed himself off. I wouldn't be surprised if he sometimes meditated with such stillness that dust accumulation was a possibility. I also stood up and fell in beside him as he walked back towards the residence cabins and vegetable gardens.

Butsujo said, "Most people come to ask philosophical questions of me, but you usually find your own answers. You have a mission of some sort when you come visiting."

With most people, I exchange pleasantries. I ask about their family or favorite hobbies to put them at ease and in a mood to talk. However, Butsujo always goes for the heart of the matter, and the truth of it, if one can be found. I suppose this is to be expected from someone who has made the seeking of truth, and helping others to seek it, the central mission of his life.

I replied, "A human woman named Lucy Moore has been asking questions that seek to uncover supernatural activities. I was wondering if you knew of her, or of any current activities that might give someone an advantage if supernaturals were uncovered?"

"I have not heard of this woman. I can't be sure what motives people have for their actions, let alone intention of future actions."

I should have seen that one coming. Truth seekers often see many possibilities, but avoid jumping to conclusions as to which is correct.

I asked, "What current events are you aware of in the supernatural community?"

With some thought and carefully chosen words, he told me of a disagreement over how the supernatural historians should portray prisoner interrogations by empaths during the Iraq war. Many were simply the world's best lie detectors, but some used their mental abilities to aid torture techniques, the politically correct term is "enhanced interrogation", by turning fear into abject terror. As in the human world, history books are the only source of information many people in future generations will be exposed to on a given event. Thus these accounts can be future propaganda for people, countries, political parties and supernatural groups involved. Although most historians try to be unbiased reporters of fact, even unconscious opinions about the morality of events can result in subtle choices of wording that imply a judgment of guilt. At best, histories are worded to reflect the majority opinion of the population, or perhaps the majority opinions from the populations on both sides of the conflict.

In Buddhist philosophy, it is inappropriate to categorize groups or individual people as "good" or "bad". This type of "us and them" mentality is what allows individuals to rationalize their actions in carrying out horrible atrocities such as the holocaust. A person has the capacity to do both good and bad acts, and the responsibility must always be on the person doing the acts, not on outside influences. That said, the reality is that there will always be situational ethics, such as how an act of violence normally considered bad may be appropriate if defending oneself or stopping a Hitler to meet the larger goal of benefitting society. However, it is a very slippery slope, which should be avoided, except as a last resort.

Butsujo also told me that there is an active discussion about cloaking devices, a technology which the supernatural community has had for years. The humans are making advances, so now there is a debate as to whether the supernatural community should aid them, allow them to proceed, or hinder them. This is a hot topic because having cloaking technology inevitably brings technology to identify when someone is using a cloaking device. The supernatural community currently uses cloaking technology to hide some of their activities from humans... and sometimes uses it to prey on humans. While an item of hot discussion, this has not yet become an issue that is polarized between the conservative and liberal campuses. Supernatural politics is more like US politics prior to the 1960s in which polarization along party lines is rare, but in recent years the degree of polarization between liberals and conservatives has been increasing. The supernaturals generally view their own politics as better than humans because traditionally each individual considers their position on each issue, and because there is a more prevalent culture of finding mutually acceptable compromise solutions.

There was another local issue at the moment. There was an upcoming vampire martial arts tournament. The traditional name for the vampire martial art is something German that has 23 constants that I can never remember, but the younger vampires call it Vampkido. The issue of the day is that one of the defense contractors in Huntsville hired a Ph.D. astrophysicist named Cindy Rory, who came in third in the last Vampkido world championships. The big game of the season locally is the NASA and NASA contractor team against the Army and Army contractor team. The NASA team chose the humorous team name of "Vampires Getting High". The Army team chose the name "The Fighting Fangs". The Army team is accusing NASA of bringing in a ringer because the job she is doing is only marginally similar to her area of greatest expertise.

The monk also told me that Fredrick Senburg was considering purchasing a new car. Frederick is one of the oldest vampires in town, and an opinion leader amongst the conservative supernatural factions. Certainly, this is a weighty decision for a senior citizen, if the term can be applied to a 450-year-old vampire, who is set in his ways and only purchases a new vehicle every 30-40 years. He probably buys a new car mostly because the old one has become so conspicuous that he can't go around town unnoticed. This is an interesting note on vampire motives, but I doubted that Ms Moore's inquiries were part of the latest car sales tactic.

None of these sounded to me like issues hot enough for anyone involved to risk exposing the supernatural community over them. However, there is always a psychological danger of assuming that other people share your own values, which is untrue surprisingly often.

This got me thinking about the nature of the supernatural political realm. Over the years, the community has become a bit more widely split into conservative & liberal groups rather than being conservative or liberal leaning moderates. This polarization is evidenced by an increasing number of issues that are voted pretty much on party lines. Finding a way to pull those sides back towards one another would benefit anyone who saw a need to get strong support from both sides. It would also be a community-building step that lessened the occasional hostilities between sides. In the grand scheme of communities, small differences of opinion were healthy and necessary, but too many big differences could drive communities and entire countries apart. The supernatural community has many members who are long-lived, wise and long-term thinking. One of these individuals may want to draw the community together purely for the long-term benefit to the community, with no immediate agenda that requires it.

The supernatural community, and the smaller communities of empaths, vampires, werewolves, ogres, etc. within it are not mirror images of the American representative form of democracy. Party leaders are opinion leaders who state and argue the case that is favored by individuals of a given mind set. These individuals are not elected. They arise based on a history of getting people to listen to them, more like internet bloggers than politicians. Sometimes someone becomes the leader of a single cause, but once one has a following they tend to be the group voice and opinion leader on many issues. Occasionally those on different sides of an issue are one race against another, but that is far more rare than liberal versus conservative mindsets.

Supernatural society is actually a true democracy, allowing every adult member to vote on important issues, in recent years via the Internet.

Butsujo, human though he may be, is in close touch with a larger number of liberal supernaturals in town than anyone else. This makes him a good weather vane, even though he is not one to lead a debate. I appreciated the time he had given me. When the conversation got down to car purchasing decisions, I decided that there was probably nothing more he could tell me. The next item on my agenda was therefore to find out what bees the conservative community had up its bonnet.

I headed back to the parking lot, and pulled off the sweat suit jacket before getting into my now overly warm car. I headed back home to prepare for a different type of meeting.

As I drove, I told my phone to dial Deirdre Smith, a young empath woman who was the personal assistant for Fredrick Senburg. I asked her about meeting with him this afternoon. The line was dead several minutes as she put me on hold, a reasonably fast turn around for arranging some type of appointment. She came back on the line and informed me that I had an appointment to have tea with Frederick at 3:30. She also requested that I pick up three cucumbers about the diameter of an old time Eisenhower silver dollar, no larger. I had expected something like that. I had never determined if this was Frederick's interpretation of the custom of bringing gifts, or his way of making people pay for his wisdom, or if he was just cheap. I was just glad it was cucumbers. He had been known to request some odd items, like ammunition for a model of gun that has been out of manufacture for a century.

I arrived home and ate a light lunch of canned soup and a half peanut butter sandwich. Then I sat down with my tablet computer and put in information from the morning's conversation as probably irrelevant facts. Nonetheless, I closed my eyes to consider past motivations and future consequences of each. I allowed this conscious exercise to slip into a meditation, which would encourage my subconscious mind to continue playing with the pieces of this puzzle.

I got up and dressed in a conservative black suit, white shirt, yellow tie and black dress shoes. Then I headed off again in my silver sedan to visit a nearby farmers market that would have the best fresh vegetables. I picked out the best looking silver dollar diameter cucumbers and headed for the far side of town.

I wound through the under-developed streets of the suburb of Madison. This area had grown faster than the major streets could be widened to handle rush hour traffic. Amongst the not so old residential areas was a large overgrown wooded area that could easily be dismissed as an undeveloped piece of land. It was marked only by a narrow gravel driveway and a mailbox. I turned up the gravel driveway. As it neared the house, the driveway widened into a concrete drive that had a branch off to a garage around the side of the house, and a concrete area in front that could park about twenty cars.

At first glance, the house is a two-story home made for a large family. It is surrounded by overgrown shrubs. The house is an unpretentious style with a brick exterior, which might be anywhere from 50 to 150 years old. At second glance, you might notice that the brickwork was a double thick Flemish brick pattern, that the window glass was unusually thick, and that multiple security cameras were hidden around the premises. I knew from previous visits that the house was much deeper than it was wide and had at least one enclosed courtyard.

As I walked up, a broad shouldered man in a white shirt and black waistcoat opened one of the heavy oak doors. I noted his size but couldn't immediately tell if he was a werewolf or ogre. The interior of the house gave an entirely different impression. There were floors of black marble, a massive crystal chandelier, white marble statues in alcoves, oil paintings in gold leaf frames, and tapestries. Two curved staircases led to a second story landing. Fredrick Senburg was so incredibly wealthy that for him to live in an opulent mansion with thirty people employed there was the equivalent of a chief surgeon who purchased an economy car with no air conditioning. I'm sure the free cucumbers were a big help.

I was met in the entryway by a young woman, who was not Deirdre, in a black cocktail dress. I greeted her and asked her name. She replied that she was an all-purpose errand runner, apparently forgetting to give me her name. She was young and pretty. I couldn't tell if she was human or empath, and she didn't give off the vibe of a vampire. She took the brown paper sack of cucumbers and led me down several hallways to a salon with a wall of heavy glass windows. The salon had furniture that was mahogany with plush red velvet upholstery. The windows looked out at a tennis court and beyond that an archery range. Frederick sat in a plush chair at a table topped with red marble. Deirdre was in the chair to his left, and a chair opposite him was vacant. Another large man loomed in a corner of the room.

I sat down and exchanged greetings with Frederick and Deirdre. I complemented Deirdre on her looks, and told Frederick I hoped he was doing well. We had a short discussion about the robotic lander scheduled to land on Mars in a few days. In Huntsville, discussing NASA missions is the equivalent of discussing the weather. Everyone is familiar with NASA.

Deirdre Smith was a woman in her early 20s. She was tastefully clothed, if over dressed for working around the home of a retiree. She had long blond hair, and a deep tan that suggested either a Hispanic heritage or significant time at a tanning salon. She still had the shapely body that nature gave young women without large amounts of sweat-drenched exercise. This was unusual for an empath. Unlike vampires for whom sex appeal was an evolutionary advantage, empaths cared most about their mental acuity. Many empaths used either a sugar high or food deprivation to sharpen their mental senses. As such, empaths were usually either anorexic or morbidly obese, seldom as shapely as Ms Smith.

Frederick Senburg was a distinguished gentleman. He was tall and thin, with a liberal number of gray streaks in hair that had originally been jet black. In deference to his easygoing retirement life style, he no longer wore ties with his immaculately tailored suits. He looked like a man pushing seventy. However, since he was a vampire, it was quite possible that the memories of his youth included knights in armor, the black plague, or the invention of gunpowder. Being conservative in his planning for the future, he probably had wealth in Swiss bank accounts, gold, and gems. He probably also had enough arms to weather an apocalyptic collapse of law and order, and enough food stores for a hundred people to survive a multi-year famine.

A serving maid brought tea and a large tray of cookies, scones, and sandwiches made from cucumber slices and cream cheese. The staff apparently had kept track of my favorite tea and type of cookie from a previous visit. Once some tea and a few cookies had been consumed, Frederick asked why I had come. I told him about Lucy Moore's activities and asked what current events he was aware of in the supernatural community. Giving out information about Lucy was a type of information currency in such exchanges. As he sat back to consider how best to answer, Deirdre excused herself to take care of other business, probably at some signal from Frederick that I hadn't caught.

Frederick was also aware of the debate over how the history books should portray empath involvement in interrogations during the Iraq war. He himself had not yet weighed in on the subject, and the debate didn't yet seem to be polarized between liberals and conservatives. I think part of Frederick's success as a conservative opinion leader was due to his ability to wait and see which way the winds of opinion are blowing before he weighed in with his own well worded and carefully considered thoughts.

On the issue of cloaking technology, the conservative supernaturals were partly neutral and partly for hindering human progress on the technology development. Cloaking technology had been the topic of multiple debates over the years because it could so readily be used to hide illegal activities. Most of the discussion had been somewhat moot, because it was so expensive that only a rare few could afford to utilize it. Again, Frederick had yet to voice his opinions on the subject.

He did bring up an issue that I had not heard about. There was currently a big debate about the impending marriage of a somewhat small, frail werewolf woman (still stronger than most human men) to a human weight lifter. There aren't any worries about children since the

25

last unconfirmed rumors of a hybrid supernatural-human was 1000 years ago, hundreds of years before the supernatural community developed individual gene sequencing technology. The issue is that the couple wants to get married with a traditional werewolf ceremony. This is a non-issue amongst liberals who have an ethos of symbiotic relationships with other species. Apparently it was a big issue for some conservatives that value traditional marriages and were worried that this would somehow bring about the end of werewolf civilization.

Sex between supernaturals and humans is common, especially amongst vampires, who use unconventional sex as a way of obtaining human blood. I've always found the conservative communities to be a bit hypocritical in the way that they apply different standards to marriage than to extramarital affairs. Most don't even consider sex with a human to be cheating on a spouse, just recreation... or a snack.

Chapter 4

The next morning, I pondered my next move while lounging in a recliner in my living room. My living room has a collection of furniture that is comfortable if mismatched, one of the benefits of being a bachelor. The shelving attached to the wall would be considered elegant, if it weren't so cluttered. Without trying, I seem to have collected samples from cultures around the world. These included Russian dolls, African masks, an English tea set complete with tea cozy, a native American peace pipe, a large crystal ball sometimes used as a focal point for meditation, and a shrunken head. I couldn't tell if the shrunken head was real or simply something manufactured for the tourist trade. I was hesitant to investigate the matter too thoroughly.

For lack of a more productive idea, I decided to go in to the office. I always considered working in an office as a rather mundane way of earning a living. Fortunately, the bureaucracy classified me as a field agent, so I wasn't bound to office hours or dress codes. I put on a reasonably new pair of jeans and a T-shirt with a collage of Star Trek scenes. There was no reason I couldn't put on business clothes, but people in the office would find it easier to dismiss my random comings and goings if I kept up the field agent routine of random dress options.

The only reason I needed to work from the office was because the office computer was on a separate physical network that allowed it to access things that I couldn't get to from my laptop at home.

My database searches and inquiries had not found anything on Lucy Moore. This screams "alias". It isn't a well built alias either. I could tell this because she didn't have a social security number, school transcripts, or drivers license under this name, as would someone with a well made alias, say in the witness protection program.

The other things I found were two more reports of someone poking around DOCS projects. These had come in via official channels, not from people that knew me personally.

The first was a report of a woman with black hair asking about anomalies in human endurance testing results. These inquiries were made outside of their work place when a woman named Lucy Moore approached some workers at lunch and identified herself as a reporter for the MIT Technology Review magazine. A quick check indicated no such person on their writing staff. The endurance tests were being tested by supernaturals first, in order to see if they would be fatal to humans. The ogre that reported this thought that it might be one of the liberal supernaturals who were often opposed to live animal testing. However, I wasn't aware of any movement against this particular testing practice.

The second report was about phone calls coming from a Huntsville phone number, which were made to St. Louis. The woman making the calls asked about an empath detective who has insights a human couldn't have gotten from the tenuous clues. The detective, who was vocal about his liberal political leanings, suggested that it could be the work of conservative supernaturals. The Huntsville phone was a disposable cell phone that was no longer turned on.

I tried to dig up more information about these reports... security camera photos, GPS data from the phone, etc. The UN has access to some interesting data, but not as much as local law enforcement, and not near as much as was out there in the security photos from most decent size companies. I have spent enough time around philosophers and supernaturals to have developed my own view of situational ethics and where to draw lines. If this little problem was to be stopped before it became a big problem, I needed to get an expert involved, preferably one with similarly flexible ethics. I knew just the girl.

ADZTK (no one knows what it stands for) is another brick and concrete building in Huntsville's Cummings Research Park. No one seems to know who pays for it, or what it does. I pressed the intercom in the entryway and asked for Summer Zen. A security guard in a glass booth buzzed me in and told me to wait in the lobby. Through the small window in a security door, I could see the computer room floor. There was a recently installed supercomputer, and a hodge podge collection of other computer equipment. On a previous visit, I had learned that they sometimes have the chips custom made for their computers. It was just the type of place you expected to find a world-class computer expert.

I waited a bit longer than one would expect someone to respond to a visitor in the lobby, before another employee noticed me and escorted me past the security doors to Summer's office. Summer was buried in some piece of computer code, apparently having forgotten that she had a visitor.

Summer Zen is the world's poster child for female geeks. She seems to have had her fingers into every aspect of computer technology I have heard of, and a few more. She is a human who is aware that supernaturals exist. I suspect she knows more than I'm aware of about many things. I have an encrypted database to keep track of how much each human is supposed to know about supernaturals, which races, etc. so that I can be cautious in not telling them more unless necessary. Summer is short, about five foot nothing, slim, with black hair, and pale skin with a number of piercings and tattoos. She wears heavy, red glasses. She seems to always be wearing black clothing and makeup that obscures or highlights different piercings or tattoos. I can never be sure which are permanent and which were the flavor of the day.

After a few minutes, she noticed someone was standing in her office doorway and greeted me. "Hey Doc!"

"Hello, Summer. How are you doing?" I replied.

"Not bad. I'm writing an artificial intelligence program to proactively give supercomputer users suggestions on how to do their work more efficiently."

"Sounds complicated."

"The AI is surprisingly simple. The hard part is figuring out how to give the suggestions to our users without freaking them out about how big brother is watching them and stuff. Target stores made that mistake a few years back when the company sent out an expectant mother package of coupons, sometimes before other members of the household were aware of the pregnancy," she replied.

"I'm glad you are trying to avoid causing the collapse of modern society," I said.

Individualized marking based on web searches and social network posts is creepy enough. I could just imagine a world where porn sites told you what lingerie and intercourse positions you spouse wants, private detectives contact you to sell their services because they already know your spouse is cheating, the divorce lawyer showing up at the door minutes after you have made a mental decision but haven't said anything to anyone. People would have a heart attack and die when they got an advertisement for funeral home services.

"Speaking of society's collapse, what brings you here?" she asked.

"I'm hurt. Can't I stop by just to enjoy a bit of intellectual jousting with a worthy opponent?" I asked.

"No, I don't think so," she replied.

"It turns out you're right," I replied. "I tried it once and people thought I was hitting on them. If I were gay, I could have had a great night with twin guys... I really need to add some female twins to my professional circle."

"Uhhh, yeah. So what did you come by for?"

"I could use your help preventing the collapse of society," I replied.

"I knew it!" she replied. "What is it this time? Cyborg werewolves? Blood tainted with vampire aphrodisiacs? A computer virus infecting military satellites?"

"A woman asking too many questions," I said.

"First you reject me romantically, then you criticize my naturally inquisitive nature. This isn't looking good for you getting my help," she quipped.

"Can I buy you something large with caffeine while we talk about it?" I asked, ignoring the trap she was baiting.

I took her to lunch at a nearby sandwich and coffee shop. We discussed trying to find out who was poking around. I had worked with Summer in the past, and I think she had official authorization from her management to cooperate to some extent. If other tidbits she got me were from her personal time, I didn't want to ask too many questions. I simply made it clear that I needed information and not evidence that would be acceptable in court. She mostly mumbled with her mouth full in response, and I didn't push her any further.

Chapter 5

Thud. The crossbow bolt hit two rings to the right of the bullseye. I reloaded. Thud. Just left of the bullseye. I had a crosswind from the left that was buffeting stronger and weaker. My aim wasn't too bad considering the winds. One advantage of living on a failed farm was having plenty of room for things like an archery range.

It isn't uncommon for people who work around science and technology to have decidedly low-tech hobbies to help them unwind. I had the crossbow, and martial arts.

I kept my focus on my target practice. I shot at targets at three different distances with a crossbow with a rifle stock, a beautiful rosewood stock, and a three notch front site, but no scope. Then I shot at the nearest target with a little pistol style hand crossbow. As I retrieved the final volley of bolts from the hand crossbow, I started to think about our mystery woman.

Who is she? She could be a human, empath, or vampire. She might be outside the community, or working for a rival country, or corporation, or someone else.

What is her motive? She might see a chance for political or financial gain. Or she may simply have a hostile dislike for the supernatural community. Humans are more xenophobic than other creatures, which is why supernaturals stay hidden. She could be a conspiracy theorist or religious nut. She could just be a good reporter or writer trying to get the great story that makes her career.

Before I could get any further in my, most likely futile, pondering, my phone rang. It was Julie Lemon, an empath in NASA's xenobiology department. She was upset about a black haired woman who had gotten into her lab. I was getting ready to walk out the door before I got off the phone.

NASA's Marshall Space Flight Center is one of their major research and development operations. Here experts in all different fields design vehicles, plan missions, and analyze samples. Julie is a Ph.D. microbiologist who joined NASA to analyze rock samples for signs of ancient microbial life. If the day ever came that we met intelligent aliens, she would hopefully be positioned to use her telepathic abilities in communicating with them.

After the usual government security rigmarole, I found myself going down an immensely long hallway of nearly identical offices to find Julie's. She was in her office, attempting to fill out an incident report on her computer but too flustered to be making much progress. Julie is a large woman, kind of like the Queen Mary is a large rowboat. She was wearing the largest lab coat NASA could provide, which did not button over her beige dress. The dress must have been custom made to disguise her girth as a section of wallpaper. She had short blonde hair, and a complexion that suggested staying away from both sun and high wattage interior lighting. I shut the door, sat down, and kept my voice and emotions calm in an attempt to calm her a bit.

"It's just so upsetting!" she exclaimed. "I was out of my lab visiting another scientist, and came back to find this woman peering at the Petri dishes that were on the lab bench at the time. She didn't seem to be touching anything. I asked her who she was. She smiled and said she must have gotten separated from the VIP group and left. She didn't give me her name, and I wasn't going to be too confrontational if she was part of some VIP tour. After she left, I noticed that a stack of paperwork was no longer neatly stacked."

Lowering her voice to a whisper, she said, "They were reports adjusted to obscure you-know-what type of activities."

"What did she look like?" I asked.

"She has long black hair, red lipstick, and bluish-greenish eyes. She was wearing a red dress, and carrying a little black handbag. I think it was a cheap knock off of a designer one, the handbag that is."

"What are you working on in that lab?"

"Nothing high profile. It's a long-term experiment. We started with some bacterial organisms that live in volcanic hot springs. Those are called extremophiles. We are gradually adjusting their environment over the course of years to make the environment more and more like the closest conditions we predict to exist at the poles of Venus."

"Is there any military or monetary value?"

"Not that we are aware of. The experiments aren't very far along. The bacteria can fairly quickly adjust to protect themselves from toxins in the environment, but they are much slower to adjust to utilize new food sources. We sequence their genome every time there seems to have been a significant change in their evolution."

"So what was in those reports?"

"Those weren't from my lab." She could have mentioned that up front, I thought to myself as I waited for her to go on. "I'm on lots of committees because there is a rule saying there must be a woman on every committee and only twenty percent of the Ph.D. researchers are women. I was looking over some reports of other projects between taking measurements in the lab. These were reports of destructive testing being done by DTS."

It made sense to me that Lucy Moore would be sniffing out data related to Greg and Nellie's work, which she was already investigating. However, how she had sniffed out an engineering report in a biology lab in a government facility was a mystery. Either she has a near psychic ability, or someone was helping her.

Julie asked if this might be the work of a liberal supernatural. I didn't follow her logic, since liberals were more likely to support sharing advanced technologies with humans and conservatives like Julie less likely. However, there is a natural tendency to suspect people different from yourself. I considered the Dalai Lama's comment that there must be many religions and organizations to match the diverse mentalities of people on earth. Supernaturals are no different.

Just then, one of Julie's lab assistants called. They had found a small smear of blood. It was on a burr of metal on the side of a vent hood right near where the papers had been disturbed in the lab. None of the people working in that lab were reporting having scratched themselves there, so there was a possibility that it came from our intruder. I asked for a sample, and Julie produced a sterile swab to collect it for me.

My next stop was to drop off the blood sample for analysis. People who are adept at some of the more advanced sciences known only to the supernatural community call themselves alchemists, regardless of whether they are human or supernatural or doing chemistry, biology or physics. The easiest way to hide such activities is in plain sight. Having piles of chemicals and laboratory equipment delivered to a home or seedy back street business would have raised suspicions that it was a meth lab. However such activities going though a high tech startup business would hardly be noticed.

I walked into the backside of the HudsonAlpha research center. The four-story atrium with marble floors, wooden columns and glass elevators was clearly designed to make an impression. To my left was a little cafe with tables to eat at set out in the atrium. Behind that on the left was the wing of the building that was a nonprofit research center specializing in biotechnology work. The wing of the building on the right was an incubator for high tech startup companies, particularly those in the biotech field.

I turned right and found the desired door of what appeared to be just another startup company with a made up name that meant nothing. It opened onto a small lobby that had been decorated in the Feng shui style. I hadn't worked with this group before, but I knew that the UN had an account with them to do DNA testing on blood from supernaturals. I told the secretary that I was there to drop off a sample and filled out a sheet of paperwork as a young, female lab tech arrived to collect the sample. The lab tech pointed out that the UN usually mailed in samples. I said that this one was a special project and asked that it be done ahead of routine work from the organization.

Huntsville Supernatural Volumes 1-3

Chapter 6

I headed home to prepare for the evenings activities. The next hour was spent sweeping and mopping out the barn. The steel frame barn is one big open room with the roof joists twelve feet above the concrete floor. It had been the last building constructed on the property and is in pretty good shape, if a bit dirty. Finally I hauled a variety of liquid refreshments and a grocery sack of food out to the old refrig in the barn.

Once that was done, I browned a package of ground beef and added the noodles and cheese sauce from a packaged mix. This was pretty fancy cooking by the standards of my bachelor life style. I knew I would be needing the protein and carbohydrates for energy this evening. I had time for a half hour of empty mind meditation while relaxing in a recliner, which was about four times as restorative as sleeping for the same amount of time.

My guests started arriving around seven. There were six werewolves, including Greg and Nellie driving their full sized, brown, diesel pickup. There were ten vampires, the younger of which drove hot sports cars, while the older drove stylish luxury sedans. A young empath couple arrived together in an old VW Beetle. One ogre showed up, driving a battered green SUV. Ogres were rare in Huntsville as there was fairly little work for bar bouncers, bodyguards, or mob muscle. A massive black human alchemist, who is a professor at Alabama A&M University, showed up driving an equally massive white Lincoln. Butsujo Sing showed up with a couple other enlightened humans driving a Subaru wagon that one of them had converted to an all electric. Christopher Lee showed up driving a Mini Cooper. Christopher is a human with Ehlers–Danlos syndrome, making him a hyper-flexible contortionist. He hides the full extent of his flexibility and works as a dance instructor and sometimes-professional dancer in local theater productions. Nearly all of them brought along their favorite form of liquid refreshment.

Several of the werewolves pulled out the heavy mats, which I would have needed a tractor to move. They worked together with the easy, unspoken teamwork that was typical of their race. Many of the group members would have liked to meet more often, but many had busy professional lives. We had this gathering scheduled for one evening every other week. I put everyone's names into my tablet computer and hooked it up to the old forty-inch flat screen I had mounted on the wall.

First up were individual bouts. The computer program chose names at random, but ensured that everyone got an equal amount of time on the mat. There is not an official set of rules for interspecies martial arts. Our group had put together a hybrid set of moves taken from Aikido, Judo, Vampkido, and Tang Soo Do. This was soft form, focusing on holds and throws. Hard forms, such as kicks and punches, were allowed in same species match ups only, and then had to be less than a quarter of the actions. We did not assign style points as did the potentially deadly Vampkido form.

The first fight was between Greg Turner and Gary, another male werewolf. They started out standing about ten feet away. Initially, they circled each other looking for the best opportunity to grapple their opponent. Gary took Greg down with a Judo throw. After that, it looked like an ultra-heavy weight wrestling bout. They went through a series of holds and reversals. Neither was able to immobilize the other, so the bout ended when time ran out. The points were tallied up, and Greg won 27 to 26.

We had developed a whole set of tactics and strategies for taking best advantage of your abilities against other species. Humans and empaths are out matched physically against the other species, but are better at the improvisational side of choosing unexpected movements and tactics. Christopher has developed a style all of his own that makes use of his ability to bend his body in seemingly impossible directions and intentionally dislocate joints at will.

The second fight was probably the most interesting of the evening. It was Christopher Lee verses Little Jimmy the ogre. The humorous name "Little Jimmy" had stuck even though Little Jimmy has a physique like Mount Rushmore. Christopher danced around Jimmy, just outside his reach, taunting him. Jimmy stayed in one place on the mat, but kept turning to stay facing Christopher. When the timing was right, Jimmy lashed out, quite fast for such a big guy, and caught Christopher by the wrist, giving the first point to Jimmy. Jimmy pulled Christopher towards him, but Christopher had other ideas. Christopher pivoted around his trapped wrist to come shoulder to shoulder with Jimmy. It looked like Christopher's arm was being bent an odd direction to do this, but it didn't seem to bother him. Christopher threw all of his weight against Jimmy, butting him shoulder to shoulder both facing the same direction. Jimmy out weighed Christopher significantly, but he moved his opposite foot out a couple inches so that his wider stance would keep him stable. No point scored, but Christopher was only trying to alter Jimmy's stance. Christopher spun back around in front of Jimmy, with his wrist still trapped in the vice of Jimmy's large hand. Jimmy reached for Christopher with his other hand, but Christopher wasn't there. Christopher had done the splits to slide between Jimmy's knees, hauling Jimmy's arm along after him. Then Christopher flipped both feet over his head in a move that was probably impossible for most humans, ending up with his feet planted on the back of Jimmy's thighs. Jimmy tried to let go, but Christopher now had his wrist with both hands. The hold was a point for Christopher. Christopher pulled with all of his strength. When Jimmy's head was nearly down to his knees, he lost his balance and fell over on his back, while Christopher jumped clear. The takedown was another point for Christopher. Jimmy wasn't fazed by this, as he displayed the ogre's famous stone faced temperament. Jimmy rolled onto his stomach then started to get up on hands and knees. Christopher was back on top of Jimmy, one leg pushing Jimmy's knee out from under him, and his elbow in the nerve cluster behind Jimmy's shoulder blade. Jimmy went back down face first with his arm thrown outward by the pinched nerve, thus earning another point for Christopher. Christopher pulled Jimmy's wrist behind his back. Normally a human isn't strong enough to hold an ogre's arm twisted, but Christopher weakened Jimmy's arm with his other thumb on the pressure point at the back of Jimmy's arm pit. Christopher knew as much about human joints as any orthopedic surgeon. The fight ended when Christopher had held Jimmy immobile for ten seconds, thus winning the bout.

After the individual bouts came the team events, two on two, and three on three. Finally, we had group matches where everyone was on their own. Those group matches always had an odd number of people so they couldn't settle into groups of two. Studies of small group dynamics in the isolation of long space missions had determined that an odd numbered group tended to be more fluid, while an even numbered group tended to pair up. Only in Huntsville, Alabama would space exploration research influence a martial art form.

After a couple hours of hard physical exercise, the mat was put away and the gathering turned into a cocktail party, if a somewhat hot and sweaty one. Nellie helped me put out trays of store bought cookies and horderves. There was no sense trying to do something extravagant for this group. What one considered a gourmet delicacy, another would find unpalatable. We just put out a variety of things and everyone would find something to eat.

I circulated around the room making sure everyone was finding a conversation. I spoke a bit to many of them, catching up on people's children and careers. These were always interesting gatherings. An empath girl was talking about the latest fashions catering to the twenty something women. The ogre was listening in and casually sipping on a bottle, looking like any guy with a light beer until you realized it was a very large bottle of bourbon. One of the older vampires was telling about how he had apprenticed under Leonardo Da Vinci, one of the great alchemists of his day. Several of the scientists were talking about a project to travel to distant planets by folding space so that you could simply step through a doorway to another planet. It sounded like the folding was working reasonably well, but controlling where you ended up was being more problematic.

Christine was off to the side by herself, looking off into the distance. That was very unusual, as vampires are very social by nature. I brought her one of the bottled "Bloody Marys" she had brought. I guessed she was middle aged, which for a vampire could be a few hundred years old. Christine worked as a detective for the

Huntsville Police Department. In addition to our little group, she also ranks fairly high in the Vampkido standings, at least on the local and regional level. She was blond, shapely and very good looking. I asked her what she was thinking about.

"I was waning philosophical," she said. "I've seen many scientific advances start out in the supernatural community, then get integrated into the population at large. One of the biggest of those was the Apollo space program."

"So what got you thinking about this?" I asked.

"Another one is being announced tomorrow night at the science museum fund raiser. It's the roll out of the neutrino based communication system. Neutrinos can pass right through the earth's core, so many communications satellites will now be obsoleted by a much cheaper form of communication."

"Why does that bother you?" I asked.

"Removing one of the most profitable applications of space flight will be detrimental to the industry," she said.

"Are you thinking of dumping your aerospace stocks?" I asked.

"Maybe in the short term. However, I was reflecting on how fragile life on earth is. We need self-sustaining colonies on other worlds to keep life from earth surviving if a global disaster were to occur on earth. You think about these things when you live long enough."

"You don't look a day over thirty," I said.

She laughed. "Dear Doctor Brown. At thirty I was a very wild adolescent. Once when I was hungry an entire clipper ship's crew of sailors had the wildest night of sensual pleasure of their lives."

I laughed and moved on through the crowd. The close proximity to her and her pheromones was starting to make me feel like a sailor that hadn't seen a woman in months. Considering that self-control and discipline were my strongest assets, I could just imagine how easy it was for her to draw in the average human male.

Chapter 7

I went to sleep pondering what our mystery woman's next move would be. When I woke up, I had a good idea where she would be. I was going to have a busy day getting prepared for it. I also needed to gather my courage for what would be coming tonight. I spent the rest of the day running to stores and digging through boxes in my house.

I sat in the parking lot for a minute collecting my thoughts and preparing for the evening. I put on the mask I had purchased for a masquerade party last Halloween, collected my courage, then put on my propeller beanie.

The Mad Scientists Ball is an annual fundraiser for SciQuest science museum. This year, the theme was "Unmasking Science" and it was a masquerade. They had a sell out crowd and had hired a private security service for the night. I knew the security team leader, and let him know I was there. I let him know that I didn't have grounds for an arrest, but may have by the end of the night, including a need to apprehend someone on the spot. Someone had given the security staff headbands with light up alien faces on spring antennas.

For someone that has a highly developed ability to perceive everything around them, a big crowd can be an overwhelming cacophony. The museum was packed. At one side of the main hall was a stand up comedian telling science jokes over a PA system. People were eating horderves and drinking. Adults were trying out the science exhibits. Everyone was talking, all at once. I was listening to multiple conversations simultaneously.

"Just a reminder that drinks at the neutron bar near the front entrance are no charge," said the comedian over the PA.

"We just don't have the budget for enough prototype engines to do those types of tests," said a middle-aged woman in pink lab coat, pink pants, pink shoes, pink mask, and pink hair. She was talking to a man in a lab coat with a pocket protector and a wad of tape on black sunglasses.

"Does a radioactive cat have eighteen half-lives?" the comedian again.

"Another couple drinks and I'll be offering to polish his rocket," said a blond woman with a lab coat tight enough to show some cleavage.

"The most important rule in chemistry lab is 'never lick the spoon'." That one got some laughs.

"Do you have any openings for prototyping engineers?" asked a man that should have rethought dressing as a rat in a lab coat.

"So Heisenberg said to the traffic cop, 'I don't know how fast I was going, but I know where I am'."

The crowd was a mass of lab coats, masks, and famous scientists with a few fictional characters, engineers, and astronauts thrown in for good measure. I was hoping my choice of lab coat, mask and propeller beanie would make me blend in, while looking non-threatening and keeping my hands free. I inched my way towards the neutrino communication display, catching more conversation as I went.

"...three kinds of blood vessels, arteries, veins and caterpillars." That one got a few groans.

"Maybe online dating will work out better for me," said a man with an inch of hairy legs showing between his dress socks and overly short plaid pants. He was talking to one of the Ghostbusters.

"I was going to talk about black holes, but the jokes all sucked."

"Liz Macey? I haven't seen you since high school."

The masked woman to my left might have been the one I met at the coffee shop the other day... Lisa. I made a mental note to look for her after attending to my evening's business.

As I approached the neutrino communication exhibit something felt suspicious. I couldn't put a finger on it immediately, but I always try to listen to my subconscious, which communicates with feelings and images rather than words. On the other side of the exhibit, a man dressed as a clown in lab coat was looking around nervously. Talking to him was a woman with long black hair in a red dress, black stockings, mask, and stethoscope. She was holding a thermometer the size of a turkey baster, which managed to look slightly phallic. She certainly fit the description I had heard.

The man took off across the room as fast as the crowd would permit. The woman followed him still trying to talk to him. I sped up trying to follow without immediately being noticed by them. Off to my left, a slightly over weight woman with short brown hair was hurrying this way. I sped up a bit more to avoid colliding with her. Now the conversations around me were just fragments that I could no longer connect with people.

"...so they hired Sherlock Ohms"

"I think he should stick with soccer, but my husband says fencing is..."

"...but the chemists periodically tabled the discussion."

My quarry ducked through a doorway with strips of plastic hung in it. I followed them; followed by the short haired woman, and a rent-a-cop decided to follow with his green, glowing, alien antenna bobbing furiously.

A few steps and there was a second doorway with strips of plastic. I went through and stopped to survey the situation. The clown and red dress woman went into a small children's area where they would have to crouch slightly. Short hair woman put her hands on my back to keep from colliding with me, then followed them. Rent-a-cop was close on her heels and started to follow her.

45

I grabbed the rent-a-cop and said, "Circle around to the right." My voice sounded like a cartoon chipmunk. Great! The archway had been full of helium.

I circled left, trying not to think about the impression I made with a chipmunk voice and propeller beanie. I went right at a branch, dead end, retrace my steps, go the other way, and on to the other end of the exhibit.

The clown and two women were just ahead of me; I fell in line as they headed past the computer lab. Off to my right, rent-a-cop had collided with an older man who had an early steam engine called an aeolipile mounted on a tray strapped around his neck like a stadium candy seller.

The next room had a row of posters displaying the electromagnetic spectrum to the right, and a collection of large displays in a grid pattern. The three ahead of me charged down the middle. I followed. Rent-a-cop went to the right. A second rent-a-cop was off to the left and headed in from that way.

Luck ran out for the clown as one of the college students doing demonstrations was coming the other direction holding a large flask containing layers of oil, water, and other immiscible liquids. The clown collided with the college girl sending a gallon of slippery liquids splattering everywhere. The two women collided with them. I tried to stop, but had no traction. Martial arts practice has given me good balance, so I surfed forward on the slippery floor without lifting my feet. I put out my hand, placing it on the back of the top person in the pile up, and began a beautiful cartwheel right over the whole pile. Two-thirds of the way through the cartwheel, my hand slipped and I came down flat on my back on the other side of the pile of bodies. Behind me, I heard the two security guards run into the pile, colliding face to face with alien antenna clattering together.

Everyone in the group tried to stand at once, groaning and finding their balance. The floor, people and exhibits were now covered in the incredibly slippery mixture. Several times someone lost their footing and brought two more down with them. No one had more than a few bruises and a wounded pride. The security guards and I finally got the whole group out of the area. We shuffled the clown, red dress woman, and short hair woman into a nearby, unused auditorium. The college girl went off to find a janitor. I wondered if the three stooges got started this way.

The evening went downhill from there. The clown was an aerospace engineer who was married to short hair woman and having an affair with red dress woman. I talked a while with red dress, but she looked older than I expected once the mask was off, and didn't fit the profile. I would put a junior UN guy on fact checking her story, but my gut said it wasn't related to the matter at hand.

I told the security guards that everyone was free to go. I didn't answer any of the guards' questions about what I was investigating. I left with my best poker face on. People tend to interpret their experiences through a haze of mental perceptions as to how they think the world is, or how they want it to be. I was sure the security guards would interpret the evening's events as them helping a UN investigation that was too secret to be told about, which was reasonably true as far as it went.

I didn't stay around any longer. I was soaked and slimy, and in no mood for idle social chitchat, certainly not with someone I was actually interested in. I slipped out the front door hoping no one would notice me, and then realized I was still wearing the propeller beanie.

As I drove home, the evening's events continued to bother me. I wasn't usually the paranoid type, and certainly not the type to jump at the first obvious clue. Like many scientists, I spent my life trying to discern the underlying truth from the outward details. I'm the guy that would figure out what was hot at the store by watching the behavior and shopping carts of the other shoppers, while completely missing the sale signs in six-foot letters. This left me wondering what my subconscious had picked up on, and whether it was anything real.

Chapter 8

I considered ignoring the phone that rang during my meditation the next morning, but I opened one eye, saw it was Summer Zen, and decided to answer it. I picked up the phone and said hello.

"Your mystery woman is named Lidia Macey," she said.

"It's nice to speak with you too this fine morning," I replied.

"Yeah, yeah. Did you hear what I said?"

"Lidia Macey. How sure are you?"

"I found her on the security videos, watched her walk to her car, and got the license. It turns out some states now sell information about people's names, addresses and car make. It's considered a source of revenue for the state government. Car companies purchase the information so that they can send out advertising customized to the individual."

"OK. Could she be borrowing someone else's car?" I asked.

"I only found one person with that name in the city where the car is registered. I found a picture of her in an online college newspaper article," she replied.

"Once again you have shocked and amazed me," I said. "Can you send them over to me?"

"They're in your email now," she replied.

"Great. I owe you one," I said.

"I'll send you a bill," she said. I knew the bill would be a favor in return.

I hung up and got on the computer, all thoughts of meditation forgotten. I was impressed that Summer had found a picture at all, although it was a crowd scene that didn't show much. I got onto the

48

UN computer and pulled up her driver's license and passport photos. She liked changing her look. Red, curly hair, or black long hair, one blond I'm guessing was a wig.

I dug deeper into her background. Adopted. Her high school grades were average. She took out loans to cover living expenses while going to cosmetology school... that one helped explain all the different looks. She worked at a salon in Mobile, Alabama for four years, then the trail went cold a month ago. There weren't any charges on her credit card to track where she had been for the past month. There weren't many pictures of her either. The only good ones were at least six years old.

I emailed a request to my superior at the UN. I asked that he have his counterpart at the FBI talk with her foster parents and if possible get copies of recent pictures of her. They could use a security clearance background check as a cover story.

I've always liked museums. They are peaceful, orderly, and thought provoking. It's a good place for quiet reflection, with enough new sights to get your brain thinking about new things. Today, I was casually browsing through the Space and Rocket Center as I mulled over recent events.

There have been a number of points in history marked by a rapid advancement in technology. These include the Industrial Revolution, dot-com bubble, and the Apollo space program. In all of these cases, there are many important innovators behind the scenes who don't get attention from the public. There are always a few people who see past the superficial events to discern how the supernatural community has aided. Usually the people that see beyond the superficial are very understanding individuals. Buddhist philosophy would define them as being on the path to enlightenment. Such enlightened individuals can accept the supernatural community and become a valuable part of it as insiders. However, occasionally a paranoid conspiracy theorist finds out about one of the supernatural species. When this has happened, the solution has not always been one of which a non-violent Buddhist would approve.

For some reason, I found myself more fascinated with the Lunar Lander than usual. I stepped back to get a better view, then stepped back again. I bumped into someone else, back-to-back. I turned to apologize and come face to face with...

"Lisa. Lisa McDuff, right?" I asked, not sounding as suave as I wanted to.

"Mike, wasn't it?" she asked.

"Fancy bumping into to you here, ah, metaphorically speaking," I stammered.

"You seem taken aback by the Lunar Lander," she said, displaying a subtle sense of humor.

"Yes. Somehow science fiction never portrays the clunky, awkward look of the real thing," I said. "Is this your first time... at the Space and Rocket Center that is?" Get a hold of yourself Mike. It's too early for sexual innuendos.

She smiled, displaying winkles in the bridge of her nose, and gave a little giggle. We started walking towards the next exhibit together.

"Do you live in Huntsville?" I asked.

"I'm visiting a friend while I consider my next career move," she said.

"Ah. Many people never find a job that feels like their place in the world. But, those that do have much happier lives." Careful, if I sound too wise she will decide I'm too old for her. "Have you ever considered all of the weird jobs in the world? The art stores sell badger hair paintbrushes. That means someone has a job shaving badgers. How do you get that job? Do you have to start out shaving bunnies and work your way up? And think about the guy who works quality control in a latex factory. Can you see him on a first date describing himself as a condom tester. That sounds like the cheesiest pickup line ever." OK, so there's not much chance I'll sound too old and wise.

We spent the next couple hours walking through the museum together, and making marginally witty remarks.

As we got out to the parking lot, I haltingly asked her if she would like to meet for lunch later in the week. She squeezed my hand a bit and said she would meet me there.

I headed for the UN offices, not for any reason but that it was a place to go until my head cleared a bit. I must have been more distracted than I thought if I was going into work without a compelling reason.

My phone rang as I was driving towards the UN building, and I put it on speaker. It was from the lab that was testing the blood sample. The man on the phone said I should come over to the lab to talk with him. His tone of voice implied that he had found something significant. I took the next exit and doubled back towards HudsonAlpha. This made me feel better, mostly because I hate the stereotype of people that have no life outside of their office.

I entered the front office of the testing lab. The receptionist was short with short black hair and vaguely Asian facial features. She was wearing a silk top cut in a traditional Chinese design. I idly wondered if she had been hired for her experience as a receptionist, or because she went with the Feng shui decor.

"Dr. Howser will see you now," she said, then whispered "Don't say anything about his name."

I was sure he had heard every Doogie Howser joke that could be concocted by five billion Internet users with nothing better to do with their time.

Dr. Howser was a balding, middle-aged man. He wore a dress shirt and pants underneath a white lab coat. His whole appearance screamed "doctor" regardless of what species he might be.

Dr. Howser asked what department I was in at the UN, as a way of checking if I was aware of supernaturals.

"Dr. Brown, you have brought me something truly unique," he said. "The blood sample you brought is from a woman who is a cross breed, from a human father and an empath mother. There have been rumors of the possibility of such an individual existing, but no confirmed cases in the hundreds of years since gene sequencing technology was first invented by a vampire alchemist."

"What else can you tell me about her?" I asked.

"Medically? Is she sick?"

"Anything. What would she look like?" I asked.

"So you don't know her." He rifled through the report saying, "Blue-green eyes, and brown hair. Genetically she tends toward medium height but could be taller or shorter depending upon nutrition as a child. At some point in her life, she will need glasses, and will develop rheumatoid arthritis."

"Will she be healthy, weak, strong?"

"Since we have no previous genetic data on a human-empath hybrid, I have no way of determining that. I can say that it's nearly certain that she will not be able to bear children of her own," he replied.

"Thank you, for your time," I said, preparing to leave.

"One more thing," he interjected. "If at all possible, I would really like to get detailed medical information on her. I can see patients as a genetic councilor, and I can recommend a female family practice physician who would be the perfect person to take care of her and do a detailed physical exam. I'm sure we can find money to cover anything that her health care coverage does not, as a genetic study."

"I'll keep that in mind, if I find her and she doesn't get herself killed first," I replied, then left.

Chapter 9

The Reflection Club is not a private club at all. It is, however, one of the world's more unique bar and grill establishments. The modest sign with gold lettering gives little indication of what is inside. The interior is full of elegant woodwork, red velvet, and leather. There is a series of rooms opening off of a wide hallway that goes back from the street. These include a dining room, a second dining/bar room where smoking is permitted, a quiet room, several conversation rooms (often with a Dungeons & Dragons game going), and several TV viewing rooms, one of which is permanently set to the science fiction channel. The entire establishment is the size of a small conference center. The chairs are chosen for luxury and comfort, unlike most establishments today, which choose chairs that will discourage people from lingering longer than it takes to eat dinner. One rule of the establishment is, no outside food or drink. The fare isn't cheap, but they keep track of past spending and give regular customers significantly better prices. Conservatively dressed waitresses know most of the regular customers by name.

On my way into the club, I passed Sylvia Davidson. Sylvia is the leader of the empath social pecking order in town. She is a very obese woman, with long brown hair. We exchanged pleasantries, then I asked her to stay another minute. She spoke with the calm assuredness of someone who is comfortable and confident in her dominant role in a group. We sat down in one of the conversation rooms. I set my tablet computer aside and ordered my favorite brand of late harvest wine and a bowl of crackers. Having them stock your favorite brands is another advantage of being a regular customer. Sylvia ordered an apple martini, which probably would have little effect on a woman of her mass.

I told Sylvia about Lucy Moore being an empath half-breed. It was clear from the look on her face that this was news to her. She said that she hadn't heard of anything happening in town that matched the description of Lucy or her actions. I asked her to let me know if she heard anything. We exchanged a few more pleasantries, then she went on her way.

I pushed back the reclining chair to relax and think. I updated my information on the Lucy Moore situation. Now I knew what she was. I also knew who she was, but not the important part. What I really needed to know was who she was working for, what she was trying to accomplish, and why.

As I had been enjoying my snack and mulling over motives, the club had been filling. Another Dungeons & Dragons game had gotten started. I could hear a number of conversations around me. One was shoptalk between several men and women, probably people in one of the companies contracted to NASA to develop satellite components. Two women were gossiping about someone else's husband. Further away, I caught snatches of a larger group discussing marriage. I was too far away to pick up if it was a conversation about homosexual marriage, or a discussion of a werewolf-human union. Supernaturals are practiced at talking in public with verbiage that tells each other what they are talking about while allowing humans to jump to the conclusion that the conversation is about something else. Further away, a tall man was having a lively discussion with a woman who had long black hair.

I went back to looking at my work, still aware of the increasing noise around me. I could now hear several heated debates. I go to the conversation rooms partly so I can listen in and get a sense of what is going on in the community. However, this was the most rowdy crowd I had encountered at Reflection. I looked around at the people, half expecting to see a motorcycle gang with pocket protectors. Everyone looked like the usual crowd, many of whom I recognized as regulars.

I considered what was causing the commotion. They weren't all arguing about the same thing, so it probably isn't a hot button issue. My feelings didn't seem to be out of line with the situation, so perhaps not an empathic projection. But then again, empaths can only enhance an existing feeling, and I wasn't in the midst of a face-to-face conflict with anyone. I noticed the black haired woman slapping her date.

Calming this type of group is outside of my abilities. I got up to leave and immediately dropped to the floor. My right leg was useless. I had been hit by an n-gun. An n-gun hit is nonlethal to humans. It makes the nerves stop functioning temporarily if it hits a limb. If it hits your head, you pass out. Some of the less scrupulous vampires use them to make people think they fell asleep, waking up with a little headache and a needle mark that is easily dismissed as a bug bite.

Now things were really getting out of hand. I could hear furniture breaking, punches landing on flesh, and glass shattering. There were bodies hitting the ground and not with the practiced tuck and roll of a martial artist. I heard the low crack of a wall stud breaking and saw a crack appear in the plaster ceiling. Most standard buildings won't stand for long with vampires and werewolves brawling in them. For that matter, with werewolves the average vinyl sided modern home may not survive a lively round of foreplay.

I struggled back to my feet, planning to limp out. I was rewarded with a large gash in my left upper arm, courtesy of a flying broken bottle. Noticing the offending bottle on the floor, I was somewhat indignant that someone had broken a bottle of my favorite dark rum.

At that point the club manager decided to take more drastic measures, with the help of a fire hose. That cooled things off, both literally and figuratively.

On a hunch, I looked around for the woman with long black hair, but she was nowhere to be seen.

Chapter 10

I closed my eyes and focused on relaxing muscles. I started with my feet, then ankles, relaxing them and allowing the tension to flow out of them as if melting down towards the floor. You don't think about how there is a little bit of tension in all of your muscles just to hold yourself in a given position, until you let go of that tension. I continued this relaxation exercise one part of my body at a time, finally ending at my face. It might have taken a minute or twenty. Time doesn't exist here.

Now I focused on the stitched up wound in my upper left arm. I willed the muscles there to relax completely. Still keeping my eyes closed, I experienced it's feeling, it's location, it's size, it's shape. Then I went deeper examining the pain. I looked at where it hurt the most. I examined what the pain was like, as though it could be given a color or a shape. I looked at the very center of the pain, as though looking at it from the inside out. Once I had examined it thoroughly, my mind knew it was there and no longer had a need to keep telling me I was in pain. It no longer registered as pain in my mind. I just felt a pressure there, as though a paperweight had been set on top of my perfectly health arm. This technique also gives a focused relaxation of the capillaries to allow more white blood cells to the wound, and thus helps the wound heal a bit faster.

Meditation that focuses on pain is usually one of the early successes of people learning meditation, provided that the pain isn't so intense that it prevents you from being able to relax and focus you mind. Likewise headaches are more difficult because they throw off your mental focus. It's also a nice type of meditation because you see the immediate result of the pain sensations lessoning. At least for me, dealing with small wounds is much easier than similarly dealing with viruses. Some intermediate meditators will seek out a bit of pain to help them focus this way, thus making acupuncture a particularly relaxing experience for them. Advanced meditators can find the most subtle of focal points, such as the tightness of skin from a few minutes in the sun or the minuscule pressure as your skin changes to develop little crows feet at the corner of your eyes.

It's difficult to say if such meditation techniques help you stay younger looking. Even if so, that would be just a minor side benefit. The real benefit of meditation is the peace of mind and clarity of thoughts it can bring you. Meditation is valuable for it's own sake, but there is even more benefit if it is combined with other types of self-reflection and improvement. Buddhist philosophy gives good suggestions of how to go about this, but even Buddha himself encouraged people to discover what is right for themselves, to discover their personal truths. Scientifically conducted surveys of people's beliefs have shown that on average Buddhist are happier than the practitioners of any other philosophy or religion.

I allowed my now calm mind to move on to other thoughts. The skirmish at the Reflection Club didn't make sense. The issues that people were discussing just weren't emotionally charged enough to bring them to blows. An empath could project strong enough brain waves to enhance a person's present feelings, although there were rules against something like last night in the empath community. Something in the air or water probably would have affected the rest of the club, rather than just that one room. The most likely answer was that our half-empath could project emotions rather strongly, but lacked the training, ability, or moral strength to control it properly.

I again cleared my thoughts with an empty mind meditation. Trying to think about nothing is a lot harder than it sounds. I'm never sure how my mind knows when that is complete, but my eyes pop open of their own accord. I got up feeling calm and refreshed, and then checked the time. A meditation session might take anywhere from ten minutes to two hours. I don't have any sense of how much time has passed until I look at a clock.

I spent the rest of the morning writing a story on neutrino based communication systems. I have to maintain my cover story as a science magazine writer, and a publication deadline was approaching.

The restaurant was busy. They were trying a new promotion having dim sum for lunch on a weekday. It was probably a day that would have been a slow lunch. The interior was a fairly elegant Chinese motif, if slightly belied by the storefront next to a birdhouse store in a strip mall. The waiters pushed around carts with small portions of various types of dumplings, meat pies, and deserts. This was a great way to sample many types of traditional Chinese foods. Many were good, although neither of us liked the tripe. We had fun trying new foods as the conversation flew by.

Lisa had worked various entry-level jobs. She had gone to a community college that had a program in newspaper production. It turned out to be a rather outdated curriculum that did everything with a penknife and opaquing brush on a light table and didn't cover computer graphic arts software. This left her with some student loans and no usable job skills.

Lisa was wearing a long pleated skirt in medium brown and a silk blouse that was dark brown. One strand of her hair didn't want to behave and kept falling in front of her face. She was too distracted by our conversation to have the presence of mind to fix it properly. I was wearing a maroon polo shirt that was tight enough to show off my pecs and biceps.

We discussed books, art, pop culture TV shows, fan films. Both of us would watch TV series on video so that we could watch them in order at a time that is convenient. Likewise we both read book series in order. We had read many of the same fantasy novels, but I read more science fiction, and she reads more detective novels. Both of us fell more on the introverted side of the fence.

A number of times as she was talking, she touched my arm or the back of my hand. I liked the way the bridge of her nose wrinkled when she smiled. A couple times I had strung together such a long run-on sentence that it only ended when I had to inhale again. We were still talking some time after I had paid the bill.

Lisa looked at the time on her cell phone and said she had to go. When we got to the parking lot, I bent close and told her I had enjoyed lunch. She gave me a quick kiss on the cheek, then ran to her car. It took me a few seconds to realize that I was standing in the middle of a parking lot and a car was waiting for me to move.

Chapter 11

Wide steps led up to the main floor entrance to the Von Braun Center concert hall. Outside the doors was a sign saying "Private Function". At the doors were two men. One was gauntly thin, an empath who could determine if you belonged in this meeting. The other was a mountain of muscle, a werewolf to enforce what the empath said. There were no tickets or secret passwords. The two knew many of the town's supernatural community by face. Those they didn't know would be asked what their business was. The empath would be able to tell if someone was bluffing about belonging in the meeting.

Normally, only a couple dozen people showed up at these town meetings. Tonight, two-thirds of the concert hall main floor seats were filled. Because empaths and vampires have extra skills in face-to-face communication, the town meetings don't use any electrical amplification of voices. Everyone sat as close to the front as they could. I sat two-thirds of the way back in the row that was currently filling up, but took the seat on the far right near the isle. The balconies were empty.

The concert hall was luxurious, with padded seats and carpet. It was of a more modern design. Thus there were multiple curved passages to either side leading to additional doors. This allowed a large volume of people to go in and out during intermission. The curved walls leading to those doors improved the acoustics of the room. The stage curtains were closed with a simple podium set in front of them.

As the meeting began, the entrance doors were shut, and an elderly werewolf stepped up to the podium. He was chosen as the mediator because he was both respected and preferred to stay politically neutral. This is not a governing body. It is an open forum to keep lines of communication open. This is valuable because it helps ensure misunderstandings don't get blown out of proportion and do undue harm. The human community would have far fewer conflicts if people on both sides of a given issue similarly spent more time talking with one another and trying to see the others point of view.

The mediator opened the floor for discussion. The first topic brought up for discussion was the marriage of a human man to a werewolf woman. The issue was brought up by an older, conservative werewolf woman. She expressed her concerns that werewolf culture would be tainted by the presence of a human who would thus be allowed at werewolf community gatherings. She also pointed out that he could be seriously injured if he tried to join in the community sporting competitions as a werewolf man would. A werewolf man, known to be a liberal opinion leader in that community, said that their premarital counseling would act as the man's indoctrination into the culture, and he could be given permanent status as an injured werewolf would in sporting events. Fredrick Senburg pointed out that it was not appropriate for vampires to comment on werewolf society, but asked if the human man had been vetted to be given knowledge of the supernatural community as a whole. Butsujo Sing replied that the man was on the path to enlightenment, interested in werewolf culture, and seemed unthreatened by the other races. The woman that started the conversation said that she thought the marriage could proceed with the caveats mentioned. This was met with a chorus of sharp barks, the werewolf equivalent of saying "aye". Sometimes it's best to just run with the stereotype. A summary news item would go out to an international werewolf publication online. Once decided, the man would be fully accepted into werewolf culture by all who had initially voiced opinions on both sides of the issue. Individual sporting competitions aside, the werewolf community had a pack mentality that was close knit and cooperative. In spite of their animalistic nature, werewolves were in some ways more civilized than humans.

Greg Turner brought up the conversation that someone named Lucy Moore is looking into evidence of supernaturals helping human scientists. Since I am human, it's considered respectful for me to allow the conversation to go a while before saying something. Several other people brought up other stories of her activities. One empath woman expressed concern that she is in a high security position with trigger-happy humans who may shoot first if she is exposed. A werewolf in a grumpy mood made a comment about empaths being helpless weaklings, which was said a little too loud so quite a few others heard it. This spawned a rash of racial accusations. I started to have dark thoughts of racial accusations myself. However, that second voice of mindfulness was letting me know something wasn't right. Friendly ribbing based on racial stereotypes was common between friends, but these comments were too hateful to be justified by the relative minor severity of the situation.

I looked around. At the back, staying a few seats away from anyone else was a woman in a black jacket with the hood pulled over her head. I could see a bit of long black hair flowing out of the open front of the jacket and over an emerald green dress. I got out of my seat, moved back a couple rows, and started moving slowly towards her. The arguments were getting louder, and people were getting out of their seats.

When I got a few seats away from her, she noticed me out of the corner of her eye and turned. Her features matched the description I had been given. The look on her face was simultaneously angry and hurt, like a high school girl that had been dumped the day before the prom. My gut said I had the right woman.

"What do you want, Lidia?" I asked.

"I want people to pay," she replied.

"Because you were put up for adoption?" I asked.

"Because there was no one there to tell me. To tell me what a freak I am. Why my emotions affect those around me," she said.

"But you know now, don't you?"

"I'm like an empath, but different. Still a freak. Probably why I was given away. What am I, anyway?"

"You are unique. Your mother was an empath, and your father was human," I replied.

Now everyone was up in arms. Many had pulled out n-guns concealed as laser pointers, car door openers, and pistol shaped cigarette lighters. A number more were carrying conventional firearms, and a few had prototype weaponry the capability of which I could only guess. The empaths were heading for cover. N-guns were nonlethal to all races except empaths, who could get permanent brain damage from them. Brain damage is a fate worse than death for an empath.

If I didn't do something to stop Lidia's angry empathic projections soon, a lot of people were going to be hurt or killed tonight. I had a concealed n-gun on my key ring, but couldn't guess how badly it would hurt her.

"You need to stop this," I said. "People are going to get hurt, or killed."

"What can I do?" she asked. "It isn't my fault they want to kill each other."

"Yes it is," I said. "You are projecting your anger and making them angry. You need to turn it off."

"I can't. I don't know how," she replied.

Great! She was perhaps the most powerful empaths I had ever heard of, and she couldn't control it.

"What are you?" she asked. "Are you here to kill me, to lock me up, to betray me? Is it all a big act?"

"I'm a regular human. I'm here to protect the supernatural community. I don't want to hurt you." I said.

"No, you just want to be nice to me, so you can stab me in the back. Well guess what, if this crowed explodes there is a good chance you will catch a bullet in the cross fire as well!" she shouted. The bridge of her nose wrinkled as she gave a malicious smile.

My hand closed over the n-gun in my pocket. People had separated into camps and were crouching amongst the auditorium seats. Those the maddest were hollering "fire" to goad others into taking action with them. Recent events were running through my head, pieces of the puzzle falling into place. If I was going to do something, I had to do it now.

I grabbed her arm, pulled her towards me, and gave her a firm kiss on the lips, catching her with her mouth open for her next accusation. She kissed me back instinctively, then remembered she was angry and tried to pull away. I had my other arm around the small of her back. I kept kissing her, while filling my mind with every possible thought of love, and probably a few of lust as well. There was no more shouting. The crowd was calming down.

That first kiss went on forever. She relaxed and pressed her body against me. Both of us forgot where we were and who was around us. As the kiss ended, she collapsed against my chest. Now the crowd was quiet. Not just friendly, but down right amorous.

I gently pulled Lucy/Lidia/Lisa, leading her away. I had to get her out of there and soon. I really, really did not want to see a couple of four hundred pound empaths having intercourse bent over the auditorium seats.

Chapter 12

Lidia (Liz) Macey, aka Lisa McDuff, aka Lucy Moore was learning the great truths of the world, one after another. I thought she was handling it rather well. This was also giving me a chance to see more of the real her, underneath her personas. As best as I could tell, the real her, the Liz, was probably closer to Lisa than to Lucy. It was also my judgment that her multiple personas were a carefully crafted move to allow her to investigate her origins, not a multiple personality disorder.

Sylvia Davidson had been in the Von Braun Center that night. She had some idea what Liz was capable of. Sylvia was also one of the most powerful empaths in town, which is why she received so much respect in the empath community.

I had been banished to the barn while Sylvia worked with Liz. I paced around like a 1950s father waiting outside the maternity ward. I imagined it must be the empathic equivalent of finding Tarzan, incredibly strong but uncivilized.

I turned around to begin my next tour of pacing and came face to face with Sylvia. She could be surprisingly quiet for such a large woman.

"Kill her," said Sylvia.

At first I thought this was a bit abrupt for a savvy political player. Then I realized that she was using the fewest words possible to make it difficult for Liz to hear her thoughts.

"Obviously, she can project." I said.

Sylvia nodded with look that said she thought I was a moron.

"Can she receive?" I asked.

Sylvia nodded yes.

"Can she control it?"

Sylvia nodded no.

I had to think a minute about that one. Lidia could walk the earth causing riots or orgies as her mood dictated. She could spend her life in some remote area, isolated from all sentient species. Any surgery or drugs that could repress her abilities would turn her into a braindead vegetable. I don't like no-win scenarios. When the odds are against you, make your best attempt at the long odds solution.

"Let me try something," I said.

I spent the next hour teaching Lidia meditation techniques. Not controlling breathing is difficult. You can control your breathing, or your body will control it's own breathing when you aren't thinking about it. However focusing on experiencing your breathing without consciously controlling it is difficult because the conscious control mechanism takes over when you think about your breathing. Once she had learned to consciously not control her breathing, I suggested that she analogously not control her empathic projections. This was more difficult since I couldn't describe what to do, but Sylvia had some suggestions. Lidia didn't have great control, but she showed enough improvement to make Sylvia hopeful.

"Congratulations." Sylvia said to me with a big smile. "You have a new room mate. I'm sure you will be a good teacher."

"I'm glad the idea has merit, but I'm hardly an expert on meditation techniques," I replied.

"You are the one she has connected with," Sylvia pointed out. "Your home is a comforting environment far from the nearest neighbor. Also, this is the plan that I am willing to recommend that the supernatural community accept."

I looked at Lidia with her eyes closed in meditation. She looked very young, too young to be facing so many new things without someone to be there for her. It should be someone who would be her friend, not just an impersonal social worker. She was also very pretty when she was being herself, especially when she smiled and the bridge of her nose wrinkled up. I liked her natural brown hair better than the black wig.

Your mind is made to look into the future. Sometimes it only looks a few seconds into the future, as when it gives you a tiny vision of what will happen if you aren't careful with a kitchen knife. Your mind also gives you predictions of possible futures, such as what your life might be like if you do or don't get married, or if you make a certain career choice. A few times in my life, I have had one of these future predictions with such a high probability of coming true that my subconscious was nearly knocking me over with confidence and certainty. Now was one of those times. I was certain that I could teach her, and certain that it would be a tumultuous experience as she explored the depths of powerful emotions like anger, hate, love, and lust. And I was absolutely certain that going down this path would result in the two of us being lovers.

Helping her learn to control her abilities would be a massive job, in size, in difficulty, and in emotional drama. Fortunately for the world and for Liz, as I was coming to think of her, I'm a really self-sacrificing guy.

Book 2
Supernatural Feelings

Chapter 1

Empath's log: Star date, uh, what the heck is a star date? OK. My name is Liz Macey. Well you would call yourself Liz too if someone named you Lidia. I'm an empath, well actually a half empath, which is... Let's come back to that later. So I just got this new gadget. It's a smart phone that can record my thoughts. When I think the words "Empath's log" it starts recording. I'm going to try an experiment doing diary entries in real time as things happen. I'm not sure if my impressions as things happen are the same as how I would write about them in a diary later in the evening. So this might be interesting. Or at least it might relieve the boredom some. Oh, Mike's calling. Empath out.

Mike Brown is my roommate, teacher, mentor, and hopefully soon to be lover. He is medium height with brown hair in a basic short men's business haircut. He is well muscled, but wears clothes that hide that fact when he is working. He came in and said we have to go. I grabbed my purse and jokingly asked him if there was trouble in Gotham City. He said that Christine Mills called. A call from a vampire police detective sounds like a bit of excitement in our day. I was wearing new jeans and a Mexican peasant blouse, which will have to do, since Mike looked like he was in a hurry. I grabbed a pair of running shoes since a crime scene may not be the best place for heels. I don't remember the Vogue Fashion Guide covering proper attire for supernatural crime solving.

"Where are we going?" I asked as we headed for Mike's boring silver sedan. Mike was carrying the rather pathetic looking, old briefcase that goes with him on all work trips.

"To a golf course." he replied.

Empath's log: Yes! Nailed it with the running shoes. Celebrate your victories where you can get 'em, girls. Empath out.

"What's at a golf course?" I asked.

"Little white balls being abused by middle-aged balding men," replied Mike, being a smart Alec today.

"I'll abuse you, when we get home," I replied.

"It's a murder scene, so someone got abused," Mike said.

"Details?"

"It's an unusual murder scene."

I understand the whole contentment and patience bringing happiness thing, but you would think he could at least express a bit of excitement. Actually, I could empathically sense that he was a bit anxious. Also, the car was moving faster than Mike usually drove, apparently intent on shaving a few minutes off the half-hour drive from our woodland home into Huntsville, Alabama. We passed a small, bright green hybrid electric car with a bumper sticker that read, "NASA is out of this world," and another that said, "My other car is a Space Shuttle." We passed a tan minivan with Apple computer stickers in the rear window, two big apples and three little apples. Huntsville is kind of an oasis of geekdom in the Deep South.

Empath's log: Liz Macey, the hard bitten crime fighter put her hand on the nine-millimeter cannon at her side and gave the crime boss a stare that could melt lead. Yeah, I could see the excitement in being a cop. But I'm not sure I could take wearing a uniform for a few years before making detective. I think someone designed those uniforms to make your butt look big. This is the first time Mike Mycroft Brown (long story) has brought me on one of his field jobs. I'm not sure if that makes me his sidekick, or a trainee intern. He'll regret it if I hear any rookie jokes. Empath out.

We went south on Memorial Parkway, past the Von Braun Center. Huntsville's conference center, arena, and concert hall is named after Wernher von Braun, one of the developers of the V-2 rocket, who then came to Huntsville to be the director of NASA's Marshall Space Flight center and develop the Saturn V rocket engines. A couple miles further south we pulled in behind a line of police cars parked at the edge of a golf course. There was a black and white military rocket on display at one corner of the golf course.

As we walked up, the forensics guy was putting away a large camera. The coroner and his assistant were attempting to pull a gurney across the green and discussing the merits of gurneys with off road tires. There were a number of uniformed officers standing around, and Christine was standing by the body, overseeing the whole operation. Christine somehow managed to look stunning in a pants suit. Christine always looked stunning. Perhaps you can be a supernatural crime fighter and shop from the Vogue Fashion Guide.

Christine is a vampire. No, vampires don't melt or sparkle in the sun. They are evolved from humans to have a long life. That evolution is nearly perfect except for needing human blood because bone marrow is the one part of their body that hasn't evolved to live a very long time. I don't follow all the sciencey explanation, but it's related to the fact that the bone marrow is most sensitive, which is why people get leukemia from too much radiation. The details of that involve vampire bodies having a different way of handling telomeres, which limit how many times a cell can divide as a natural defense against cancer, but also limit how long the body can live... which is about where I fell asleep during one of Mike's supernatural science lectures. Since vampires need human blood to stay alive, they have to prey on humans either by being stronger or by being sexually alluring. A little natural selection, and you get vampires that are drop dead gorgeous, emit human pheromones, and have strong, wiry muscles.

I opened my senses, looking at body language, listening to inflections in people's voices, and listening to what my empathic sense was telling me. No one seemed too upset about the death of this man, who was in a bright orange jumpsuit. The upper and lower sections of the body were at an odd angle to one another. Some of the uniformed officers didn't want to get too close to the body, but they were more afraid of Christine. I don't think they knew Christine was a vampire. She just has two hundred years of practice letting men know who is in charge. Christine noticed my presence but didn't say anything.

Christine filled us in, "Keith Voss went to jail for assaulting his girlfriend. He slipped away from a work crew yesterday. This morning he was found here. It looks like his body was cut in two. When they go out on work crews, the zipper of the coveralls is sealed with a blue tie wrap. The tie wraps in that shade of blue are only sold to law enforcement. The tie wrap and coveralls are still intact. How do you cut a body in two without removing or cutting the clothing?"

Mike spoke up, "This is a lousy place to dump a body, in sight of a busy street. The murderer must have been forced to dump the body here in a hurry. Do you know where he was killed?"

"We haven't found the primary crime scene yet," said Christine.

"Wait a minute," I piped up, "How do you know he wasn't killed right here?"

"He has red clay on the bottom of his shoes," Mike pointed out.

There was no red clay in sight on the golf course. Crime shows often have the forensics lab find something really unusual on the body that tells them exactly where it came from. There is red clay about an inch below everything within fifty miles. That didn't limit the possibilities much.

The coroner announced that Keith Voss died late last night. I wondered if the coroner knew about supernatural species? It would seem logical that a coroner could help cover up certain suspicious deaths. When he and his assistant lifted the body onto the gurney, I got a strong whiff of dead corpse.

Empath's log: Liz Macey, the hard bitten crime fighter, ran to the edge of the golf course and breathed hard to keep from loosing her breakfast. OK. At least I managed to avoid that embarrassment in front of Christine. I think I'll take coroner off my list of potential career choices. I can earn enough money to put food on the table as a beautician, but I'm not nuts over working constantly on my feet for the rest of my life. Also, it seems like the world's only half-empath should have a more iconic career option. Empath out.

Mike and Christine agreed to work on different angles of the case. Christine would investigate the usual crime stuff, like who would want to kill Keith Voss. Mike would investigate how the body got cut in two. Mike officially works for the United Nations as a liaison to the supernatural community, and sometimes policing it. I think this undercover James Bond thing is kind of cool, although he really needs a hot sports car. I know he carries a concealed n-gun, which can interrupt nerve impulses. I don't know if he has any other cool gadgets.

Mike said he needed to organize his thoughts about the death. He suggested walking across the street to sit at a picnic table in a small park. As we crossed the street, he took my hand and asked if I was all right. Mike is a really kind and caring person. The first time we met, I looked into his eyes, stumbled, and literally fell into his arms. A short time after that was an incident where he could have shot me, but instead he kissed me. That incident occurred because I didn't know how to control my empathic powers, and people could have gotten hurt. The supernatural community could have had me killed or isolated, but instead Mike convinced them to let him try to teach me control through meditation and other practices. Perhaps the fact that he isn't a supernatural only makes him foolish enough to think he can.

We walked over to a small park. There was a memorial for people killed in action, and a large jungle gym. Only a couple children were playing while a pair of mothers chatted on a bench near the climbing equipment. Mike set his tablet computer and a keyboard out on the picnic table. I know he usually likes to think at coffee shops, which is where I first met him. However, he was trying to keep me from being around too many people for two long, as it was going to be a long day regardless. I appreciated that he was thinking of me, but I also felt bad that he was constantly organizing his life around me.

Mike went to a web site I had seen before. It was an email hosting service that people pay for in order to get extra services like no advertising and extra security. It was a legitimate email site, although not very popular. Once in his account, he went to another area, typed a second password and got to the hidden, unadvertised layer of the site. It was an online portal to the supernatural community. The supernatural portion of the site had a Voodoo theme with Voodoo dolls as buttons for various types of information. The separate theme for the supernatural portion of the site was supposed to remind people which area they are in to avoid sending sensitive information to the wrong people. I watched the children playing and listened as Mike narrated his search efforts.

Mike was talking to himself as much as to me as he said, "Selective cutting? No, that's about trees. Selective grinding? No, that's about dentistry. Cutting flesh? Here is something about plasma surgeon's tools that cut flesh but not bone. Here is a reference to hair being cut by a malfunctioning cloaking device, which some supernaturals use to hide their activities. Cutting titanium with high pressure water."

"Cut class. Cut corners. Cut the cheese," I suggested to lighten the mood before he got too frustrated.

Empath's log: What would it be like to be a surgeon? You deftly cut into a body, doing things that would make many people cringe at the thought. Then again, there would be days you have to tell the patient's family that their loved one had died in spite of doing everything known to man or werewolf. I think that would be just too devastating for me to handle. Empath out.

As Mike packed up his mobile office, I looked at the monument and asked him why people join the military. It had never been appealing to me. With two seconds thought, Mike came up with a well-worded lecture on the subject. He's good at generating encyclopedia articles on the spur of the moment. He talked about some people wanting a very structured environment, a way to get out of a bad neighborhood, and a way to pay for college. There is also a streak of self-sacrificing altruism in human nature, people that are willing to die to protect the constitutional freedoms that America is founded on, and people who just want excitement and adventure. I can see how sitting in an office would not be the right career for someone, but going to war to avoid it seems like a bit much.

We walked back to the car and headed out. The next stop was Dreamland Bar-B-Que Ribs, one of a number of good local bar-b-que chains. In the parking lot was a pickup with an odd looking contraption in the back. After staring for a minute, I realized it was a moonbuggy. The moonbuggy race is a competition for engineering students with requirements similar to those of the car that was taken to the moon. They design a pedal car, which must fold up to fit within a certain amount of space. The pedal cars then race on a bumpy cement course at the Space and Rocket Center, which is designed to simulate the surface of the moon.

The interior of Dreamland was a rustic décor featuring rough-cut wood. There were various antiques, license plates, and sports team memorabilia on the walls. College football is big in Alabama, especially the rivalry between Auburn University and the University of Alabama. The décor also included an experimental rocket model about two feet long, which seemed a bit out of place. I could just imagine some redneck trying to use a Stinger Missile for duck hunting.

We got a takeout order with enough ribs, corn, and banana pudding for five people then headed home. Home is an old stone farmhouse nestled in a woodland grove with some with some overgrown fields that apparently failed to be sufficiently profitable.

We got home just minutes before Sylvia Davidson arrived. Sylvia is kind of the unofficial head of the empath community in town, and one of my teachers. Sylvia is incredibly obese, and was wearing a layered blue dress that might have doubled as a pavilion tent at a renaissance fair, with heavy blue eye shadow to match. Some empaths, like Sylvia, use a sugar high to enhance their empathic abilities. She polished off three orders of food and the tail end of the ribs and pudding that were too much for me to eat.

I was born to an empath mother and a human father. Supernaturals and humans aren't supposed to be able to have children, but no one told nature that. I'm the only known example. Humans have only had gene sequencing technology for a couple decades, but alchemists have had that technology for centuries. Alchemists are the scientists that are supernaturals or humans that are insiders in the supernatural community. I'm the only scientifically proven half-breed in the centuries that gene sequencing has been available.

I was put up for adoption. I don't know if my father even knew about me. Being raised by humans left me to figure out the empath thing for myself. I can sense other people's emotions and project my emotions to them. Unfortunately, I couldn't figure out how to not project my emotions more than a little on my own. There was a lot of emotional drama in my high school years. If I was mad, everyone got mad. If I lusted a boy, he couldn't help but to lust me as well. This created a number of bad situations. By college, I had learned to distance myself from other people and must have naturally projected the introverts desire to be left alone.

My ability to sense when people are lying allowed me to pick up clues that there are other empaths, and other supernaturals like vampires and werewolves. This also led to some anger issues because there was this whole supernatural community and I wasn't part of it but should be. I followed those clues to Huntsville, Alabama with it's larger than average supernatural community to find some answers. There was some drama when my empathic projection almost started a riot, and then an orgy. A less understanding person might have locked me away, but Mike convinced Sylvia that he could make some progress teaching me to control my abilities and integrating me into the supernatural community. Mike Brown is a normal human, but an exceptional one with his Ph.D. in physics, meditation abilities, and martial arts experience. Before Mike took me in, Sylvia told me in private that they would do all they could to help me learn to control my abilities, but if they failed she would consider killing me the most humane option. I've never told that part to Mike.

Mike kissed me on the cheek then went off to change the oil in the mower and cut back weeds the size of small trees, while I had my lesson with Sylvia.

Empath's log: I dated Mike a couple times before he knew I was an empath. After I started living with him, the relationship development came to a halt at the kissing friends stage. I know Mike doesn't want to take advantage of me when he is my teacher, but come on, we're both adults and we would both enjoy the arrangement more if we spent some time together in bed. I've been flirting with him verbally and letting him get extra glimpses of skin. He's the first man I've ever met that could resist my empathic lust projections for more than ten minutes, although I know it arouses him. Empath out.

"Let's discuss selectivity. How do you send an empathic projection to one person without affecting others?" Sylvia asked as she began our lesson.

"I thought projections were equal strength in all directions," I said.

"Yes, but not everyone is equally susceptible to them," she replied.

"So can you target human's without targeting werewolves?" I asked.

"Not like that." she said. "A person who is very focused on something is less receptive. However, people occasionally check their surroundings in order to keep track of what is going on around them. A little flicker of their eyes usually accompanies that flicker in their attention. When they do that they are more receptive to empathic projections. If you project in half second bursts when a person's attention falters, you can project mostly to a single person in a crowded room."

I spent the next hour trying to send out little flickers of empathic projection. Some of these were emotions, which could be sensed by humans, or supernaturals, or sometimes other mammals. I also tried sending individual words or a short sentences, which could be received by another empath, my empathic smart phone, and on rare occasions can be heard by someone else who has a close personal connection with an empath.

An hour of this left me emotionally and mentally exhausted. I fell asleep on the couch minutes after Sylvia left.

I woke when Mike kissed me on the cheek and said, "Time to wake up, Sleeping Beauty."

He had made dinner. Well, kind of. He microwaved two meals in black plastic trays, and poured glasses of milk. I was still groggy and he let me eat in silence.

After dinner, Mike pointed out that we needed to dress up a bit for our evening's activities. I put on a light dress in multiple shades of green. It had one short sleeve with a diagonal neckline, and a diagonal hemline, leaving my left shoulder and my right leg bare. Mike put on beige dress pants, a white silk shirt with open collar, and a tan sport coat. I felt the curve of his pecs underneath his shirt as I gave him a little peck on the lips. He might pull off the James Bond thing yet, if he would ditch the glasses.

"So, am I going to see someone get their throat ripped out?" I asked as he drove.

"No biting in Vampkido," he replied. "The vampire martial art form is judged both on physical blows and on style. There are extra points assigned for grappling an opponent in a sexually suggestive position."

"Sounds like bitchy ballerinas," I said.

"I'll let you decide that for yourself," Mike said with a laugh.

"How many people will be there?" I asked, starting to get worried about controlling my empathic projections.

"Tonight's tournament is for beginners only, so there will be a fairly small number of spectators," he replied. "It's a good opportunity for you to practice holding your empathic projections in check around people who are excited. Just let me know if you feel it's time to leave."

We drove to a warehouse by the airport. A company that had reduced the size of their Huntsville operation owned the building. Someone must have an arrangement with the company to use it, without too much explanation as to how it is being used. The hunky vampire guy at the door seemed to know Mike and barely glanced at me. It's kind of cool to think of us walking calmly past the iconic horror film villain.

We walked up the stairs to a second storey balcony that looked down on the warehouse floor. There were folding chairs along the balcony railing. The balcony was large and the audience was small, so everyone had a front row seat pulled up to the balcony railing. Vampires are big into good looks and style, so everyone was dressed for a ritzy evening on the town. On the warehouse floor, a sixty foot diameter round ring had been constructed. The sides of the ring were eight feet high. Within the ring was a collection of obstacles up to five feet high. The ring floor, walls, and obstacles were all covered in what looked like an inch of gray foam rubber.

Contestants were called at random. First up in the ring were Theodore Edwards and Wendy Bowman. On deck were Nicki Lewis and Marta Rodriguez. After that Timothy Stokes and Paul Doyle.

"They let men compete against women?" I asked Mike.

"Don't try to apply your own cultural thinking to other cultures...or species," he replied. "Vampire women can handle themselves just fine in a fight."

Theodore and Wendy were positioned at opposite sides of the ring. They were dressed to look good, similar to ice skating outfits but without the flesh colored tights underneath. Theodore was bare-chested with tight black shorts and back running shoes. He was medium height with short black hair slicked back to mirror the sleekness of his shorts. Wendy had a baby blue short sleeve top, bare midriff, baby blue skort and running shoes. She had an athletic build, and was nearly the same height as her opponent. Wendy had medium length blond hair in permed spiral curls that made her look good and kept the hair out of her eyes.

A buzzer signaled the beginning of the match, and both of them started running. They made beautiful leaps onto and off of the obstacles. At this point, I was still thinking it fit more in the bitchy ballerinas category than the martial arts genre. Both started altering their path to create close passes between the two. On one of these passes they went by one another just as Wendy had both feet on the ground and Theodore was in the midst of a leap. At the last second, Wendy's arm shot out, clothes lining Theodore under the chin. His head snapped back and his feet kept going. He hit the ground with a loud thud and I thought I could feel it in the floor of the building. That blow could have killed a human, but the wiry vampire, with nice pecs I might add, spun back up to his feet and reversed direction to chase his lovely opponent.

Wendy made the beginner's mistake of pausing to see how Theodore recovered from the fall. That bought Theodore a couple seconds so he was now right behind her. Wendy dodged around obstacles, but didn't otherwise utilize them. On one of her sharp turns, Theodore went straight and accelerated past her. As he passed, he gave her bottom a loud slap, thus earning a style point for Theodore. Wendy didn't immediately realize that Theodore was ahead of her. She ran right into his arms. Her feet kept going as he lowered her towards the ground in a lover's embrace with his open mouth on the side of her neck. Theodore didn't extend his fangs and was surprisingly gentle with her. The crowd cheered at the jugular vein move.

Wendy kicked one foot off the ground, throwing her body over Theodore's. She landed behind him, temporarily immobilizing him in a half Nelson as she ran her tongue up the side of his neck to his ear, bringing another cheer from the small crowd of spectators. Theodore spun out of the hold and two faced one another. The fight was now a series of Aikido-like holds and reversals. Every movement was carried out to its full arc and extension, thus bringing a beautiful if dangerous rhythm to the fight. Several times one of them broke a hold by throwing their leg in a circle peaking straight up in the air as a vertical split. A couple times Theodore put a foot on one of the obstacles to accelerate his sideways movement.

Empath's log: I feel the adrenaline building in my body. My heart rate is faster, and my skin is flushed. I have to keep my focus to keep from sending out empathic projections. Breathe. Become aware of my body, the feel of my dress, the chair, my shoes. Now I expand my awareness to the battle below, smell, light, and other spectators. I think I feel the floor bowing as Sylvia Davidson sits down in a chair behind us. Her movements don't mirror those of the other spectators. She's here to check on me, not watch the event. Most of the spectators just leaned forward, anticipating the end of the fight. Empath out.

Wendy flipped Theodore to the ground with a Judo throw. On his way down, Theodore kicked one of the obstacles to give himself a sliding landing. Wendy leaped on top of him, but Theodore tugged on her, adding to her sideways inertia so she overshot sliding flat on the ground. Theodore was coming down on top of her even as she came to rest with her legs underneath an overhanging obstacle from mid-thigh down. Theodore had his chest across her with his elbow on the ground so she was trapped on her back with one elbow pinned to her side. He wasn't putting weight on her, and she could have gotten out if she could slide out from under the obstacle. As it was, her one free arm just couldn't do enough. Theodore ignored the one free hand trying to push, twist or punch him. He lovingly stared into her eyes and idly played with a strand of her hair. The buzzer sounded because of Wendy being immobilized. Theodore won the match, not by superior strength, but by superior use of the obstacles and getting more style points.

The next match was between the two women, Nicki Lewis and Marta Rodriguez. Their match started out with incredibly beautiful leaps into the air. Both of them tried to rack up some style points with series of rather erotic holds. First I felt myself blushing deeply. Then I gave Mike a punch in the arm because I could almost see the sexual fantasy forming in his head. He winked at me, and I blushed some more. Once one of the women thought she had the advantage, she gave her opponent a sharp elbow to the face. After that, the fight became more vicious and brutal than you would expect from any pair of men. Both were panting hard. Vampire muscles have a better strength to weight ratio than human muscles, but their endurance is worse. Marta won, but they both looked so bloodied that it looked like a lose-lose situation to me. Both would probably kick back a pint of blood and be practically unscratched by morning.

The next bout was between a pair of men, Timothy Stokes and Paul Doyle. Their fighting styles were distinctly different. Timothy relied heavily on a variety of fast kicks. Those kicks could have been bone crushing if they had landed squarely, but trying to kick Paul turned out to be about like trying to kick smoke. Paul's ability to dodge and use his opponent's inertia reminded me of an anecdote about how fighting the inventor of Judo was like trying to fight an empty jacket. I thoroughly enjoyed watching the two shirtless men with their chiseled muscles glistening from the sweat. I had heard that vampires give off human pheromones for sexual attraction when they exert themselves. This seems to be an evolutionary adaptation to shake the focus of a human opponent and attract willing victims. I must have been picking up those pheromones as I began to idly fantasize. By the end of the bout, I was rooting for Paul, who gave a graceful bow to the audience and blew a kiss in my general direction.

I was enjoying the event, and being surprisingly successful at controlling my empathic projections. However the strain of that empathic control was starting to wear me down. As we waited for the next fight to begin, I began to yawn and shake my head to stay awake. Mike mercifully suggested that it was time to go. As we packed up to go, I noticed that Sylvia had already left. A few seconds before we would have been out of the viewing area, Mike's phone rang.

Mike's end of the phone conversation got my attention. "Ghost? How big?... No I doubt it's an astronaut ghost. Who was nearby?... Well, that's a new one for the transgender community. We'll be there in ten."

As we were about to walk out the door, Mike noticed Christine talking to another woman. Christine was in an evening dress. She obviously had evening plans that didn't involve police work. Mike and Christine talked a minute, and then she said she would meet us at the Space and Rocket Center. We pulled out of the parking lot with Christine's baby blue T-Bird right behind us.

Chapter 2

As Mike drove the few miles to our next destination, I closed my eyes and imagined an invisible plane, like a sheet of glass, slowly moving from my toes up to my head. As the plane moved across each muscle group, I consciously let go of the tension in the muscles. Once my entire body was relaxed, I visualized a blank, white wall right in front of me, stretching out infinitely in all directions. This type of relaxation and empty mind meditation is like a super power nap. It washes away fatigue, allowing you to be alert and functioning hours longer before you need to sleep.

We passed the vertical Saturn 5 rocket replica and a large glass walled building with a real Saturn 5 running the length of it. The next freeway exit allowed us to double back and into the parking lot of the Space and Rocket Center. It's not as big as the Disney attractions, but the center and the adjoining space camp are a Mecca for space enthusiasts.

It was after hours, but the main building had been rented out for a private function. The person on the front desk waved us by when Christine and Mike flashed badges. I didn't know Mike even had an official badge. I suppose it comes in handy for situations like this. For that matter, how many situations like this are there? A couple images of crossdressing ghosts came to mind, and I started to giggle. Christine ignored me and Mike gave me a sideways glance, no doubt wondering if I had had too much for one day.

We crossed a foyer with brightly colored tile. Suspended from the ceiling was an early airplane that looked like it belonged in a steampunk movie. We went up a flight of steps then entered a massive hall that had a Saturn V moon rocket lying down in sections. It was up on scaffolding so you could walk right under it. I immediately clamped down on my empathic senses as I was hit with a massive wave of humanity with their emotions running high. Around the edges of the hall were tables with punch and cookies and some party decorations on the walls. There were posters and fliers concerning issues relevant the community of gay, lesbian, crossdressing, and a few things I had never heard of.

The occupants of the room drew your attention far more than the massive rocket suspended above your head. They were milling around in animated conversations, most with drinks in hand. A few were making out in corners of the room that weren't nearly well enough concealed. Some were readily identified, such as pairs of gay men in flamboyant silk shirts with their arms around one another. However, there were some that I couldn't identify as man or woman even with my empathic senses catching their emotional state. This was a new experience for me. Men and women think differently and use their emotions differently, on top of the range of introvert, extrovert, emotional, analytical, etc. I can always tell when someone is romantically intrigued with someone else, and up until now I could always tell male from female without needing my eyes to provide clues. I was also picking up a lot of angry self-entitlement vibes in the room and only a few that were completely at peace with who and what they were.

We were met by a "woman" who was six foot one, dressed in a vintage gown, and looked like she was no stranger to the bench press. She identified herself as Annie McBride and took us to a desert table part way down the hall on the left. Standing there were a few guests who were more upset than the rest. First to talk with us was a medium height woman with a pale complexion and short, straight black hair. She was dressed in running shoes, jeans, and a flannel shirt. She was probably an A cup or smaller and I'm pretty sure she wasn't wearing a bra.

"We were getting desert. There was a soft light over in that doorway. By the plants," she explained. "It was transparent. Barely visible. A man, medium height, dark pants, white shirt. You saw right through him. Could barely see him at all."

"His features were slightly blurry. You wouldn't recognize a face even if you had known him," This came from a second woman in a floral print party dress that would have been in style in the 1950s. She stood a step behind the first woman and kept a hand on the first

85

woman's shoulder at all times, even when they were dismissed by Christine and moved off to join the other guests. The empathic story was that it was an interdependent relationship, but one that worked well for both of them.

The other guests that had seen it gave pretty much the same story. One was sure the ghost was wearing a large Western style belt buckle, which was out of place with the black and white outfit. Apparently the ghost moved its arms then winked out of existence, if it had existed in the first place. It got boring listening to the same story in different words, even twice, but Mike and Christine stayed focused on every word and nuance of body language. Noting similarities and differences between witness accounts was an important part of their job.

Empath's log: What would it be like to be a rocket scientist? You would spend all of your time trying to plan for anything that could happen, and a few more just in case some physics theory or science fiction novel was right. I may not be your average social butterfly, but I don't think a life of technical details is right for me either. Empath out.

Having interviewed the witnesses, Mike, Christine and I conferred off to the side. I told them that all of the witnesses were telling what they believe to be the truth. The conversation continued with the premise that these people did see something. It's nice to work with people who respect your skills. Mike and Christine are able to come up with a few ideas of things that would look like a ghost, like holograms and projection on a sheet of glass. They don't seem to be giving any thought to the idea of it being a real ghost. Apparently a lot of the world's ghost stories are actually hoaxes to keep humans away from places the supernaturals don't want them. Most of these have stopped since it became popular culture for young people to investigate ghosts following role models like Scooby Doo and Ghost Hunters. These days, the supernatural community scares people away with signs warning of mold, chemical spills, radon, etc.

Christine got a call then said, "That was the night coroner. He's an apprentice alchemist, who likes to call people with important news. I think it's partly because he gets lonely on the night shift. The body found on the golf course was indeed cut in half. What's more interesting is that the wound was partly cauterized. Also, it was inflicted while the victim was still alive."

Mike got that far away look that means he is thinking out an idea. I know it's useless trying to get him to talk about it until he is ready, so I tried to make myself useful.

"If this was done with a big sheet of glass, could there be marks where it was slid or rolled across the floor?" I asked.

We started looking around. There were no marks on the floor. Behind the nearby doors was a service hallway that was not open to the public. There was nothing of interest in the hallway. Mike estimated where equipment would have to be located to generate a hologram, but several of those locations had enough dust that they couldn't have been touched in months. I was examining the baseboards and floor along the walls, when I found something interesting.

"Take a look at this," I called to Christine and Mike. "There are leaves from this big potted plant on the floor behind it. If you stand next to the wall, you can see that the plant was sliced along a line."

Mike looked at it from next to the wall, from above, and kneeling down, then said, "Actually, I think it's cut in a gradual arc in two directions, like a section of a large sphere."

Christine pointed out, "A sword blade would only arc in one direction. Also, the cuts are too clean to be done by a single slice of even the sharpest katana. Note how the ends of the cuts are slightly singed. You could devise a device with a curved heating element to cut like this, but none come to mind. Anything meeting that description would be pretty conspicuous. It would look like a curved light saber."

We scratched out heads over the plant mystery for another minute then headed back through the party crowd towards the reception desk.

Empath's Log: I could be a party planner. It doesn't need a lot of technical skills, just a sense of style, contacts with caterers, and the ability to organize things and keep them on schedule. I suppose the downside would be having clients that are self-righteous, bitchy prima donnas. I could just see myself getting mad at a client when emotions are running high and empathically prodding their fiancé to break off the engagement, or starting a riot of angry people at the party. I've seen what happens when my emotions make a room full of people angry, and it's not pretty. I better keep thinking about the whole career path thing. Empath out.

The perky college girl working the front desk was excited to be helping. I bet she couldn't wait to describe the evening's events on some social network site. Christine got a copy of the evening's sign in sheet and the video footage.

"What are you looking for?" I asked Mike as he was going through the sign in sheet.

"I'm looking for anything suspicious," he replied.

"What can be suspicious about a name?" I asked.

"People don't pick false names the same way they name a baby. Someone choosing a false name will pick one overly common, or subconsciously pick one similar to a fictional character, or make some other mistake."

"I think you are grasping at straws," I said.

"Here is a false name, Itzhak Baumstein III," he said.

Empath's log: Rats. I put my foot in my mouth, but he could have been a bit more tactful in pointing it out. Empath out.

"How do you know the name is false?" I asked.

"Itzhak Baumstein is clearly a traditional Jewish name. However, Jewish names seldom have Junior or the third in the name because Jews consider it bad luck to name a child after someone who is alive thus seldom naming children after their parents," he replied. Mike carries an impressive amount of weird, trivial information in his head, but sometimes it comes in handy.

We found the section of security tape that matched the sign-in time for Itzhak Baumstein III, but it didn't show much. The camera was mounted high up in the two-storey lobby, and poor quality. All it really showed was a man with short black hair. He was wearing black pants and a white shirt. His face couldn't be recognizable from that angle. You couldn't even tell how tall he was.

We drove home and collapsed on the couch. Mike sat on the end, and I leaned against him. It had been an exhausting day for both of us. Mike had kicked his intellect and problem solving into high gear, which is sometimes more tiring than physical activity. Today had been the most hours I had to keep my empathic abilities in check since coming here.

I started to relax and snuggle against Mike. He had his arm around me in a way that was cuddly but not trying to feel me up. I rolled to face him, now in each other's arms. I looked up into his eyes. He told me I had done a good job today. I gave him a little kiss on the lips, intending it to be a thank you for the compliment. He kissed me back. We spent a few minutes kissing. I was just living in the moment and enjoying the physical sensation of his touch. Then I though this might be the time and sent a bit of empathic lust projection his way. Mike broke off the kiss, told me good night, and then went off to his bedroom.

Empath's Log: So that's his game. He wants me to learn to have a relationship without using my empathic skills to manipulate it. I could go to him and apologize and probably spend the night making love, but I'll be damned if I'll give him the satisfaction. I'm still feeling a bit put out that he was withholding sex to teach me a lesson. I thought only women were allowed to do that. Empath out.

Chapter 3

The next morning, Mike was busy writing a story. He does science news articles for an online publication called ScienceBlog. Of course his real job is working for the United Nations, but the science reporter job on the side makes a good cover story when he wants to poke around and ask questions discretely. This morning he was writing an article with an overview of research activities aimed at genetically engineering viruses to tell the body to lose weight. Get a cold and lose twenty pounds. I bet you need one heck of handkerchief.

I took the morning to relax and read. I needed some time to clear my head after the previous day's overload of other people's emotions. Today I was reading a historical fiction novel by Benerson Little. It was engrossing and more than a little bit racy. I started picturing myself as the plucky heroine and Mike as the captain, and all those ropes, and… OK, I'm having trouble focusing on the book. I skipped back a couple pages to the last place I could remember reading and put in the bookmark.

I moved to the back deck and sat down cross-legged to meditate. I allowed my body to relax from toes to head. I focused on the sensations of my body, breathing, heart beating. I let my mind close in on itself with a sense of timelessness. Then I felt my consciousness expand outward, with part of my mind just observing this. That observation, being aware of what you are feeling and your subconscious, is what Buddhists call mindfulness. I could feel the slightest movement of air on my skin, heard leaves rustling, and the ever present hum of appliances in the house. In my mind I got an image of Mike sitting on the couch… not doing anything romantic, just sitting there. It occurred to me that it was more important to be in the same room or home with someone than to be lovers. This is why people have relationships and get married, or at least should be why they get married, not because of idyllic walks on the beach and witty conversation. I never really got that before. Although, being lovers wouldn't be all that bad. As I started to consider that, I heard more leaves rustling. I opened by my eyes to see a pair of squirrels humping in the yard. Oops, the whole managing my empathic projections thing is still a work in progress.

I came into the house to find Mike sitting in a recliner working on a computer. He wasn't saying anything to me, but he was there if I needed him. I was glad he was.

"We have mashed potatoes, gravy, and a full beef tenderloin which should be big enough for eight people." I said.

"That should do for the four of us," Mike said. "I have a case of dark ale that Greg and Nellie like."

"I get the bit about werewolves not liking green vegetables, but why not milk?" I asked.

"Most mammals loose the ability to digest milk after infancy. European descent humans have a mutation that allows us to digest milk our whole lives. Most humans in Asia and Africa are lactose intolerant as adults," went another of Mike's impromptu lectures.

"I know I've been around werewolves and they look like muscular humans. Is that it?" I asked.

"They are better evolved as hunters… stronger, better sense of smell, equally intelligent, and a natural tendency to cooperate in groups. Most have a passion for hunting and tend to use modern weapons," he replied. "Around humans they will wear colored contacts to hide their yellow eyes and shave and dress to look human. Most live and work as part of human society. Greg and Nellie are destructive testing engineers, which means they blow things up for a living."

"Talk about a blow job," I joked.

"Greg and Nellie are here," Mike said as we heard the sound of a diesel engine in the driveway.

I took a look at Greg and Nellie Turner as they walked in from their big, brown pickup. Greg has brown, curly hair, a barrel chest, and the exaggerated pecs and biceps of a weight lifter. He is average height, but seems to be shorter just because of the proportions of his unusually broad shoulders. He was wearing jeans and a khaki shirt with four pockets that looked like it belonged on safari. Nellie is perhaps an inch taller than Greg with long brown hair and a thin face. She has taught herself to move with tentative movements that make her seem a bit frail. Her mannerisms help hide the fact that she is actually very strong and an accomplished martial artist. She was wearing simple black slacks and a white top that had red stitching around the frilly collar and cuffs. The oversized collar on her blouse helped to make her shoulders, which would be respectable on a man, seem slimmer. Both of them still had brown contacts in to hide their bright yellow eyes. Out of habit the two of them scanned our small yard and adjoining woods for a couple seconds, perhaps checking for onlookers or checking out the local game animals.

Mike answered the door and made introductions. I had glanced at Greg and Nellie in a group, but had not met them socially. I have been in seclusion at Mike's old farmhouse while I learned to control my empathic abilities better. I'm just now starting to get out and introduced to many of the people in Huntsville's supernatural community. I feel a bit bad that the martial arts nights that Mike used to host have been moved to another location so that I won't be subjected to that many adrenaline filled supernaturals until I'm ready for it.

"How long have you and Greg been together?" I asked as I prepared the potatoes and Nellie thickened the gravy.

"We've been married four years now. We met in college when I went to my first local pack meeting at Michigan State University," she replied.

"Are you required to do things for the pack?" I asked.

"No.   Most local packs are more of a social club that sometimes organize events, particularly hunting trips that are only open to werewolves," she replied.

"How many are in the packs?" I asked.

"A pack is an informal group consisting of all of the werewolves in the area.   There are usually a couple hundred in a medium size city like Lansing or Huntsville, although they seldom all show up at once. The packs in New York or LA are perhaps smaller, since most werewolves don't like big metropolitan areas with little access to woodlands. There are a few big concentrations in Alaska, Montana, Siberia and some other places."

"Are there multiple packs or pack rivalries in some places?" I asked.

"Almost never," she replied.   "Werewolves are naturally cooperative so there is little rivalry to cause packs to split up into smaller groups. In that way, werewolves are more civilized than humans."

"That's certainly a different culture. Empaths tend to choose careers where they won't routinely be in big groups to avoid the mass assault on their empathic senses," I said, displaying my newfound knowledge of empath culture.

"Yes, empath culture seems rather odd to werewolves," she replied.

"Thanks for helping with the food. Mike doesn't cook much that doesn't require removing cellophane and pushing microwave buttons." I said, as we brought the last of the food to the table.

We had an enjoyable meal. The conversation ranged from current NASA missions to favorite books. Greg told a funny story about a werewolf who mistook the smell of a Yorkshire terrier for a fox in heat. I talked a bit less than the others, but avoided empathic projections, and managed to use what I was sensing to steer the conversation away from delicate subjects. It could have been any

93

dinner amongst human friends, other than the occasional topic of conversation, and Greg draining entire bottles of ale in one casual swig.

After dinner, we moved to the comfortable, if eclectic, furniture in the living room with our drinks in hand. Mike seems to have an aversion to matching furniture, or perhaps he's just a typical bachelor. I sat next to Mike on the couch. We were sitting close enough that the side of my leg touched his. The physical contact was turning me on way more than it should at my age.

Mike brought up the subject of different ways to cut things. After discussing common things like knives, water jets, and lasers, they went into a discussion of technologies only known to the supernatural community. These included force fields, sonic blades, and some theoretical work on incontinuities in the fabric of space itself. Those that seemed capable of selective cutting on different materials included some strong chemicals and ones based on constructive interference of electromagnetic fields. Greg and Nellie went on to tell us lots of work stories about interesting ways they had seen pieces of equipment exploded, folded, and mutilated in their destructive testing work.

Chapter 4

Thursday morning I got up later than usual. I wasn't hung over, but I was moving slow, and the world was a bit blurrier than it should be. Mike was awake and had cleaned the kitchen. He greeted me as I came into the room. My keenly honed mindfulness senses observed that voices that would be chipper at most times can be obnoxiously annoying at too-early hours of the morning. I was considering telling Mike what to do with his "very good morning to you" when his phone rang.

I listened to Mike ask some telling questions like "Are you sure it's his blood?" and thus guessed that it was Christine. I was hunting up my shoes before Mike got off the phone. A couple minutes later, he handed me coffee in a travel mug and a bagel with lox wrapped in a napkin and we were off.

As we drove onto the college campus Mike was doing his Obi Wan Kenobi impression saying, "The University of Alabama in Huntsville. You will never find a more introverted hive of scientists and engineers. We must be cautious."

I shot him my "too early in the morning" glance.

We pulled up at the curb behind a row of police cars in front of a construction site. The sign on the site said "Future home of Alpha Omega Epsilon" and had the same emblem I had seen on a dilapidated two story house just off campus. The site consisted of a concrete foundation with a few steel beams sticking out of it. There were mounds of dirt and pallets of construction materials strewn about apparently at random. We walked across the muddy construction site to where Christine was talking to a familiar looking CSI guy. I wondered what it says about your life when a swarm of police officers seems like familiar territory and they don't pay any attention to you either?

"What made you decide to look here?" Mike asked.

"Keith Voss was in jail on a domestic assault charge. He assaulted his girlfriend who lives right there," she said pointing to the sorority house on the next lot. She went on to say that they had searched the area because one of the sorority girls claimed to have seen a guy that fits his description hanging around.

You could see a roughly man shaped impression in the dirt where one might lay to peer at the windows on the west side of the sorority house. The impression had a wide line of dark red stained dirt. You could see where something that had been adjacent to the body had been dragged toward the street, then the drag marks were obscured by too many footprints. He had apparently been laying between two pallets of construction materials that wouldn't be needed for another week or two. The forensics guys would have to do a genetic fingerprint, but Christine was sure it was Keith Voss. Mike was inclined to trust Christine's vampire sense of smell for blood, unless it turns out Keith has a brother who has also been eating jail food.

Mike looked at the blood on the ground, which was a big splotch, but you might be able to imagine it being a slightly curved splotch. Mike tried putting his arms out, but decided the radius of arc was too small. Then he grabbed a board off of a pile of construction material and tuned around in circles holding the board out in front of him. He took a couple steps and tried again, as Christine and I watched and tried to figure out what mad scheme he was hatching. When he had satisfied himself, with a circle that had the end of the board passing over the blood patch, he put the board down and started staring at the weeds where the end of the board had passed on the other side of the circle. After a couple minutes, he motioned for Christine and I to come over.

"See where weeds have been sliced," he said while pointing to a line in the weeds. "The radius of the sphere is larger here than at the Space and Rocket Center."

"It doesn't affect the construction materials," Christine pointed out.

"No. Only living organic matter," said Mike.

We spent a few more minutes walking around the perimeter of the circle, then decided there was nothing more to see here. Mike asked if they had interviewed people in the sorority house. Christine said that was next, and asked us to come along. She was looking at me, so I guessed she wanted my truth sensing abilities along.

The sorority house that Keith had been watching was a large red brick building with enough marble accents to make it sufficiently pretentious. From the outside, you could see that a number of the residents had decorated their windows with various items such as bows, the silhouette of a surveyors transit, band logos, a Star Trek emblem, and a rainbow flag.

As we approached the building, I mused aloud, "An engineering sorority. How does that work? Do they invent mechanical push-up bras?"

Cynthia Jibbon was medium height with jet-black hair in tight curls and large, black glasses that managed to make her look more attractive by comparison. She was dressed meticulously in the sorority girl role. There must be a dress code that keeps the sorority girls traveling in small groups with similar outfits. Being an experienced beautician, I guessed that her hair texture came from a tiny percentage of African in her genetics, but too small to show in her facial features or complexion, other than sporting a nice tan. I got the sense that Cynthia was trying very hard to fit in at the sorority and to cover up her rural Alabama accent.

Cynthia sat up straight at the front edge of her chair and clasped her hands nervously as she said, "No, I haven't seen him. I thought he was still in jail."

"Where were you the night before last?" asked Christine in her official police business voice.

"I was in my room here, studying, alone," Cynthia replied.

"Can anyone verify that?" Christine asked.

"I had dinner with Cheryl and Amanda at the cafeteria. We walked back to the sorority house together. After that I was in my room alone the rest of the night. My roommate had gone on a date with her boyfriend and didn't come back until morning," explained Cynthia.

"I know you already talked with the police about the how Keith Voss assaulted you, but I'd like to hear it again in your own words."

"Keith was my high school boyfriend. He was OK, if not the sharpest tool in the shed. I told him I wanted to break up. I'm trying to make something of my life and just don't see him fitting in. He got mad. He wanted to know if I was seeing some college guy, which I wasn't. This was in the campus bookstore. The argument got a big ugly, and he shoved a display rack over on me, giving me a pile of bruises and cut on my arm that required a few stitches. Campus security held him until the police got here. He always was a hot head who would steam and hold a grudge."

Christine looked at me, and I gave a little nod to indicate she was telling the truth. Christine asked a few more routine questions, then sent Cynthia on her way.

A junior detective name Joe arrived. He talked to Christine, acknowledging that it is her case, but asking if he could help to get a few hours away from some paperwork at the precinct. Christine told him to interview every girl with a room on the west side of the building to see if anyone had noticed anything in the construction site the night of the murder.

The housemother called down twelve girls. Mike and I waited until all of them had filed in. I felt the barrage of emotions in the room. One girl was ecstatic as she twisted a new engagement ring on her finger. A couple others were whispering back and forth about one of them breaking up with her boyfriend. There were plenty of emotions in the room, but none exhibiting anxiety at being questioned by the police. I whispered this to Mike and we left.

Empath's log: What about being a teacher? I could sense when students are confused and need more help. But what age group would I teach? Small children? Wiping noses and tying shoes. Teenagers? Lots of emotional angst there. College students? Still emotional and acting on those emotions. If I wanted to teach something I'm good at, it could be at a beauty school. Still seems a bit of a mundane career choice. Thinking about all this emotional angst in people, I can see the attraction of having a lover who is older and more stable in his emotions. Mike certainly fits that description. Empath out.

When the demands of life don't intercede, Mike has a short period of silence after dinner. He just sits in the living room, or sometimes outside. He doesn't read or watch TV. He will just sit and let his thoughts wander. After a while, he may meditate. I've taken to sitting in silence with him, although I get fidgety before he does. Today he may have been thinking about a murder, but I wasn't.

"Mike?" I asked to get his attention, and judge his mood. I didn't want to annoy him by using my empathic senses on him.

"Yes," he replied, in the voice of a man willing to give me his attention with all the patience in the world.

"I know you use meditation and mindfulness techniques that come from Buddhism. Do you consider yourself to be Buddhist?" I asked.

"Many of the Eastern Buddhist denominations are rich with rituals, symbolism, and traditions. In the U.S. you more often see Skeptical Buddhists. These are people who agree with many of the core principles of Buddhism, but don't pay attention to any of the cultural rituals or symbolism. I fall in that category." Mike believes in introducing a topic.

"Do Buddhists believe in a god?" I asked.

"No. Buddha himself was quite clear that he is a teacher, not a god. Buddhists do believe in working towards becoming a better person, the ultimate level of which is called Buddhahood. Some people incorrectly refer to this as becoming a god, but it is most certainly not a god as Christians describe god."

"I like that. I don't consider myself to be religious. I find Christianity to be repulsive. I hate the thought that there is an all knowing, all-powerful god that sees every atrocity committed on earth, has the power to do anything, but does absolutely nothing about the atrocities. I can't for the life of me figure out why Christians would characterize such a god as a loving god. Or why they can dismiss all of this with some glib little saying." This was the first time in my life I have verbalized this thought.

Mike pointed out, "Many people consider a large percentage of religious stories to be fairy tales, not absolute truth. They participate in religion to be part of the social community, not because they agree with all of the beliefs. That is why congregations are often fairly homogeneous in race, income level, and political leanings."

Mike continued on with the subject, "There are two main branches of Buddhism. In one people try to live a good life based on their principles, but only holy men meditate routinely. In the other, called Esoteric Buddhism or Vajrayana, individuals engage in meditation, martial arts, and other activities to better themselves."

"What type of principles of Buddhism do people believe in?" I asked.

"My favorite is that you should not believe anything because a book or person told you to. You have to determine the truth for yourself," he replied.

"That's a tall order," I said.

"No one said it was easy," he replied. "There are much easier steps along the way. The Noble Eight Fold Path is the Buddhist equivalent of the Ten Commandments. There is quite a bit about dealing with sadness and suffering in Buddhism, probably stemming from its origins in very impoverished areas. Also, Buddhists tend to strive for long term contentment rather than short term pleasure."

"I really like that idea, since emotional extremes are not private around an empath," I said. "But why is Buddhism considered a religion if it doesn't involve a belief in a god?"

"Buddhism is a philosophy for how to live your life. As such, it fills the same role that religion fills in your life. It gives you a set of values that help you make decisions and choose how to behave. Buddhist monks help people find their truths and path. In some of the Eastern denominations, the group sessions resemble a religious service so much that you can't tell how it is different from any other religion unless you understand the meaning behind all of the symbolism."

"I can appreciate the value of helping people decide what to do," I said. "I'm a good beautician, but I don't want to do that forever. I've been thinking about what I would like my life to be like."

"You will have to decide that for yourself. However, I will point out that many people will prioritize what is most important, second most important, etc. in their life. Depending upon the person, the most important thing in their life may be a particular career, living in a given location, a marriage, obtaining wealth, or something else."

I didn't reply to that, but I immediately sensed that it was a very important point.

Empath's log: Mike suggested figuring out what things are most important in my life. I know money is not. I would rather be happy than rich, and even I am smart enough to realize that having money beyond what is necessary for food and shelter doesn't make you happy. I don't have a desire to live in another country. That would be another whole culture, society, and laws to be anxious about. Relationships, careers, and personal beliefs are going to be much harder subject for me to think out. It occurs to me that I am more comfortable right here, right now with Mike than I ever have been with anyone else. Empath out.

Chapter 5

Friday morning, Mike was called by someone reporting an incident on Redstone Arsenal. I couldn't go along because I don't have the security clearance, but I didn't want to sit at home. I put a couple books in a backpack and had Mike drop me at Bridge Street, an outdoor shopping mall made to resemble an old time city street. I could sit on a bench by the pond there and read until he could pick me up again. The following is a description of Mike's visit to the arsenal as best as I can describe it from what he told me.

Our hero did an academy award worthy job of impersonating a United Nations bureaucrat as he drove a stodgy sedan towards the top secret military compound. A frumpy set of business casual clothes hid the rippling muscles that had pleasured many of the world's most beautiful women. Just the night before he had... oops got distracted again there. Better get back to the story at hand before I find myself writing a completely different type of story.

Mike showed his identification to the gate guard who raised an eyebrow at the U.N. badge but waved him on through without question. It took him another twenty minutes to reach his destination. Traffic was backed up by a remote controlled land mine destroying robot inching it's way along a main road. Someone would probably get in trouble for driving that on the base roads, but it wasn't Mike's problem. Mike left his cell phone, brief case, and pocketknife in the car. Just before he slammed the car door, he remembered to remove the cartoon Iron Man emblem from his key chain. The emblem concealed an n-gun, a technology unknown to the human community at large.

He entered the building, showed his credentials, and was passing through the metal detector when the head of special project security showed up. The security chief, Laura Nelson, was a woman having a bad day. She had been overjoyed when she got a promotion a few months ago, moving from a low-level administrator position to being the head of a security team. Yesterday, she found out that a piece of experimental equipment had disappeared, and it dawned on her that she could be sitting in the scapegoat chair. After investigating all day, she was nearly in a panic when one of the senior science advisors, actually a vampire, suggested working through U.N. security rather than the senior management in her own organization. She jumped on the idea with no regard for whether she was breaking protocol. She made a call to the U.N. that evening. The vampire, who was placed there to keep an eye on these projects, made his own call to ensure it would be routed to Mike's department.

Mike spoke with Laura standing in an alcove in front of the restrooms. The wall of the alcove was painted with a picture of skunk peaking out from behind the NASA emblem, the unofficial symbol of special projects, which is also known as the Skunk Works. She explained that she wanted this matter handled discretely, but didn't go into the details.

Laura took Mike to meet with the project technical lead, Dr. Sylvester, known behind his back as Sadsack Sylvester because he sadly moped through life as the eternal pessimist. Today Dr. Sylvester was more pessimistic than usual. He might have been considered a security risk if anyone thought he had the nerve to touch a firearm, but everyone that knew him had him pegged as equally spineless. Sylvester explained that a device had been missing a number of days. It took a while to realize it was gone because researcher A thought B had it who thought C did, who thought A had it but wasn't currently in the mood to talk to A. Mike asked about classified material tracking paperwork, and was informed that they don't enter experimental devices into the system until they work well enough to be named whatever it is they are trying to create.

Mike asked what the object was. Dr. Sylvester started to talk about light refraction, and Mike cut him off to say "A cloaking device."

Sylvester sadly replied, "Yes".

Mike said, "A malfunctioning cloaking device that can sever organic matter."

Sylvester nodded even more sadly.

Laura asked, "Do you know where it is?"

Mike said, "No, but the good news is that we are already on the trail of the person who has it." His audience perked up visibly, before he went on, "The bad news is the device has already killed one person."

Laura slumped down in a chair, and Sylvester leaned against a lab bench. Both had visions of public relations nightmares dancing in their heads.

Mike asked quite a few more questions of the two and of others working in the same lab. Nothing of value came from the questions. The most useful thing he got was a list of everyone that had been in the building in the past month, even if all they did was wield one of NASA's state of the art toilet plungers. He also got a picture of the device, which looked like a large brass belt buckle with some dials and switches on it.

Cloaking devices have been used by the supernatural community for some years. Now the humans are independently inventing them. A vampire alchemist keeps an eye on them and gives the project little nudges to keep things safe, and help them succeed. The human science community is ripe to develop this technology, and even has some innovative ideas. Thus there is no point in trying to prevent it, and the best option is to keep things moving along smoothly. It was a fairly cushy desk job for an alchemist approaching retirement.

Cloaking devices refract light using constructive interference of electromagnet waves. However, if some constructive interference should occur at the wrong frequency, such as the resonant frequency of lipid molecules that form cell membranes, they can be damaging. This is why organic matter is ripped apart along the sphere of the devices reach without damaging other materials.

Mike picked me up from Bridge Street late morning. He had already made arrangements to meet Christine at Beauregards, a local restaurant a short distance away. The restaurant appeared to be several storefronts connected together. Each table had a paper towel roll to serve as a napkin dispenser. Although the menu was not large, the food was very good, particularly the chicken wings. Christine seemed to particularly like the wings. She had a drip of bar-b-que sauce coming down from the corner of her mouth, which was easy to imagine as a drip of blood on the thirsty vampire.

After we had eaten, the conversation turned to the investigation at hand. Christine said they hadn't turned up any evidence of Keith Voss having connections to the arsenal. Also, he would have been in jail at the time it was stolen.

Mike described the cloaking device. He also pointed out that the cutting radius seems to be getting smaller on the malfunctioning device, so it may eventually slice through the person wearing it.

"What do you call a quadruple amputee at the front door?" I contributed to the conversation. "Matt."

Next came the fun part of the conversation, brain storming about what may be going on. There were a lot more ideas than answers. What if Keith Voss was stalking Cynthia Jibbon? What if Cynthia wanted to kill Keith? What if someone else wanted to kill Keith? What if Keith was a not so innocent bystander who was just in the wrong place at the wrong time? Could there be a political motive? What about a financial motive? Becoming invisible could be very valuable for a diamond thief or bank robber. What is the connection between the sorority house and the Space and Rocket Center?

By the end of lunch, I was starting to get weary from keeping my empathic projections in check for so many hours. We headed home so I could rest and Mike could do some computer work.

Empath's log: I should put a home in the country on my life's wish list. I need the time away from people to relax and let down my mental guards.   Keeping that mental control is apparently more difficult for me than for full blood empaths. Empath out.

Chapter 6

Mike doesn't work a regular schedule, and doesn't necessarily get weekends off. However, if you don't have a good idea what to do next, it can be useful to do something else and take your mind off of a problem. Saturday noon, we took a picnic to the botanical gardens. They were having an open house and inviting people to get out in the nice weather.

We casually strolled into the botanical gardens. The botanical gardens are uniquely Huntsville as well. There are pieces of space junk acting as children's play areas and tool sheds. As we entered the bonsai garden, we saw Christine in the distance, flirting with a young man as they headed towards the butterfly house. I guess being a vampire means that your picnic basket can walk on his own feet.

I enjoyed the bonsai garden. Those dwarf trees have so much character as they reflect the essence of how trees can grow on wind swept coastlines. The result is a mix of cute and the gnarled character of an ancient tree.

We took a path to the right to find a shady place to eat our picnic lunch. We passed a children's climbing area that looks like a lopsided house, and went further along the path to find some privacy. We stopped at a bench by a small pond. People have a view of southern areas being a jungle of voracious insects, but there are fewer mosquitoes in Alabama than I had encountered on a visit to Minnesota. Perhaps it is too hot here and the mosquitoes go down in flames like the loser of a WWI dogfight when they wander into direct sunlight.

We ate our lunch in silence. Mike ate his sandwich slowly as he looked at the vegetation around him. I recognize this as another type of meditation. It's an exercise to perceive details of the world around you. The idea is to see things as they really are, rather than looking through your preconceived notions of how things are or should be. I finished eating then packed the remains of the meal back into the tote bag we had brought it in. The tote bag had a logo identifying it as being from the Huntsville Simulation Conference.

I began to engage in the same awareness meditation. I took in the trees, sunlight, and ferns. I could see how the leaves moved in unison as a gust of wind caught them. Then I saw some undergrowth movement that was out of place. It didn't match the wind motion. I stayed still, but focused my attention to the area around the unexpected movement. A shadow moved from tree to tree. A few fern leaves drifted to the ground as if sliced by an unseen blade. In my peripheral vision, I could see Mike shifted his head slightly. He was seeing the same thing.

Mike spoke, but didn't look aside at me, "What do you think of that ghost at the Space and Rocket Center".

I knew he was baiting our unseen visitor, so I played along by saying, "They just opened a display from the space shuttle Columbia disaster. If there are ghosts associated with the space program, that would be one place to find them." Our eavesdropping shadow moved a bit closer to us.

Mike slouched a bit and started casually running his fingers through the grass next to the bench as he said, "Poltergeists are often associated with intense emotions. There were certainly some interesting emotional vibes at coming from the LGBT community members."

I was trying to keep the conversation going as Mike started to fiddle with a stone he found on the ground, "Yes. I can usually tell male from female emotional patterns, but there were some emotions in that room I had never encountered before."

Some tall grass fifteen feet in front of us was flattened by an unseen footstep, and Mike immediately threw the stone with enough force to make a major league pitcher proud. The stone disappeared, as we heard the sound of it hitting flesh and a voice saying "ouch".

Mike lunged towards the sound. There was the sound of twigs snapping and footsteps running away from us down the trail. Mike was in close pursuit.

I grabbed up the tote bag and set off after him. Now I wished I had read all of the details in the user manual of my empathic smart phone. I took my best guess at the function I wanted.

Empath's text: Christine. In pursuit of Keith Voss assailant. Empath out.

A sapling ahead of Mike quivered as if struck and the black ghost of our quarry became visible. He made an incredibly sharp right turn by placing his left foot five feet up on a large tree. The move reminded me of the movements in the Vampkido tournament.

A few seconds later, my phone empathically gave me Christine's reply, "Where are you?"

I considered saying "by the trees" but was afraid Christine might be able to literally kill me with sarcasm.

Empath's text: Christine. Path to right, by pond. Turning right, heading back towards entrance. Empath out.

The shadow stumbled. Mike jumped into the air, intending to come down on top, but at the last second threw his arms out and rammed into two medium size trees. The shadow man had gone invisible. A spherical area of weeds and low hanging branches had been sliced out, including curved gouges into the tree trunks inches from where Mike had caught himself. I realized one of us could be killed or have a limb amputated by that malfunctioning cloaking device.

Mike staggered and felt his arms to see if he had broken anything or just bruised them badly. He was already looking for the shifting foliage of invisible man's trail, now twenty yards away.

Christine came running in from the right at an inhuman speed. I saw her take one glance at the sliced foliage ahead of us, ignoring Mike.

The cloaking device flickered off for a few seconds and we got a view of the back of a medium height man with short black hair as he turned sharp left, away from Christine, and put on a burst of speed.

I caught up with Mike, and skidded to a stop. I put my hand on his back and started to ask if he was hurt badly. He took off running before I could get the words out. He went straight, the direction he had been going, rather than following Christine to the left. I wasn't sure where Mike was going, but did my best to keep up.

Mike was ten steps ahead of me as he came up to the path leading back to the entrance, and skidded to a stop behind a tree on the far side of the path. He couldn't outrun a vampire, but he could set up an ambush if our mystery man again headed out of the botanical gardens.

I tried to stop and hide on the near side of the path, but stumbled on a tree root and ended up on my hands and knees in the middle of the path. Christine was running right towards me with a shimmer in the air in front of her.

Mike broke cover early and lifted me to safety as he abandoned the ambush idea to help me. The cloaking device, again malfunctioning in cutting mode, sliced a corner off of Mike's pants leg and drew a thin line of blood as it grazed his ankle.

Christine had to abort a couple of her own takedowns due to the random flicker of the malfunctioning cloaking devices cutting action. She lost invisible man when he hit the parking lot and there was no more foliage to give away his location.

We caught up with Christine in the parking lot. It took very little conversation for us to agree on two things. First our man was a vampire with Vampkido training. Second, there was nothing more we could do right that minute.

My mind and heart beat were still racing as Mike drove home. The afternoon's excitement was simultaneously exhilarating and terrifying. This left me pondering whether I would want a job that was both exciting and deadly, or if safe and boring was a better compromise. If there is something in between, it wasn't coming to mind.

We got home and both plopped down on the couch. The emotional exhaustion was stronger than the physical exhaustion, which had started to recover on the car ride.

Mike said, "I'm glad you didn't get hurt."

I said, "I'm glad you didn't get hurt either."

I looked at him feeling a swelling of love and desire. I left myself completely open, keeping my mental guard up so that he would not get any empathic push from me. It made me feel more vulnerable than I had ever been.

Empath's log: He's kissing me long, soft, and deep. My body is on fire desiring him and I know he feels the same way. He cups my breast through my dress. I feel his pecs, which are hard and well defined. I unbutton his shirt. Kiss. I help him take my dress off. More kissing as his hand gently slides my bra strap off my shoulder and rubs my nipple. He kisses his way down my neck to my nipple. Now his hand is sliding down my stomach, and into my panties, and .... Oh ... Oh ... Empath out.

Empath's log: Allow me SOME privacy. It's not like it was my first time. I slept with a few guys in college. As an empath, if I want a guy and he even notices me, I can fill him with sexual desire, and it's not like it's that hard to get college guys into bed in the first place. Although in college I hadn't realized I was enticing them empathically. But Mike was different.

Mike kissed, touched, caressed, massaged. We would do it a while, then he would stop, more caressing, and do it in a different

111

position. Once I realized that was the game, I gave him some of my best moves as well. We must have been at it nearly forty-five minutes before we couldn't take it any more and both climaxed a minute apart, which is like four times as long as any guy my age ever took with me.

I know girls who are into older guys. I always had the feeling that they were a bit shallow because older guys have better paying jobs. But after making love with Mike, I'm getting on that bandwagon in a hurry. Empath out.

Chapter 7

That evening, we were eating ice cream and snuggling on the couch. I was still thinking about vampires.

"How do vampires get blood without leaving a trail of dead bodies?" I asked.

"Vampires are aware of the benefits of blending in with human civilization, and using the system to their advantage." Mike explained. "Think about all of the blood banks that have to dispose of blood with a surprisingly short shelf life. There are vampire employees there that collect the blood for sale to the vampire community. The vampire that controls the local blood supply often becomes quite rich. There are also doctors that treat diseases that require frequent blood transfusions, and some of those patients are vampires paying to get fresh blood. There are probably some that prey on the homeless, lost hikers, etc."

"None of those sound relevant to the sorority house," I pointed out.

Mike thought about that and said, "Blood isn't the only thing that motivating vampires. They are as intelligent as humans. With that intelligence comes all of the same desires, emotions, needs, and neuroses.

"Great! Bipolar bicep bragging blood monsters," I quipped.

Mike went on, "We need to figure out what his motivation is? What do the space center, the sorority house, and the botanical gardens have in common?"

"Do they have to be connected?" I asked. "The botanical gardens might have been trying to find out how much we know."

"OK. What about the other two?"

I thought a minute, trying to visualize a picture of both places. "What about the flag?" I asked.

113

"What flag?" Mike asked, obviously interested.

"The rainbow gay pride flag in the second floor window of the sorority house," I explained. "Perhaps our vampire has a fetish for lesbians."

Mike thought about that for a few seconds, then immediately texted Christine, to give her my theory.

Empath's log: Bingo! Take that, brainiac boyfriend. The beautician empath solved the case... hopefully. Empath out.

It's Sunday morning and the world is quiet. I put some big cushions down on the living room floor and sit down lotus style on them. Mike has been describing mindfulness meditation, one of the more difficult types, and I want to try it. I close my eyes and go through the now familiar body relaxation. I start from my toes, up through my spine, and out to my fingertips, willing each part of the body to relax. If there is a twinge or itch of a bug bite, I note it but don't move to do anything about it. Finally, I relax my neck and the muscles in my face. I then use the empty mind trick of visualizing a blank, white wall. I shift my point of view to look up the face of the wall in all directions, then pull back to see myself in front of the wall as if outside by body. Now I visualize an object, my favorite pair of hair cutting scissors. They are silver with a swiveling loop for my thumb. I look at them from all angles. I note the wear on the grip, the scratches on the blade and flat surface from multiple sharpenings.

Mindfulness meditation is a technique to listen to the right side of your brain, your subconscious mind. That part of the brain communicates with pictures and emotions, but not words. I try to visualize my shears with pictures only, not using any words. This is to get the brain communicating in pictures, the right brain's territory. Now I relax and let the image go where it wants, rotating or zooming in or out. Now a series of tenuous images flickers by, a half second each. There are scenes of groups of people, then images of individual people that I know as they looked during some emotional confrontation. I notice that the images are just slightly off color. I've never paid much attention to the belief in auras, which always feels a bit like quackery. However, it occurs to me that a color might be the right brains convenient way to tell you what it is sensing about a person's emotional state. I also realize how flat and lifeless the world is without the overlay of the emotional landscape. This brings me to the realization that I like being an empath. I've been viewing it more as a burden, or disability. At some point as I'm considering these things my eyes have opened and I'm no longer in the meditation state. However, I feel a sense of accomplishment at having gotten some result from the mindfulness meditation, even it only lasted a few seconds.

I don't think it matters what color people say an aura is supposed to be. It only matters if your subconscious communicates that way and what colors it associates with a given emotion. I wonder if Christine has an aura color? What color is cynical?

Later Sunday afternoon Mike was reading the Sunday paper. Actually, I think he skims the Sunday paper and only reads the comics in detail. Anyway, he hands me the paper to look at an ad. There is a concert tomorrow night at the Von Braun Center featuring gay and lesbian themed songs. Mike calls Christine and they agree that the concert may be a place to catch our man, if we haven't caught him already.

On Monday morning, Mike got a list of male vampires working on Redstone Arsenal from a database that his department of the United Nations maintains. We headed into town to meet Christine at the police station and discuss it with her.

In spite of being fairly new, the police station has an impersonal government look about it. I wonder if someone has a system of interior design meant to make suspects feel uncomfortable, or go with stacks of papers and cups of stale coffee? No wonder police officers lose their sense of humor after working in a building like that. Or maybe the office is meant to be depressing enough to make officers want to go out on patrol.

We sat down to discuss the arsenal list in a conference room, complete with half filled cups of stale coffee. Christine and Mike seemed to feel they have a duty to go through every name on the list rather than quickly focusing on the likely ones. They went through a list of twenty-three names. Carlos Montoya is a night shift technician in the microgravity laboratory at NASA, which is one building over from the special projects building. Jim Young is an electrical engineer at NASA special projects, which means he had a small part in the cloaking device project. Theodore Edwards is a night janitor at special projects. Tommy Bidet is an accounting clerk for the Army Materiel Command, but doesn't have security clearance or access to special projects. Daryl Smyth is a supercomputer system administrator, who is a contractor with CSC assigned to the Space and Missile Defense Command. William Burns is a senior administrator with special projects. William is the one who encouraged them to get Mike's office involved. This went on and on. I may have dozed off.

They decided to pay a visit to Carlos Montoya, Jim Young, Theodore Edwards, and William Burns first. These were the four that routinely work in the Skunk Works building. We headed out in Christine's work car, a dark blue Crown Victoria. Someone had worked hard to make the unmarked cars used by detectives look as much like a police car as possible.

Mike called Laura Nelson, the NASA security person he had already met, to find out which of them were at work today. It turned out none of them were. Many government employees work nine-hour days, then take a three-day weekend every other week. Today was apparently the off day for special projects. Laura gave Mike a few suggestions of places a couple of them might be if not at home.

Christine called the manager of Reflections, a private club where Jim Young is a regular. We headed there first since we knew he was there, and he had direct access to the prototype cloaking device. Jim Young was watching science fiction channel at Reflections.

Reflections is kind of a cross between a posh bar, and an English private club. The nondescript entrance hides a plush interior with a variety of rooms. One was a swank bar, one was a quiet room, a couple are TV rooms. A couple rooms could be reserved for groups, which usually meant Dungeons & Dragons in Huntsville's rather geeky environment.

The manager at Reflections gave us a hard glare of warning then offered us the use of his office for our business. He was no doubt remembering a brawl that Mike and I had been involved in a while back. That was a rare occasion since Reflections was usually the most civilized of establishments, in spite of its multi-species clientele. I made a mental note to be careful what I said around the manager. I didn't want him knowing that the brawl had been caused by me before I started learning to control my empathic projections. I had gotten mad at my date. A little uncontrolled empathic projection and everyone was mad at everyone else. At that point the whole place was a powder keg that blew within minutes.

The club manager led Jim Young and our group to his small office off the kitchen, then left, closing the door behind him. The office had enough chairs, but was pretty bare. It had only the bare essentials to keep paperwork for the club. Apparently, their management believed in minimizing administration and spending as much time as possible around the club.

Jim Young completely breaks the vampire stereotype. He is short and dark haired. He walks with his shoulders hunched in rather poor posture. He has a geeky laugh and the halting speech patterns of an introverted engineer. He apparently wears enough cheap cologne to ensure that women being attracted to his pheromones won't interrupt his focus on engineering and science fiction.

Christine identified herself as both detective and vampire, and asked him what a young alchemist was doing hanging around humans. This served multiple purposes. First, it let him know he could talk about things known only to the supernatural community with him. Second it let him know we already knew something so he wouldn't try to deny everything. Lastly, it got him talking on a safe subject, thus getting over the hurdle of not wanting to talk to police.

Jim apparently had a stock answer to this question memorized, "We allow the normal humans to develop technologies mostly on their own. This allows them to explore variations on the technology that we might not have thought of. They have already come up with some solutions to emitter design problems that require less power than the system used by supernaturals. The supernaturals never did succeed in creating a portable device."

"Why make a portable device first if it is more difficult?" Christine asked. A good detective feels out the situation because that often leads to an understanding of motives.

"It's not about ease or likelihood of success." Jim explained. "It's about money. A portable device is more useful to the military, so that is what they are willing to fund."

"So why have NASA develop it, instead of the Army?"

"There is a lot of cutting edge physics involved in the design. NASA has the largest concentration of physics expertise in the world. Apparently some of the key concepts are adaptations of things they have learned by studying how the sun's gravity bends light from distant stars."

Christine subtly turned the conversation by asking, "What is your role in the project?"

Jim explained, "As a low level engineer, I have access to everything in the verification and testing process, but I'm not expected to do the primary design work. That allows me to see everything that is going on without influencing the design, unless there is a serious safety flaw in a particular approach."

"Have you done testing on the belt mounted prototype?" Christine asked.

"Yes. I was doing verification that the amount of power consumed matched the theoretical calculations. However, they took me off that a little over a week ago. Now, I'm verifying the circuitry calculations again, which seems unnecessary." Jim explained.

Christine and Mike watched his reaction closely as Christine said, "The device was stolen about then."

Jim Young exclaimed, "That's terrible. The current prototype is unstable. If the calibration gets knocked out of adjustment, it can be dangerous. The lead developers are working on a feedback based auto-calibration to prevent this from happening in the next prototype, but haven't found a good solution yet."

"You are surprised." I said. I was behind Jim where Christine and Mike could see me nod if he was lying. Jim took my statement as a question, but the others knew that I was informing them that he is genuinely surprised by the news of the theft.

"Of course, I'm surprised. Why hasn't anyone investigated it?" he asked.

"Why do you think we are asking you all these questions?" Christine asked. A good detective knows when to take advantage of someone's emotional response by rattling them a bit more so they don't have time to plan an answer. That tactic was automatic for Christine, even if we already know he is innocent. Maybe it will reveal something else. Jim didn't have anything to say to that.

"Who do you think would want to steal it?" Christine asked.

"Of course, the government is worried about unfriendly countries getting a hold of it." Jim said, pointing out the obvious.

"How much would it be worth?"

"In an open bidder situation, a lot. Millions at least. However, spy networks find ways to get leverage on people through blackmail, sexual favors, or some other promise." Jim explained. He had apparently read plenty of spy novels in addition to a stream of security awareness junk mail.

"Is there anyone who seemed to take interest in projects beyond what is required for their job?" asked Christine. Mike was staying quiet, knowing that she had been getting information out of people since long before he was born.

"No one who talked with me."

Jim Young didn't have anything more useful to tell us. We decided to check out Carlos Montoya next.

Carlos Montoya wasn't at home. He owned a tiny house in a residential neighborhood behind Farley Elementary School. Some young vampires live very cheaply until they can build up enough money to live off of their investments. The grass was mowed and there were no letters in the mailbox, so he can't have been gone long. There was a dog barking at us from behind his door. Christine or Mike could get GPS data from someone's phone if there was enough evidence to justify it, but Carlos didn't yet seem that urgent when there were others to visit.

Theodore Edwards was next. He lived in a nice looking gated community of townhouse condos, nestled on a steep hillside at the east end of Airport Road. Airport Road does not have an airport, unless you count the grass top of a former landfill where people fly remote controlled model planes.

The facade of the townhouse was done in multiple colors of brick with white frames around the windows and doors. The doors were painted a deep green. The designers had made sure every unit wasn't identical. Some had bay windows. Some had an extra awning over the door. A couple were single storey units, but most were two storey. Apparently visitors could park on the street in front of each unit, but the residents must have had parking in the rear of theirs. Theodore's was a two-storey unit with no bay window or extra awning. We could hear a television in the front room.

Christine knocked, waited a minute, and knocked again. Mike was starting to ask what we should do when an engine roared to life behind the building and we heard the squeal of tires as someone left in a hurry. We were back in the car with Christine starting the engine when we saw a motorcycle swerve around the half opened gate at the entrance and the gate began to close again. We got up to the gate, but it wouldn't open. Christine honked in frustration. The manager came out of the apartment nearest to the gate to see what was going on. After much head shaking and muttering over the malfunctioning gate, he hand cranked it open. By that time, we had been delayed by fifteen minutes. The manager did confirm that Theodore was one of three residents who had motorcycles.

Christine was in a foul mood as she drove us back to the police station where Mike had left his car. We couldn't be sure that Theodore Edwards was the man on the motorcycle, or that he was running from us, or that the gate was rigged to delay us, but it seemed like too much of a coincidence not be kept as our working theory. We made a plan to watch for him at the concert that night. I suggested going in disguise so we wouldn't scare him off immediately.

Chapter 8

I was in my element as we got disguised. I was wearing a multi-layer emerald green dress that buttoned up the front with a high collar. I also had a padded bra with extra padding stuffed in the cups to change my proportions. I put on green eye shadow and mascara. I chose a dark red lipstick. A wig of long, red, wavy hair finished the effect to make me look completely different.

I came out to the living room where Mike was, struck a pose, batted my eyes and used the cheesy southern drawl you only hear in movies to say, "I know y'all are going to adore tonight's cotillion."

Mike responded with his own exaggerated southern accent, "Why missy if you weren't the grand niece I'm escorting to this evenings shindig, I'd be offering you a mint julep and trying to take advantage of the situation."

Mike was wearing a white suit coat, striped shirt, and a string tie with an octagonal cut agate. I did a Hollywood worthy makeup job accentuating lines in his face to make him look twenty years older, then added a gray wig with a pony tale which made him look thirty years older than his real age. I finished it off with a very realistic looking gray goatee.

Empath's log: Being a licensed beautician comes in handy when you need to whip up a disguise. Hey, it happens more often than you might expect. Empath out.

We arrived a bit early for the concert and took a walk around the building. The auditorium is at the north end of the building, and exhibition halls on the south end. One hallway leading west to parking and the backside of the exhibition halls was blocked off with a sign indicating that there was construction in progress as a new wing was being added. We headed back towards the auditorium to keep an eye out for Theodore Edwards.

Christine walked right up to us before we recognized her. She was in a long, black sequined dress, wearing a wig of straight, black hair, and dark eye shadow. As always, she looked stunning in anything she wore.

The auditorium has a main entrance at the back, a stairway to the balcony and entrances at various rows along the sides of the main floor. Mike went left, Christine went right, and I went to loiter in front of the balcony entrance. None of us saw him. We all went in to our seats as they were announcing last call. Mike and I were at the back left of the main hall. Christine was at the back right.

Empath's log: I don't think I would want to be an entertainer. Crowds aren't easy for me to handle, even when no one is paying attention to me. What about being a makeup artist? I already have most of the skills. It could be exciting being around the entertainment industry, and going from one project to the next would be less boring than many jobs. On the down side, the odd hours could get old. I think I need some measure of stable home life to relax and let my empathic guard down. Empath out.

The music was interesting. Some were love songs that were very beautiful. Some were very angry themes that didn't appeal to me. I don't have anything against people being gay or lesbian, but I treat people as equals and feel that some of the perceived persecution is imagined. I've never had a deep conversation on the subject with someone. As my control over my empathic abilities improves, I hope to have more close friends, which I could never risk previously.

I thought I was doing well not projecting my emotions in the crowded auditorium, but a bit of the strain may have shown. Mike took hold of my hand, and I realized I had been all tensed up. I did a quick relaxation exercise and found the empathic block could be an easy acceptance of my environment, rather than a forced shielding of myself. This was actually a breakthrough for me, but now wasn't the time to dwell on it.

I began sensing more of the people around me. There was the usual mix of enjoying the music, being amorous towards their date, boredom, and a few disgusted with aspects of the performance. I felt a few that were having erotic fantasies about the performers. I couldn't understand the words or images in their head, but the emotions were clear. I started focusing on those individuals. I felt their love, kindness, lust, a faint signal of lust combined with thirst... bingo a vampire. Focusing on that one only, I could tell it was a man, but about as far away as I could distinguish in this crowd. Anything further away was a low level white noise of emotions that I couldn't untangle. The current song was love song between two women, full of sexual innuendos.

Empaths can't sense direction, but they can get a sense of distance by the strength of the emotional signal and visual clues. I focused on that. I saw a young girl three rows up from us fidget in her seat and felt the strength of her boredom; at about half the signal strength I can distinguish. That means lusty, thirsty vampire man was the distance of about six rows from us.

I whispered to Mike what I was feeling and estimated he was twenty to twenty-five feet from us, which could be in any direction. Mike discretely texted Christine, breaking the house rule about cell phone use. Then he pushed himself up higher in his seat and started looking around at people about the right distance away.

It was the last song before intermission. Right as they were singing what sounded like the final phrases, Christine got out of her seat and walked across the back of the auditorium to stand just behind us. She must have seen something or someone as the doors opened for intermission. She didn't run, but walked very quickly. We followed her as quickly as possible, but the auditorium seats weren't made to be exited gracefully.

Christine was about thirty feet ahead of us, and Theodore about that distance ahead of her, at the door to the backstage area with a "performers only" sign on it. Theodore knocked on the door then switched on the malfunctioning cloaking device. He was slightly visible as a mostly transparent shadow if you focused on looking in the right spot. The door had just started to crack open, when Christine called Theodore's name. He abandoned the idea of going backstage and bolted to the left out into a hallway. Christine slipped off her heels and ran after him. We followed and I snatched up Christine's shoes.

There was no chance that we could run as fast as two vampires, but we followed all the same. They headed left, then left again to go towards the south end of the building that would be mostly empty at this time of night. We lost sight of them, and Mike took a reasonable guess that Theodore would head for the construction area.

We stumbled into the half built wing of the building and found Christine standing still in the entrance, looking around for a sign of her quarry.

I felt his minds presence, and whispered, "He's here".

Theodore's cloaking device malfunctioned making him visible for a few seconds. He tapped it. It flickered. He slipped out of site behind a palate of construction materials and yelled, "The weak starve to death!" Later Christine explained that this was a traditional Vampkido challenge.

Christine said, "I can't fight Vampkido in this dress." and looked back at us. Mike realized what she wanted a second before I did and unzipped the back of her dress. The dress and her purse dropped to the floor and she took off at a run.

Christine is stunningly beautiful in or out of anything. She was wearing matching sea foam green bra and panties that looked like something out of the Victoria Secrets catalogue. She had on a garter belt with gray stockings that ended at the ankle and had stirrups going under the arch of her feet. Ankle stockings with stirrups worn with high heels were the hot upscale fashion that year. Both of us stared at her gorgeous departing posterior for a couple seconds. Mike's mouth was hanging open a bit. I slapped him to remind him which woman in the room he had a chance of going to bed with tonight.

The wing under construction would be a dangerous place for a Vampkido fight. It was a big open room with exterior walls and roof, but no interior walls. There was scaffolding in various places. There were pallets of construction materials and more piled in stacks that didn't look all that stable. There were temporary workbenches with tools on them, and extension cords running everywhere. There were a couple partly built walls that consisted only of steel studs. It looked like there would be a central atrium with a glass roof, and a number of huge potted plants had been stored in that area.

Theodore ran through the room, bouncing off of obstacles with incredible agility. Christine was right behind him. They looked like a couple of squirrels playing tag in a stand of trees, with no concern for what would happen if their footing missed. Theodore may be good at Vampkido for a young vampire, but Christine was at a pretty high level in the sport with a couple centuries of experience on him. In a fair fight, Christine would mop the floor with him, but this wasn't a fair fight. Theodore had the malfunctioning cloaking device making him go invisible at random times, and was desperate enough to take dangerous risks.

We heard a pile of steel studs topple over onto the concrete floor. Mike had his n-gun out, but it didn't have a very long range and he didn't want to hit Christine. Theodore came running directly at us, but made a sharp right turn at incredibly high speed by grabbing the corner of a piece of scaffolding. He made the turn, but toppled the scaffolding in the process. Christine had to cartwheel to her left to keep from being crushed by the scaffolding, then switched direction to cut him off. A nail gun toppled off of a workbench and nails machine-gunned around the room. I dodged left and hid behind a pallet of cement bags. Mike jumped to the right.

Theodore and Christine ran through the unfinished atrium and the cloaking device flickered. Branches rained down off of a couple of the plants.

Mike hollered out, "Theodore, turn off the cloak. It is malfunctioning. It could cut your feet off."

Theodore made a half completed wall of steel studs into a slalom course, then changed direction by pushing off with his foot four feet up the wall. Christine cut inside his turn, then had to stop short to keep from having her arm sliced off by the flickering cloaking device. She had figured out that the cloak gave off a short static buzz just before it flickered.

Theodore came back towards where I was hiding. I could feel his elation, and realized that he noticed Mike and I were no longer blocking the exit. There was a long piece of half inch steel pipe on the floor by my feet. I put my right foot behind it and slid my toe under the pipe. Right as he was about to pass me, I shoved my leg forward as hard as I could. The steel pipe connected with Theodore's shin, and stopped so abruptly that my own ankle got a good bruise where it was against the pipe.

Theodore hit the floor with Christine coming down on top of him. The fight was now a series of holds, reversals and takedowns. Finally Theodore came down flat on his back. Christine came down right on top of him, with her knees on his biceps and her hands on his thighs.

Even when a vampire loses, he has to lose with style. Theodore Edwards stuck out his tongue and ran it slowly down the crotch of Christine's panties. Not many people have the audacity to do that to their arresting officer. Not to be outdone, Christine slammed her forehead into his groin. He put up very little resistance as she pulled handcuffs from her purse, which I handed her, and cuffed him.

I helped Christine zip her gown. Her pheromones were in full force now. Every perfume maker on the planet would give their first born for that scent. It is the most potent human sexual attraction scent on the planet. Unfortunately, this highly reactive modification of human pheromones is unstable and thus degrades less than an hour after it is produced.

I'm not into other women, but Christine's pheromones were affecting me as well. I have resistance to empathic bombardment, not to chemical stimulus. I had to resist the urge to feel the curves under her lingerie. I could enjoy a night in bed with her. I have some blood to spare as long as she sucks it out of my... my subconscious interjected with a strong mental image of the exit door.

Ok, going. I stepped outside into the cool night air and unbuttoned my collar. The effect started to wear off, but I still wasn't sure if that was good, or if I had missed out on something fantastic. I wondered just how many humans had awoken from a night of sex, drinking, and blood sucking wondering just what had come over them. For that matter, how much different would it be waking up from an orgy caused by an empath's emotional manipulation, other than the memory of having sex with a four hundred pound empath?

Christine passed me on her way out, pushing Theodore Edwards in front of her. She mumbled good evening, but didn't slow down. I'm sure Christine knew what her scent did to me, and avoided giving me any opening to pursue that temptation. When we got home an hour later, Mike and I played out some of those lustful fantasies, then I fell asleep in his bed.

Chapter 9

After the previous night's excitement, it seemed like there should be some great ending, like riding off into the sunset. However, all I felt was a sense of serenity, almost bordering on melancholy. I got up in the morning. The house was quiet. It was the same house, but somehow everything felt different, or perhaps I was different. I wondered if this was some sort of vampire pheromone hangover, but that didn't feel right either.

Mike spent the next few hours on his computer and multiple phone calls. I got the gist that it was all about the apprehension of Theodore Edwards, but couldn't tell exactly what was going on. Mike distractedly ate anything I put in front of him. I was tempted to feed him some dead crickets, but it felt like crossing some sort of line. Besides it might trigger some Buddhist oneness thing and cause him to become one with the cricket. Cue visions of a man-cricket hybrid from a cheesy science fiction film. OK, I was still a bit loopy.

Mike finally got off the phone and computer. He sat at the table having a cup of coffee, and I joined him. That brought both of us back to focusing on the here and now. There's nothing like caffeine to restore your humanity. I suppose that says something about humanity.

Then Mike told me what he could about the case. Because of the cloaking device, it was a national security case. Because of Mike's involvement, it was a United Nations matter. Because Theodore Edwards is a vampire, it is a supernatural case. Because of Keith Voss's death and Christine's involvement, it's a city law enforcement matter. However, some powerful players, perhaps all, would prefer that the matter be kept as quiet as possible. For the time being, Mike was out of the loop.

Empath's log: Last week, I helped Mike with one of his cases. This felt like a turning point in my life. I'm much stronger at controlling my empathic abilities. I don't know what career I want,

129

but I wouldn't mind helping Mike out again. I got an immense sense of accomplishment from catching a fugitive. I do know that living with Mike is the most at home I've ever felt. Empath out.

It was late in the evening, although still a bit early to fall asleep. Mike was reading a book although I got the feeling he wasn't very focused on it. You know what they say in the Army. Never pass up a chance to eat, sleep, or have sex. Come to think of it, I think that must be the Navy motto.

I struck a pose in the doorway, putting my hands against the doorframe and sticking out my posterior. I called out to Mike, "Hey sailor, wantta show a girl a good time?"

Book 3

Supernatural Apocalypse

Chapter 1

The stockings were too short, only coming half way up the thigh. This left an inch of skin showing between the stocking and hem line, creating an optical illusion of the skirt being shorter than it was. Cleavage? Check. Three-inch heels? Check. The raincoat was slightly shorter than the skirt hemline. Ruby red lipstick? Yep, it pretty well screamed "cheap hooker".

I checked myself over one more time in the mirror, then walked out onto the street and headed down the block. I put a "couldn't care less" dazed stare on my face, with eyelids partially closed.

He was leaning against a building with the sole of one foot against the wall. He was smoking. He also had a faint smell of blood about him. I leaned on the building next to him, both of us facing the street. I reached out my hand, and he gave me the cigarette. I took a deep breath and handed it back as I slowly blew the smoke out through my puckered lips.

"I wish I had something stronger," I said out loud to no one in particular.

"That can be arranged," he said.

I looked directly at him for the first time. My face lit up and I said, "Yeah?" Then I bit my lip with an expression of worry and said, "No, I better not."

I started to slowly turn away from him. He put his hand on my shoulder and gently but firmly pulled me back around towards him. I do believe that constitutes assaulting a police officer.

I gave a cat-like yowl and slapped at his face like a girl with no idea how to fight. I made sure one palm landed flat on his nose so it would hurt. He pushed me away, and I grabbed the sleeves of his jacket pulling both of us down onto the sidewalk. As we rolled onto the sidewalk, I came out on top. I weakly pounded at his chest and stomach. It didn't hurt him, and wasn't supposed to. What it did was let me feel which pockets had small bags of drugs in them. I grabbed at those pockets, then dug in with my fingernails. When he pushed me off, the pockets ripped and drugs spilled out across the sidewalk.

He rolled over in preparation for getting up. He flattened back onto the concrete as my elbow jabbed into the middle of his spine, and the cuffs were on before he knew what was happening. I pulled the little revolver out of the waistband at the back of his pants. The angle at which he leaned against the building had told me it was there before I walked up to him.

I raised my voice a little and said "Unit two, I have a pickup for you." A little beep of my cell phone told me they were on their way.

Then I noticed two packets of blood on the pavement along with the drugs. I scooped them up and clicked the button that turned off the voice transmission from my cell. I stuck the blood packets against the dealers face and eye then said, "See this? What is it?"

I slipped the blood packets into an inner pocket of my raincoat. He started talking immediately, probably wanting to cut a deal for giving up his supplier, "It's called Apocalypse, or just A. I was told to put a drop of it on my jacket and not mention it unless someone asked about blood. No one has."

"What does it do?" I asked.

"I don't know. I thought it was for those silly teens that get off on vampire movies," he replied.

Listening to the tone in his voice, my gut said he was telling the truth. The conversation was ending there anyway, as a battered unmarked van pulled up and three more officers piled out to read him his rights and bag the evidence all over the ground. I unloaded the pistol and bagged it correctly so that no one else's prints could be on it. It was a cool night and no one made any unnecessary conversation.

The officers were just happy to have a valid excuse to go back to the police station after being cramped in the surveillance van.

As I pulled into the parking lot at my apartment building, the gate opened automatically as it sensed the small electronic tag on the dash. I checked my smart phone. No motion sensor hits inside the apartment. There was nothing unusual on the live cameras in the hall and inside the apartment. I wasn't expecting anything, but it's a good habit to check. No, I'm not paranoid. I just know what truly scary stuff is really out there. I walked into the building, casually unconcerned as usual.

I walked into the apartment and put the Sharper Image cooler on the sleek, quartz counter top. The kitchen was done in stainless steel and birch. The design was clean and modern. Only a counter divided the galley kitchen from living room. The living room was in gray and red with furniture that was both modern and comfortable enough to have sex on.

I pulled my ice tea bottles out of the cooler and put them in the dishwasher. I plugged in the cooler to recharge. Then I pulled the bags of blood out of the false bottom in the cooler. I inspected them carefully, but they seemed like perfectly ordinary clinical blood bags. I sniffed at them. The blood type matched the label, and it smelled like ordinary human blood. I thought about putting the blood in the false compartment in the refrig, but decided to leave it in the cooler compartment.

I dropped some mail on the desk in the spare room, then headed to the bedroom. The bedroom was done in light green. It was stylish but not so feminine as to be off putting to a male guest. I left the light off and checked out the south view through the sheer curtains as I peeled off the hooker outfit. I wouldn't have picked a south view, but view was a low priority as I had this apartment custom designed during the building renovation. It was an old mill building converted to apartments with some sections of old brick walls and beams exposed to give industrial style accents. My apartment was adjacent to a service crawl space where pipes and wires ran through the building. I had a secret door at the back of the closet that gave an emergency exit into the service area.

The bedroom also had a second double door closet concealed behind blank wall panels. It was the full width of the wall, but only a foot deep. That one concealed a variety of manacles, ropes, riding crops, and everything else an S&M aficionado could want. I'm not really into S&M, but finding a submissive is one of the better ways to find someone who will allow you to bite them. That's right, I'm a vampire. You got a problem with that?

Chapter 2

I got up late the next morning. No one expected a detective to arrive in the office first thing in the morning after a night sting. I showered, then remembered to get iced tea going. I made the tea up using bottled, raspberry flavored water. I was still wearing only a bath towel.

I got dressed in a deep blue dress that I had just received from a New York designer. It was a shame to put the shoulder holster with my sleek Beretta over the dress and a Navy blue jacket over that. The police issue Glocks were ugly and bulky, making them difficult to conceal. Plain-clothes officers were allowed a bit more latitude in selecting side arms.

I thought about the drug dealer carrying blood bags as I ate a bagel and juice. First things first. I had better find out what the stuff is.

I put in a call to Dr. Daniel Howser, Huntsville's expert on blood. An overly pert receptionist's voice told me he was not available. I identified myself as a police detective. Then overly pert told me he was out of town on vacation, and would be unreachable as he did some crazy endurance run through the Alps. I had heard of those runs. Some years half of the entrants drop out with frostbite and hypothermia and someone died every once in a while. Howser was a useful resource. I hoped he didn't do something foolish and end up dead.

"Oh damn," I said out loud as I realized who I would have to go to.

I called Paul Ackerly, who answered his own phone, and told him I'd be there in half an hour. Some expertly applied makeup, a couple bottles of ice tea in my cooler and I was out the door.

The day was sunny, and comfortable. I lowered the top on my powder blue Thunderbird and headed out. No, vampires don't burst into flames in the sunlight. We are evolved from humans to have a longer life span. That evolution isn't quite perfect, specifically in the bone marrow that produces blood. So vampires have to consume a bit of human blood to stay healthy. You can get blood from humans through violence or seduction. Natural selection created vampires that look human, are athletic, and very beautiful.

Paul Ackerly is brilliant, but I don't like dealing with him, partly because he is a socially inept dweeb, and partly because he works at the cities sewage waste processing plant. I pulled into the waste plant, and slipped a blood packet from the hidden compartment in the cooler into my purse. I told the receptionist he was expecting me, and I knew the way. She waved me by, apparently not anxious to escort someone to that part of the building. I didn't give her my name, and she didn't ask.

Paul is a human alchemist, the name for scientists that are insiders in the supernatural community. He is middle aged with black hair turning gray. I wondered if he bought those black glasses with tape already on them. His white lab coat was badly stained, with what I really didn't want to know. I think he keeps some particularly disgusting things simmering at the front of the lab bench just so no one will bother him. The lab fridge had a sign saying "Human waste samples only. Don't eat the leftovers."

Paul looked up from his work and said, "Ah detective Christine Mills. What disturbance in the Force brings you to my lair?"

"I need you to analyze a blood sample," I said, trying to keep it professional.

"Dr. Howser is our local expert on blood genetics," he replied.

I replied, "Yes, but Dr. Howser is out of town, and I'm mostly looking for foreign substances."

He said, "OK, I can have a preliminary report in under an hour."

I handed over the blood packet, and said "Good. I'll wait." I sat down on a steel stool, which to my surprise was not covered with papers and disgusting sample vials.

He put on fresh rubber gloves, then pulled blood samples out of the bag with a sterile needle. He filled two vials and dropped them in a centrifuge that roared to life with a loud hum. He injected smaller amounts into a couple machines that I couldn't identify.

I checked some things on my smart phone while he worked. He kept up a dialog, perhaps half to himself. Twenty minutes later, his diatribe increased in volume, apparently to include me in the conversation.

"At first pass, the blood seems fairly normal." he said. "It is type A Positive from a human male, Caucasian, in his late twenties. He is reasonably healthy, other than drinking a bit much. There are not any of the more readily identified diseases, or genetic anomalies, although Dr. Howser could do a more detailed genetic analysis. However, there is a foreign substance, which I am isolating now."

I signed at his need to tell me a bunch of unimportant information, then went back to my phone as I waited for the important part.

He seemed to finish with several of the machines, then moved to a desk against the wall with a large monitor.

"Here is the chemical structure," he said.

I walked over to look over his shoulder. Yep, it looked like a geometric but asymmetric pattern of lines and letters. For all I knew, it could be a building floor plan that some drunk architect had scribbled on a cocktail napkin. Ackerly was apparently running it through some sort of search algorithm.

"The exact structure is not previously known to science," he said. I couldn't tell if he was talking to me or had forgotten I was present.

"It has a nAChRv pharmacophore match, which means it will be addictive to vampires," he continued. I caught the second half of that, and figured it was probably the only important part.

"Able to permeate the blood-brain barrier. Partial similarity to a number of known psychotropic agents," he droned on in mad scientistese.

He looked up at me and said, "That's it. It's a mind altering drug that is highly addictive, but only for vampires."

"What does it do to their minds?" I asked.

"I can't tell with this equipment," he said, "It would take a major drug testing lab months to work out the details. Or you could stick a vampire in a prison cell and give them some to see what happens. But make sure it's someone you don't like. I can't give you any reliable estimate on what dosage will kill the subject either."

He put all of the scientific analysis results on an archaic CD disk and took ten minutes to type up his summary. He had some point about how data lasted longer on archival quality CDs than on flash drives. I walked out of the building with the disk in my purse, just under an hour from when I walked in. I still thought he was a dweeb, but I had to admit that some other lab might have taken weeks to tell me a lot less.

Mark Blout was the detective heading up an investigation of illegal drug activities in Huntsville. He was the one in charge when I was helping out with last night's drug dealer arrest. I headed back to the station to talk with him. Since this drug targets vampires, I need to be more involved with his investigation, without letting him know that vampires exist or that I am one of them.

Mark was his usual self. Five-o-clock shadow at ten in the morning. Eyes blurry until his third cup of coffee. Tattered sport coat. Shirt that looked like it had been slept in for three days. I've never seen him in a clean shirt. I'm presuming he presses his shirts by wadding them up and putting them under the doormat for a few days. Mark is local boy who is a decent enough detective. He isn't a genius, but he knows the local culture well, and he is good at reading people.

I casually leaned on the desk across from his and said, "Good morning, Detective Blout."

He grunted. He must be in a good mood. He's probably still having fantasies about seeing me in that hooker getup.

"One of my informants mentioned something about a new drug on the streets," I said.

He looked at me. I took it as a sign that I should continue.

"This is your case, but I was wondering if you mind me following up on some leads until my work load picks up."

He took a swig of coffee, possibly hoping to evolve into something capable of human speech.

He said, "The group meets at one in conf B. There are rumors of dealers targeting a new group of customers. We don't know who." Presumably, he made that entire speech without injuring himself.

"I'll see you then," I said. I headed off to contact my informant network.

By one o-clock all I had was a report of someone seeing bags and vials of blood at a club, which I could have guessed already. All I told the other officers was that I had heard reports of a new drug called Apocalypse or A.

Apparently last night's sting on the drug dealer was part of a larger plan. They think they are getting close to mounting a raid on the local drug boss, who controls the supply in town. I heard about a few of the tidbits of evidence. The evidence they have thus far is too weak to get a conviction, but they are hoping a raid that captures a large amount of incoming product will take care of that. I offered to participate in that raid when the time came.

I spent the rest of the afternoon testifying in court about details of a bust I had made the month before.

That evening I had a boring but edible microwave dinner. I changed into matching turquoise athletic shorts and a fitted t-shirt. Over that went a sweat suit with a sleek cut in gray with a pink piping. I filled a fresh travel mug with raspberry iced tea and headed out.

I really enjoyed the martial arts nights hosted by Mike and Liz. It always has an eclectic mix of vampires, werewolves, empaths, ogres, and exceptional humans. The best martial arts instructor I ever had taught me that a reasonable ability in many fighting styles was more important than perfection in one when you find yourself in a real fight.

The year was 1816. I was an impetuous, young forty-year-old leaving home for the first time. I wanted some excitement and adventure, so I made my way to Charleston. I got a job as a waitress in a dingy pub by the waterfront.

It was called the Pig's Head Tavern. The sign above the door was a carving of a pig's head and a large mug of ale. There were no words on the sign because most of the customers were illiterate. No matter how we cleaned, the walls, floor and ceiling were stained dark from tobacco and cooking fire smoke. The lighting from oil lamps and the fireplace was dim. There was a constant cloud of smoke in the air whenever customers were present, which was most days with a few starting at noon and a packed house after dark.

The tavern owner was a big man named Clyde. He had a twisted nose from having it broken too many times while evicting unruly or nonpaying customers. His evictions usually tossed them well out into the street, and if possible into a pile of horse dung. I gave Clyde his due respect, but always looked him square in the eye. He hired me as a serving wench because I was pretty enough to catch the eye of customers, and tough enough to deal with them. Clyde gave me a small room above the tavern, free meals, and a pittance of additional pay above what I got from tips. He never tried to take advantage of me. His wife, Midge was a small, round woman who cooked the food in a small kitchen at the back of the building. Clyde and Midge lived in a small building at the back of the property that had been converted from a stable into living quarters.

There were two whores who rented rooms on the second floor. They gave Clyde a small cut for being able to ply their trade in his establishment and occasionally getting his help dealing with an abusive customer. One was named Clara, and I can't remember the other's name. They were rather plain looking women. Clara was a bit over weight and the other was getting a bit old for such work. However, the Pig's Head wasn't the place for top tier prostitutes, and these two seemed to give the customers a good value in the form of enthusiasm and willingness to act out the part that the customer wanted them to play.

Of course vampires are used to keeping secrets. None of the people there ever knew that I was a vampire, how old I was, or that I already had three college degrees, conferred under three different names I had been going by at the time. I had already gotten a fair amount of instruction and experience in sexual acts, since that is one way to get blood from people. Many vampires will spend a time being a prostitute when they need the money or are in the mood. Vampires are immune to sexually transmitted diseases. Many customers are drunk enough that they don't realize you have taken some of their blood, or will consider the occasional bite as part of the fun in a round of rough sex. Nonetheless, I learned a fair number of new tricks from the whores at the Pig's Head.

I had also gotten a fair number of lessons in hand to hand combat by that point in my life, since force is the other option for a vampire needing to feed. I had evicted a couple unruly customers, and the rest knew not to go beyond the bounds of what was socially acceptable. Of course, in that time period in that type of establishment, a serving wench was expected to put up with a fair amount of groping and pinching as long as the customer left a reasonable tip. I played along a bit as long as they stayed within bounds. The customers got what they wanted, I got good tips, the tavern was packed and some of them shelled out the money to give the whores some business. People today might view it as barbaric, but the economic system of the time worked.

As I waited tables, I started learning all I could about the various sailing ships that came and went. There were fisherman, who would have smelled disgusting if you could smell anything beyond the tobacco smoke. There were merchants who made trips across the Atlantic in the summer months. There were Navy ships, many of which had seen action in the War of 1812. There were also coasters, smaller ships that shuttled goods from the large seaports to small towns up and down the coast, and a short ways into the larger rivers. The ones I was most interested in were the larger coasters. They had ocean-going vessels and made trips as far north as Newfoundland in the summer and sometimes as far south as Panama. The golden age of piracy was long gone, but the large coasters were still most likely to be skirting around tariffs, or encounter hostile ships, or occasionally be hostile ships.

One summer night, I got off work well after midnight. It was warm in my little room and I couldn't sleep, so I went for a walk along the waterfront. I was watching for drunken sailors passed out in alleys, who wouldn't miss a bit of blood when they woke. I wasn't watching the rest of the foot traffic as well as I should have been. I went into a promising looking alley, but what looked like someone slumped in the alley turned out to be trash heap.

I turned around and found my way out of the alley blocked by six large sailors. They were foreign merchants, with the rough demeanor that usually meant military veterans. Of course, they intended to rape me. For a vampire, sex is just part of shopping for groceries, so it wasn't like I would be traumatized by being raped. I might well get a chance to feed in the process. The problem was that they would be likely to kill me to cover up their crime. I could fight off two or three men larger than myself, but six were long odds.

There was no sense giving them a chance to surround me, so I walked up to the nearest one. I landed a hard kick in his groin, then a fist to his throat. He was doubled over, so I put all my weight into forcing his head into the cobblestones. It made sickening crunch, so I'm pretty sure I killed him. The second one grabbed me in a bear hug. I knew some wrestling moves, but I couldn't move and his huge arms were crushing the breath out of my chest. I sunk my teeth in. He didn't cry out, but I got a good drink and injected venom into the wound. He let go as the high from the venom took effect then he staggered back against the wall.

Now there were three at once on me and hands grabbing me more places than any wrestling move accounted for. The fourth was apparently looking for something to club me with. It occurred to me that this might really be the end of my short life.

A shadow detached itself from the wall. The sailor getting ready to bean me with a cobblestone slumped to the ground. The other's looked around, but couldn't see the cause of their compatriot's sudden slumber. One of the ones holding me went flying backwards into the darkness and disappeared with a loud thump. A second drew a knife and turned away from me to face the unseen menace and a couple seconds later also slumped to the ground. I landed a couple blows on the last one holding me, then he suddenly flew sideways into a wall.

The shadow again detached itself from the wall, and a small voice said, "Unharmed the young lady is, I hope."

"Yes, thank you," I said. I didn't know who this was, but I had no intention of disrespecting someone who could toss around large sailors like Sunday laundry.

As we stepped out onto the street, I saw that he was a small man. He must have been four inches shorter than me. He pulled off his black robe, and turned it inside out, putting the black lining on the inside. He donned the robe again, which was now blue with an embroidered picture of a golden dragon and small, twisted trees. What surprised me most was his face. I had heard of Asia, but had never met anyone from that continent.

I took him back to the tavern and fed him, mostly as an excuse to ask him questions. His name was Michi Ito, but the Americans he knew called him Mitch. He was some type of clergyman, who was traveling around the world to bring back knowledge of lands little known to his own people. It occurred to me that Asians must have a much different idea of the clergy given his fighting expertise. I had never heard of a Buddhist monk.

Mitch was currently working as a deck hand on the Endurance, a small clipper that was one of the larger coasters. He had impressed the captain with his agility in scaling the highest rigging and had been hired on to work for his passage and food. He was also teaching the crew hand to hand combat. That particular ship was rumored to occasionally smuggle goods, and to get into scraps that a more conservative merchant would not. It was also one of the better armed of the coasters.

As soon as I heard about the ship and his role on it, I immediately asked what I could do to come along with them, and learn fighting techniques from Mitch. To his credit, Mitch took me seriously, when most people would have laughed at a barmaid wanting to be a sailor. He told me that the ship did not take passengers, but that the cook had gotten thrown in jail that day and would probably not leave with the ship in the morning.

By that time, the sun was starting to come up. I stuffed my three changes of clothes and few belongings into a pillowcase and accompanied Mitch to the ship. He introduced me to the captain, Jack Brown, and I immediately asked for a job as ships cook. One of the crew made a lewd remark about what he would like to do with me in the galley, and I decked him. The captain hired me on the spot, and we left with the tide an hour later. I never had a chance to say goodbye to Clyde, but he had a couple times commented that I wasn't the type to spend my life as a tavern wench, so he wouldn't be surprised. I had tossed my apron on the bar, which was all the resignation that was needed.

Mitch and I spent the next two years on the Endurance. Between cooking and learning martial arts from Mitch I worked

145

fourteen to sixteen hour days. Mitch had only been on the ship a couple weeks, so I quickly caught up on what I had missed. He started by teaching us to fall in various ways and not get hurt. Then came ways to block a blow, then dodges. Then came myriad types of sparring. Sparring at long distance was some sort of karate, although all the martial art forms didn't have names like they do today. We went through fighting when you are a foot or so apart, grappling close (pretty similar to today's Judo), holds on wrist and throat, using obstacles to your advantage, fighting blind, fighting while you are on the ground, and probably more I'm forgetting to list here. He taught us to disarm opponents, and use a staff, but he never used a knife or sword. He seemed ideologically opposed to the use of edged weapons. All of this was done on the rolling deck of a sailing ship. Most of the other crew participated in at least half of the lessons, but I never missed one. The captain watched every lesson intently, but never participated since he felt it was inappropriate to give crewmembers an opportunity to fight the captain. I'm pretty sure he practiced the moves in his cabin. After two years, I could get some decent blows on Mitch, but couldn't defeat him in a fight even when I used a vampire's speed and strength. I think Mitch must have realized there was something exceptional about my physical abilities, but he never said anything. There were indeed a number of interesting adventures during that time, but I'll have to tell about those some other time.

One fall, we intentionally beached the ship near New Orleans, so that we could do repairs on the hull. Mitch said his goodbyes, then bought a ticket on one of the first steamboats to travel north to the small town of St. Louis. I decided it was time to be on my way as well. I never saw Mitch again, and never found out if he made his way back to Japan. I've had many martial arts instructors since then, but none as good as Michi Ito. Now that I'm old enough to take a longer view of my life, I sometimes think it would be great to spend thirty years learning from a true master like Mitch.

The ogre was a foot taller than me, and three times my weight. I could have gone straight to tactics for handling a larger opponent, but I get few chances to face ogres and wanted to learn more about their

146

abilities. Most ogres depend upon their size and strength alone, but Little Jimmy was also a fairly skilled fighter. We circled around one another. Jimmy kept his right hand out towards me and turned to keep me on his right quarter. He kept his left hand back by his chest, ready to launch a left cross that can pulverize a cinder block.

I launched a series of blows and kicks all from long distance. I gradually increased the tempo to see how fast his reflexes were. He blocked nearly all of my attacks with surprisingly fast arm speed. He moved his feet very little. I couldn't be sure if he was really slow on his feet, or if his fighting style just depended upon a stable footing and little footwork. The group had invented their own scoring system for inter-species martial arts. Successfully blocking an attack earned a quarter of a point, so Jimmy had gotten a couple points from my failed attacks.

I considered other options for defeating Jimmy (nicknaming him Little Jimmy was rather moronic humor in my opinion). Other than their size and strength, ogres are little different from humans. The species of ogre is defined mostly by their inability to have offspring with humans.   Ogres tend to take jobs as bouncers, bodyguards, and football players. With a human twice my weight, I can lever them around if I get hold of a wrist. Jimmy's on guard position had his left elbow almost back to his ribs, obviously in hopes an opponent would underestimate his reach and come too close. I made a series of feints towards him, hoping he would extend his arm so I could grab it. Eventually he did grab for me. I grabbed his wrist and pulled it downward with all my weight. I found my feet dangling off the ground as he effortlessly held my entire body weight off the ground with his completely outstretched arm.

I swung my left leg from as far back as it went to as far forward. That gave enough inertia to get my leg over his head and put his neck in a scissors lock between my knees. He turned his head towards me so my knees would be squeezing on the sides of his neck where it didn't do any good. He reached his right hand out and pushed down on my shoulders. My back could bend backwards only so far before I had to let go with my legs. I flipped and landed face down on the mat with a jarring belly flop. I rolled out of the way just before his pile driver of a fist smashed into the mat where my jaw had just been. I wondered if he was holding back some of his strength for our little practice bout. It certainly sounded loud enough to crush my skull. The big dimwit might kill me just from being too dumb to know his own strength. That gave me a bit more determination to stop feeling him out and take him.

I feinted closer now, trying to draw his left cross. When the blow came, I used all my speed to move closer to him, slamming my back into his chest. As the blow went past my collarbone, I grabbed his arm and used his own momentum to keep him moving on into a Judo flip. He landed on the mat on his back. However, he still had a hold on me as well and pulled me down onto the mat next to him. He rolled over incredibly quickly to pin my shoulders like a college wrestler.

Jimmy won the bout fairly. However, I had learned quite a bit about the ogre's abilities. In the long run, the experience would be far more valuable than having won the bout. Over the years, I have become comfortable enough with my martial arts ability that I sometimes give less than my best and allow an opponent to beat me, just so they will underestimate me the next time we meet.

The audience applauded. The usual mix of humanoid species was standing around, half for the martial arts practice and half to schmooze over drinks and snacks. On the next mat over, Mike was fighting a werewolf named Gary. Mike is an exceptional human, who works for the United Nations as a liaison to the supernatural community in Huntsville. Liz was mixing up another bowl of punch. Liz is an empath, who is Mike's live in student and girlfriend. The student-teacher-bedroom relationship thing doesn't bother me. Mike was wound pretty tight, so Liz has been good for him.

The evening progressed about as expected with martial arts practice giving away to a social party. I asked a few select individuals if they had heard anything about new recreational drug activity. I told the other vampires and Mike more of the details so they could be on the watch for it. I got drawn into a long conversation about Vampkido, the vampire marital art, and was one of the last to leave.

It was starting to rain as I was driving down Mike's long driveway. I saw Gary Halvorson walking back to town. The passenger window rolled down with a muted hum, and I called to him, "Hey Gary. Get in. I'll give you a ride." I hoped the big lug wouldn't shed on the upholstery. I'm not a dog person.

As best as I could tell, Gary was a happy-go-lucky guy who bounced from one job to the next. He was currently restoring an old Indian motorcycle. The restoration was apparently a work in progress, as evidenced by the bike left in Mike's barn and Gary walking back to town.

"Are you still living on the north side of town?" I asked.

"Yeah" he replied, "I'm renting a room in a house a couple blocks behind Krispy Kreme. I'm surprised more police don't live in that area, what with a doughnut factory just down the street and all."

I retorted, "It's pretty low rent when even the cops can afford to live in a better neighborhood."

I decided to change the subject by asking, "Are you still working as a bouncer at that bar across from the courthouse?"

"No, I quit. There were too many weekend shifts and I wanted more weekend time for the motorcycle club and hunting with the pack," he replied. "I'm still looking for a new gig."

After a slight pause, he said "If I may ask, what is that smell?"

We both had a bit of the scent of ode de exercise about us after an evening of martial arts. None the less, I was getting ready to flatten his nose with a hammer fist for making fun of the way I smelled when he went on.

"It smells like a pharmacy in here," he said.

I jerked the car off the road and slammed on the brakes. I reached behind the seat and pulled the second bag of blood from the cooler, then shoved it under his nose.

"Is this what you are smelling?" I asked.

"Yeah. It smells like drugs. I hope you haven't been drinking that stuff," he replied.

"No kidding?" I replied with my best sarcasm. "OK. You just got your new job working as a consultant to the Huntsville Police Department. Give me your cell number and I'll call you when I need your nose."

"Just my nose?" he asked, grinning and showing off a not unimpressive bicep.

I gave him a smile and a voice that was both sexy and sarcastically sweet as I said, "Honey, if I take you to bed, you won't be able to walk when I need you to work the next day."

Chapter 3

Friday morning, I slid the home gym out from under my bed and unfolded it. I'm sure I paid twice as much for an apartment friendly gym, but public gyms are a bad idea for a vampire. Someone might ask questions about a woman who is stronger than a man twice her weight. I do quite a few exercises with a moderate number of reps. I always follow the same sequence so I can run on autopilot and let my mind wander. The exercises got my heart beating but didn't really push me physically. Then I headed out for a five-mile run along one of the greenways that Huntsville has along side small streams that swell to handle storm runoff. After five miles, I felt like I had been run over by a truck. Vampires are made for speed and strength, not endurance.

I showered, dressed, ate a light breakfast, made more raspberry iced tea, and put a note on the shopping list to get more bottles of raspberry flavored water. I took some time at the computer in the second bedroom. Like most vampires, I make contingency plans for wars, pandemics, natural disasters, and fast getaways. Those might be long odds for humans to worry about, but if you live a few hundred years you can expect to experience most of them. I checked on my investment accounts in several countries. Even if you don't go for big money jobs, putting a little money aside and investing wisely for a couple hundred years adds up.

Finally I checked a number of web sites for drugged blood. I checked law enforcement, pop culture, and supernatural sites. There were a couple vague rumors of a Columbian drug cartel taking an interest in blood supplies, but nothing on social sites. By going through the NSA, I can search private posts on social media sites, even narrow the search by age, race, location, and economic status demographics. Peer pressure is a key marketing tool for illegal drugs, so nothing on social media means they haven't done a big product launch yet. Even illegal activities are marketed like a Silicon Valley startup, if you know how to recognize them.

I spent the day going around town to talk with people about drug activities and a new blood product on the market. Bar tenders are some of my best contacts. They tended to know an awful lot more than the evening news about the towns social structure, trends, affairs, etc. I also talked to people who ran homeless shelters and a number of youth activity programs. In a small city, a big network of acquaintances can be a detective's best friend. Today, the only thing I got were some tips on teens who were thought to be doing drugs and areas that dealers are working. No one had heard of a drug called Apocalypse or A. The fact that I got nothing about a new blood based drug, even at a Goth bar and a club with a VIP room that caters to vampires, means that we had caught this thing right at the beginning, before they had figured out how to market it to the right crowd.

Having checked on the word on the street, it was time to talk to the power brokers. As I headed home to change for the evening phase of this operation, I called Gary and told him to dress formal. I hadn't brought him along during the day because people in those areas are more likely to talk when they felt it was confidential. This evening's social function would be the sort of place where it is easier to blend in with the crowd if I'm hanging on the arm of some guy. I checked the time and estimated how long it would take to change and pickup Gary. We would be getting there fashionably late but not unreasonably so. I sped up a bit and headed home to change into a filmy green dress that I thought was one of the better styles to come out of Milan that year.

I was invited to a party at Frederick Senburg's mansion tonight. I was going to skip it to spend the weekend in Nashville with an occasional lover who enjoys getting bitten. However, I decided that a chance of stopping this drugged blood thing before it got started was more important. Frederick usually serves blood to his vampire guests, so I planned on getting a snack there.

Tonight Frederick was throwing a party in honor of Milese Wendt, a young vampire woman who just graduated from law school. It was an opportunity to introduce her to the movers and shakers in town. Milese is the daughter of Teresa Wendt, Frederick's head cook. Of course, he needs a vampire head cook to prepare meals to a vampire's taste. Frederick gives his staff free room and board and perks like this party. Perhaps he has a bit of a soft heart, but I think it's mostly because the miserly old billionaire knows that it's cheaper than paying them enough to afford their own home.

I picked up a platter of cheese slices at a deli, then headed towards Gary's place. Gary was renting a room, and apparently most of the garage with motorcycle parts spread out on the ground, in a house in a very affordable neighborhood. Huntsville doesn't have gang war zones, but has a few neighborhoods like this where half the houses have bars on the windows.

Gary was standing in the garage staring down at the parts of the dismantled Indian. There was another old Harley off to the side, in one piece if not functional. To my surprise, Gary had on a nice looking black tuxedo with a dark red cummerbund. I had expected a sport coat and plaid tie. Gary explained that he sometimes works security at high society functions.

Frederick's mansion is hidden in the middle of the Madison suburb. We drove up the gravel road in the wooded area that hides Frederick's mansion. Most mansions are wide and shallow to make them more impressive. His is a bit smaller than average, as mansions go, across the front but much deeper to hide the true scale of his wealth. The front is brick and designed to almost look like it is simply a large house. I parked, then grabbed the cheese platter. The old skinflint makes all of his parties pot luck.

As we walked towards the front doors, the first surprise was that no one was standing outside the door. As we stepped past the porch columns we could see that the door was cracked open slightly. I held up my hand to indicate that Gary should stop where he was. I stepped forward very quietly and peeked tentatively into the doorway. All I could see was a leg on the floor, and it wasn't moving.

I ran back to my car without pausing to indicate what Gary should do. I ran as fast as a vampire woman could while wearing three-inch heels, which is to say slightly faster than the fastest human sprinter. I popped open the trunk, pulled out a belt with a sleek Browning nine millimeter pistol and extra clips, and slung it over my shoulder. I tossed my heels in the trunk. Then I lifted the trunk floor to reach the spare tire compartment and pulled out two N-guns. At that point, Gary got to the car, probably not running his fastest.

I handed one of the N-guns to Gary. He checked the guns power level and said, "Neural inhibitor pistol, model 37a in brushed nickel with birdseye maple grips. You have good taste in weapons."

N-guns are one of the technologies that the supernatural community has not shared with the humans. They don't have a very long range, but plenty for hitting anything in a room of the mansion. The guns operate at the frequency of brain waves to cause people to pass out. It does no permanent damage, except for a chance of brain damage when used on empaths.

I glanced at the case at the back of the trunk that held a sniper rifle and a riot gun, but decided that might be overkill.

We headed back towards the house, leveling guns to cover one another. Cops are trained for that. Gary seemed to be doing a better job than I would expect just from someone emulating what they saw on TV. At some later date, I might remember to ask him about that.

In the foyer we found two of Frederick's guards, both werewolves. Neither was moving. We didn't have time to stop and check if they were alive when whoever had beaten them might be still in the house and ready to attack us from behind. The inside of the building was much more opulent. There were smashed marble statues and splintered inch thick walnut paneling. Whoever did this had been tossing werewolves around the room. My bets were on drug-crazed vampires. Gary sniffed at some blood on the wall and confirmed that he could smell the same drug.

We headed further back into the house, with guns at the ready. There was nothing in the formal living room or study. The formal dining room had smashed chairs and plates of hors d'oeurves scattered around the room, but no bodies.

The kitchen was in rough shape. There were pans and utensils strewn everywhere. There was one body on the floor. It looked like one of the female servants. She didn't have fangs and she wasn't big enough to be a werewolf or ogre. Thus she had to be either human or empath. You couldn't tell without a genetic test or feeling them in your head. A vampire can't tell the difference in the taste of the blood. In this case, there wasn't any blood to be had. She was drained completely dry. There were also small traces of blood around the edges of the counter. It looked like the cook had been cooking a dish made with the drugged blood. Some drug crazed vampire had even licked the drops of blood off the counter top.

Off the kitchen was a pantry the size of a small house. Things in the pantry had been knocked over, but it didn't look like anyone had tried to open the packages. However, an enormous amount of damage had been done to a metal door at the back of the pantry. But there were no tools, so someone had beat on the door with very strong fists. Someone was in such a frenzied mental state that they couldn't come up with the idea of going to get some sort of tool, not even a butcher knife from the next room. From the plaque above the door, it was a refrigerated wine storage locker, probably the size of a small bus. Gary and I were discussing how the door was damaged and hypothesizing about there being more blood in side, when we heard a couple metallic clanks and the door started to slowly swing open.

Inside was Deirdre, a young empath woman who worked for Frederick as an administrative assistant. I'm sure Frederick used her empathy skills to give him an edge in business negotiations. Deirdre was sitting on the floor of the cooler with her back resting against a shelving unit. She had sustained a number of injuries before locking herself in.

I grabbed some clean kitchen towels off of the nearest pantry shelf and started binding the wounds that were still bleeding. I had to swallow down a bit of blood craving as I smelled the blood on her. It was about time I drank some blood, and there wasn't a safe source in sight.

"What happened?" I asked as I attended her wounds.

"I think it was the blood. Before the party, Frederick told the staff to bring him fruit juice during the party, even though he would ask for a blood cocktail in front of the guests. He's been sicker than he lets on. The vampires present got more and more excitable, all except Frederick. When the vampires started trying to bite everyone, Frederick tried to get all of the non-vampire guests and staff together. Frederick and the non-vampire guards were trying to protect the group as they made their way to the storm shelter in the sub-basement. The cook's assistant, Shelly, and I were at the other end of the hall and couldn't get to them. We were attacked. I hit them with a projection of depression with enough force to collapse a vampire into a sobbing heap at close range, but they didn't even slow down. I broke free, and ran in here. I knew that killing Shelly would occupy them for a few seconds so I could get to safety, but there was nothing I could do to save her. I ran in here and wedged a steel cooking spoon in the latch mechanism. They beat on the door. They were too far gone to speak. They only growled and screamed like animals."

Deirdre should have been helpless with the number of vampire bites I saw injecting venom into her. She should have been in a complete daze of orgasmic bliss. She must have been really scared to muster enough adrenaline to cut through that. A number of the bites on her were in the wrong places, where no blood would have been gotten. Vampires are experts at drawing blood dozens of places on the body, and not this sloppy, at least when they are in their right minds.

I asked Deirdre how many vampires were in the house that night. She was too addled to count, but named off Frederick, the cook, the cook's daughter, two security staff and about eight guests. I didn't expect her to have a perfect count in her current state. While she was naming these off, Gary handed her juice and cookies like they give you at a blood bank. I should have thought of that.

I considered Gary and I trying to protect Deirdre, look for other survivors and detain a dozen drug crazed vampires. The odds weren't good. I quickly decided this was time to call for backup. I wanted to keep this in the supernatural community if possible, so I would have to get creative. The Huntsville area has three-hundred thousand residents, but only a few hundred supernaturals. That wasn't enough to have a supernatural police force or jail, but there are some who are marginally in the business.

I pulled out my cell and started dialing numbers into a conference line so I would only have to explain once. I called two werewolves who are on the part-time S.W.A.T. team, Mike Brown with the United Nations, a couple security people from the arsenal, and Little Jimmy... I was ready to take a bar bouncer in the present situation.

I got most of them on the line, then gave my spiel "Hi. This is Christine Mills, vampire with the Huntsville Police. We have a security situation in Huntsville's supernatural community, and I'd like to keep it in the community if possible. There is a new illegal drug on the market, spiking blood supplies. It makes vampires turn into bloodthirsty maniacs. This evening it was given to vampires, probably without their knowledge, at a gathering at Frederick Senburg's place. We have one injured, one dead, possibly more of both and we estimate a dozen vampires still under the influence, hopefully still on the premises. We are going to move the injured to the small security office on the left side of the entryway, protect that position and try to use the house security system to find out more. If you can respond, we could use your help here. Use non-lethal force if possible, but be prepared to do more."

Most of the others on the call gave an immediate "on my way" and hung up. Mike said he would call a doctor also. I'm used to the police dispatchers knowing when an ambulance is needed from the description of the situation.

Gary carried Deirdre while I covered us with both N-guns. We made it to the security office without seeing anyone. The two werewolf guards in the entry were breathing, but we couldn't tell how bad their injuries were.

The house security system had a screen showing open doors and windows. There were cameras covering grounds, exterior doors, and some common areas but no bedrooms or bathrooms. I could see a vampire in an upstairs hallway. He was sitting in a little ball shaking like a drug addict with withdrawal. There weren't any security cameras in the storm shelter, but there was a line for the sub-basement on the house phone.

I called the sub-basement and got one of the people in the storm shelter. There were about two-dozen people locked in down there. They had some injuries, but none critical. They also told me Frederick Senburg had been killed as he helped cover their retreat. I told them to stay put until more security people got there.

Deirdre seemed to be feeling better and had moved from the floor to a desk chair. Since we had time to wait for reinforcements to arrive, I thought I'd occupy her and get some background information.

"What has Frederick been working on lately?" I asked.

"Local politics has been slow, but he is a member of the Council of Vampires," she replied.

I had forgot he was on the Council of Vampires. The vampire race doesn't have a rule making government, but the council watches out for vampire interests in international politics, science, the media, etc. They have actually promoted the popular culture of vampire movies and books. That is to hide the truth inside a barrage of false expectations. If someone sees a vampire's fangs but they don't burst into flame in the sunlight, the assumption is that it is someone with Halloween false teeth not a vampire.

"What has the Council been doing?" I asked.

Deirdre replied, "The big one lately has been artificial blood. There have been some blood substitutes invented in Europe that can carry oxygen thus keeping a human alive in an emergency. However, vampires need the blood bank system to survive. Agents of the council have manipulated the artificial blood test results to make it appear not as good as it is. They even make the bad results such that they will drive scientists towards a product that can feed vampires as well as being an emergency blood substitute.

"All the world needs is more junk food made out of stuff you can't pronounce," I said, both lightening the mood and displaying my natural sarcasm.

Vampires have spent thousands of years manipulating human culture to provide a blood supply. Vampires invented the medical practice of "blood letting", an ancient practice of curing illness by bleeding some blood out of the patient, which then fed local vampires. More recently, vampires have been behind the creation of a system of blood banks to store human blood for emergency use, which incidentally does save many human lives. Vampires were also behind the development of the anticoagulants that keep blood bank blood usable for a long time, and the false scientific evidence that it goes bad quickly. The expired blood, which is really perfectly good, must be destroyed for health reasons and the local vampire community intercepts that supply to feed themselves.

Blood from animals is too different to properly nourish vampires. Vampires are evolved from humans and need human blood to live so long. Empath and ogre blood is fine, but those are pretty rare species. Werewolf blood is slightly less nutritious, and our venom doesn't work on them so the werewolf feels like a hornet is stinging them. Primate blood has been tried out of curiosity, scientific investigation, or desperate necessity. It doesn't nourish us, and you don't want to know what happens when you bite a gorilla.

Frederick being a member of the Council of Vampires complicated the situation. Over the next couple weeks, hundreds of vampires would converge on Huntsville to attend his funeral and elect a new council member.

At that point our reinforcements started arriving. First to arrive were Forrest Jones and Hunter Greene, the two werewolves on the police force. They and Gary started searching through the first floor, with me watching the security cameras. Once I gave them a heads up when they had passed a stairwell that had no signs of life, then someone came down the stairs to catch them from behind. The drugged vampires might be sobbing or catatonic, but they could instantly explode into a killing machine.

The guys took to hitting them with N-guns and tying them up while unconscious. That put them at a bit of risk if they got attacked before the N-guns had time to recharge. There are heavy rifle N-guns that can shoot several shots in rapid succession before waiting for the ultra capacitors to recharge, but no better range. The short range and recharge time are the down side of N-guns.

Then Doctor John Bowie arrived. He is an empath medical doctor who treats all of the supernaturals in town. It's hard to hide being a different species from your doctor, so you need a doctor you can trust to know your real species. Doc Bowie, is pale and so thin he could be mistaken for a demonstration skeleton.

The doc slapped a wide bracelet on Deirdre, which told him more than a battery of hospital tests. The bracelet is another piece of technology that hadn't yet been shared with the human population. He sealed a couple cuts almost instantly and told her to eat, rest, and drink plenty of liquids. Maybe supernatural medicine isn't that much different from human medicine.

One of the werewolf guards we found in the entry was coming around. Doc checked him over, and told him to take painkillers for the headache. Then he started on the other werewolf guard. They put him on an ornate antique table as a make shift operating table. The doc pulled a suitcase from his car and setup a contraption that gave a portable sterile field as well as giving an MRI image of the internal organs while he did a delicate brain surgery on the spot that would have been nearly impossible with human medicine. Gary made sure that no one bothered the doc while his hands were inside of the patient's head.

Mike Brown arrived, then Little Jimmy, and one of the arsenal security people, a vampire, at about the same time. They got the survivors out of the storm shelter, and brought them to the foyer.

I heard more of the details of the party from the survivors. Frederick was the first one to realize something was wrong. He tried to act discreetly before all hell broke loose. He sent the guards that weren't vampires to lock down the exits, then come back to the group. Apparently the two we found in the entry way didn't make it back.

The remaining non-vampire guards and Frederick herded the guests towards the storm shelter, protecting them from the vampires. They fought their way down one flight of stairs, then another. The storm shelter in the sub-basement, below the first basement, was a good idea. However, the armory was in the first basement. The vampires, still lucid enough to use tools, grabbed the first thing they could reach inside the armory door, swords. Frederick had an eye for top quality weapons, some of which were the best ever made and hundreds of years old. Of course the old guy probably bought them hundreds of years ago at more reasonable prices than the tens of thousands of dollars medieval weapons are worth on the antique market today. The retreating group had only steps left to get to the storm shelter, when two of the vampires lunged simultaneously at a werewolf guard who was occupied with a third vampire. Frederick jumped in front of the werewolf. He parried one of the swords, but the other sword went through his heart.

The doc started analyzing the drugged vampires, who were solidly bound. They had neural evidence of addiction, aggressiveness, and impaired decision-making. He started a log of blood chemistry, and neural activity in order to start mapping out how long the drug stayed in their system. Huntsville doesn't have a jail for supernaturals. Nor is there a hospital ward, so Doc Bowie tends to setup home care when possible. It was decided that bedrooms in the mansion would act as a hospital and the patients kept restrained until the effects wore off. Doc took charge of that and arranging for nurses to be there as necessary. Fortunately, Fredericks plan to seal off the house worked and we found all of the drugged vampires. The one that got as far as cracking open the front door must have decided to head back to the massacre in the kitchen.

There was a lot more investigating to do, but it had been a long day already. As I was taking Gary home, I detoured to a particular fast food restaurant to get us both some food. I gave the correct phrase with the order and slipped an extra twenty in, so they would slip a bag of blood in with our food. Gary took a whiff and told me this blood was drugged also. Damn. I usually keep some blood on hand, but had just gotten to the point of running out and getting more. If I didn't get some blood soon, I would start getting weak and anemic.

We could have turned around to talk with the restaurant staff, but they had just closed so it could wait until morning. When I got home, I only wanted to collapse, but I had one more urgent item this evening. I sent emails with the appropriate hidden meaning to explain the drugged blood problem. I sent them to every vampire I knew in town, and to the elders of the other races in town. I pointed out that it might be a good idea to hire werewolves to help monitor the blood supply.

Chapter 4

Saturday morning with nothing to do is a luxury that detectives don't always get. I was up at seven for a light breakfast and brisk workout.

At a little after eight, I made a belated call to the guy I was going to spend the weekend with in Nashville. I apologized for not showing up last night, and made a joke about work being murder. He wasn't very upset. The advantage of casual sex relationships is that people don't get too bent out of shape about these things. The disadvantage is that it isn't much of a relationship, only slightly more personal than hiring a prostitute.

Just to be sure, I checked the concealed compartment behind the crisper of my refrigerator. Nope, no blood there. Vampires have to jump through more hoops to obtain blood today than they did hundreds of years ago. It's also more trouble switching identities, especially if you wanted the identity to hold up to a credit records check at least, or Defense Department security clearance at worse. It used to be much easier being a vampire.

The year was 1788. I was twelve years old, but I looked more like ten. One of the down sides of vampires living so long is that it takes us a bit longer to mature.

My dad was working as a doctor in a small rural town in Massachusetts. Most of his patients were humans, but there were some vampires in town who bought the blood dad obtained from bloodletting, a practice that would continue for about another hundred years. This made dad one of the more influential, and well-connected vampires in town.

One day I came by my dad's doctor office after school as usual. Dad had sent his nurse home early, and was busy packing things up. He gave me a note and told me to run home to mother as fast as I could. One of the vampires in town had gone too long without blood and accidentally killed the young woman he had been secretly sleeping with. The vampire had been caught and would probably be tortured for information about other vampires. In those days, most people were still quick to believe in vampires, ghosts, witches, and much more.

I ran home along a back street to our small farm on the edge of town. We settled there so we could raise some of our own food, thus hiding differences in our diet, and to have ready access to an escape route. As soon as mom read the note, she and I started packing a wagon. Mom didn't waste any time deciding what to pack, so she must have had a plan memorized. A couple hours later, dad arrived home dragging a large sack that would have been too heavy for a human to move. I learned much later that the sack contained recently buried corpses. There wasn't much in the way of forensics in those days, but they could at least count bodies.

Just as the sky became completely dark, dad lit the house on fire, and we galloped away. Dad had left a note in the doctor's office saying his family had the black plague, and he would do what he must to protect the town from it. The townspeople would see the burned corpses and assumed he had chosen to die with his family. We would be away clean as long as the captured vampire died from the torture before he gave our names. Even if he did give our names, they would probably never find us.

We went as fast as the horse could pull the wagon through the night. As morning approached, we found a wooded spot to hide. It was far enough off the road that travelers wouldn't readily see us. We had been too filled with adrenaline to sleep at night, and all slept in the shade under the wagon much of the day. Dad used the remaining daylight to search the area around out spot to make sure we weren't too close to anywhere anyone was living. Mom and I searched for the very driest wood that would give off little smoke when burned.

We ate bread during the day, then lit a small file to cook after dark. From our position behind a small hill from the main road, Dad guessed people would be more likely to see smoke during the day than firelight at night. We could only hope there was enough of a breeze to dissipate the smell sufficiently.

I thought that evening's long conversation was the most exiting I had ever had. We decided our new last name would be Hodges. I got to choose my own first name, and chose Meredith, which we pretended was to honor a Welsh friend of Dad's from his boyhood. I would be nine years old. I would look a bit big for my age at first, but would again look younger than my classmates by high school. We invented a new family history, along with little anecdotes. Dad would again be a doctor, and mom and dad chose new ages for themselves as young as possible. They had been putting a mixture of talcum powder and ashes in their hair to look as old as they should be after living in the Massachusetts so long. I had been described as a late life miracle baby born to a woman of fifty. Actually mom and dad had switched identities before and were in their late eighties when I was born. Vampires have a very hard time conceiving babies and carrying them to term.

In the morning my parents washed the gray out of their hair. We started an ongoing game of asking each other our names, how old we were, where we were from, etc. Dad took a change of clothes and most of our coin money in a carpetbag, then started walking to Boston to get us forged paper documentation of our new identities, and a medical school diploma under the new name. He left the horse behind since mom and I would need it if he didn't come back. If he didn't arrive after three weeks, we would move to Charleston and mom would find work there. I was worried, but mom assured me that dad could take care of himself. He came back two weeks later, and we set out to find a new life.

We traveled to South Carolina before starting to look for a new place to live. We would stop in various places and dad would talk to the local doctor and vampires about where he could find a town that needed a doctor. We settled in Augusta Georgia, which had a little over two thousand residents at the time. I was in awe at the big city of Augusta after living in a small town. It had stores that carried fashionable clothing items, some of which had come from Europe. It had an impressive capitol building, important looking diplomats, and a militia contingent. I would go through school there until I went off to college. My parents stayed in Augusta for thirty years, about the longest a vampire could conceal their age from a human population.

I caught myself reflecting on my past, and made a mental note to give my parents a call. It has been a few years since we talked. Keeping in close touch has a different meaning when you live hundreds of years. My parents are now in L.A. where they have become very wealthy operating a blood bank.

I called Gary and asked if he was available to tag along with me this weekend. He understood the importance of the situation. Also, he needed the money since he had been out of work for a while.

We had a couple leads to follow. One was the fast food restaurant that had the tainted blood. We also still needed to interview everyone who had been at Frederick's place last night. Normally, those interviews would be done immediately, but we had been spread too thin, and there were too many people to talk to. Sometimes, you just can't help it.

I like being comfortable when I work on weekends, so I put on a Navy blue pants suit with a forest green silk blouse, and low pumps. I wanted to be comfortable, not look like one of the town's homeless.

I picked up Gary at his place. He had on a wrinkled white shirt, perhaps the same one from last night, and a checked brown sport coat with pants that didn't quite match the coat. He had gotten a small smudge of grease on the sleeve of the coat tinkering with a motorcycle part before I got there. I noticed how the jacket fit and asked to see the pistol he was carrying. It was an N-gun a bit older and more worn than my own, but the same amount of firepower. I gave him a warning scowl about getting too trigger happy, but didn't tell him not to bring it. He certainly looked the part of a TV detective.

166

I decided to head for the fast food restaurant first. Getting the drugged blood supply off the street was more pressing than working out events after the fact. I had an understanding of how the fast food distribution worked, although I didn't know the people. The store was managed by a vampire, who probably made more money than any other fast food manager in town. The counter and cooking employees were young supernaturals, mostly vampires, getting their first taste of the working world. I had once heard that the store owners gave the employees a small cut of the blood profits.

We parked and went in. The restaurant chain, named Duck Fries, was a cheesy version of the average fast food restaurant. The décor was done in green camouflage with a few low cost plastic decoy halves nailed to the wall for decoration. It didn't smell all that good to me, but it must be popular with the southern redneck community given the number of overweight customers in overalls and camouflage. I wondered if the whole chain was a front for blood distribution or just this one franchise.

I walked up to the slightly overweight man minding the cash register, and said "I'm detective Mills with the Huntsville Police Department. I'd like to speak to the manager, please."

The overweight man said, "You're looking at him. A couple of my employees didn't show up for work this morning."

I noted that vampire employees would certainly get their blood here, and may be off on a bender. I filed that away, since following solid leads to the source of the problem took precedence over running down every person who might have been dosed. I asked, "Is there someplace we can talk in private?"

The manager had us go around to an employee entrance door by the restrooms. He left a pretty raven-haired woman to mind the register and met us at the door. I got a little whiff of his pheromones as he let us in, so I knew he was a vampire. If he recognized me as one, he hid it perfectly. The manager didn't have a separate office, but he took us to a storage room that was empty.

I introduced myself again, "My name is Christine Vanessa Mills. This is Gary William Halverson." Those weren't our real middle names. Using a full middle name that begins with V or W is subtle way of letting another supernatural know what you are without compromising yourself if it turns out they aren't. It wasn't necessary since I had identified him, but using a familiar ritual often puts people at ease.

He replied, "Nice to meet you detectives. I'm Fred Valentine Miles. What can I do for you today."

I replied, "I know that you deal blood. That's not a problem, but drugged bags of blood have begun showing up in town. The drug is very harmful to vampires. I picked up a bag of tainted blood here last night."

He seemed truly alarmed and said, "I'm so sorry about that. Of course, I'll give you a refund or exchange." I guess being a good store owner was second nature to him. He went on, "I just heard about this when I checked my email this morning. I hadn't had a chance to get someone to inspect our current supply."

"Where do you get your blood?" I asked.

"We normally get expired blood from the local blood banks. However, this week we got a shipment from a new source. It was a salesman named Peter Mulgrew. He was offering blood at half the normal price. He said it was excess from a charity blood drive in New Orleans that they wanted to unload."

"Do you have contact information for this Mulgrew character?" I asked.

"Yes," he replied. He dug out a business card, which only had an email. It was probably an address that couldn't be tracked or wasn't real in the first place.

"Can you describe him?"

He thought a minute then said, "He was a short guy, about five foot three. He had a sharp nose, and short black hair. He didn't have a beard, but looked like he had shaved the night before. He was driving a beat up refrigerated truck with no markings. It looked like it was an old truck with the original company name painted over."

We asked a few more questions, but didn't get anything useful. Gary checked out the blood they had on hand. Everything he had was drugged. The manager assured us that the blood would be destroyed immediately and no more would be sold from that batch. They had sold a couple dozen units from this batch.

Gary and I headed back to the police station. He wasn't in a chatty mood, and I wanted some quiet to think while I was driving anyway. More units of blood getting out create more problems. As I was threading my way back east on University Boulevard, I decided that this was going to blow up too much to keep the humans completely in the dark.

Back at the station, I left Gary to relax with a cup of something resembling coffee, and went to check on Mark Blout's team. Most weren't working on the weekend, but they had been working various shifts to keep an eye on the drug dealers leading up to a big raid. I found Jesse Washington at his desk. He was one of the cops I liked best. Jesse was a tall black guy with sculpted muscles, a deep voice, and a shaved head. I sometimes thought he got married just to fend off all of the women wanting to get him into bed. I would never proposition another cop, but if Jesse ever made a move on me, I'd have a great romp with him, with or without fangs.

The Huntsville police force is a bit enlightened in their willingness to let various detectives work in the ways that are best for them. Many still work with a partner. Mark Blout works with a larger group of junior detectives, probably in part to pump up his ego. It took a little bit of arm-twisting for the captain to let me work alone. I got his approval when a budget cut forced us to forgo replacing a retired detective, and instead I got a bit of extra budget for working with outside consultants, informants, bounty hunters, etc.

I told Jesse about the new drug on the market. I told him it was either made to look like blood, or had a bit of blood in it. I mentioned them selling it to the Goth crowd, teens into vampire movies, and some fetish types. I told him I had a sample of the blood, which an informant had obtained for me.

I gave him the description of Peter Mulgrew. Jesse seemed certain it was Benny Marsden, who up until recently had been a fairly minor cog in the drug distribution machinery. He also mentioned that Benny sometimes used the alias William Stewart. Mulgrew? Stewart? Only in Huntsville would you find Trekkie thugs. I made a mental note to interrogate anyone calling themselves Shatner or Bakula.

Jesse said he would pass the information on to Mark. He asked me to attend their group meeting on Monday. He also asked me not to spook the drug rings too much so that it wouldn't jeopardize the big raid they were planning.

After that, I got the blood bag from my cooler, tagged it as evidence, put a big "keep refrigerated" note on it, and hand delivered it to the duty forensics person. I knew they would take a while to get much of an analysis, but I needed the credibility to show that I wasn't making up the drugged blood story.

I headed back to my desk, where I found Gary with his chair leaned back against the wall with his eyes closed.

"Let's go get lunch." I said. We drove a short distance to a cheap buffet. The food wasn't fantastic, but it had enough variety that we would both find something palatable. The meals that most restaurants sell are balanced with meat, starch, and vegetables for a human diet if too large a portion size to be healthy for humans. They aren't ideal for a vampire or werewolf. Supernaturals tend to cook their own meals or eat at buffets.

Over lunch Gary asked, "Did you find out who our drug weasel is?"

"Yes, but we don't want to jeopardize a major crime bust, so the little snake walks free for just a little bit longer," I replied.

"So what do we do now?" he asked.

"We still need to interview the guests from that party last night, and any of the vampires who have sobered up enough to hold an intelligent conversation without trying to bite us. If I think I can get some useful information from them I'll talk to them even if they are trying to bite me," I said.

"They'd be lucky guys if they got to bite you," said Gary.

"People who get bitten by me are lucky too, unless I decide to kill them afterwards," I replied. I can flirt with the best of them, and give him something to think about too.

I pulled the discussion back on task by discussing the people who had been at Frederick's house the night before. Teresa Wendt, the cook, will be a good person to ask where the blood came from, once she sobers up. Shelly, the cook's assistant, was dead. There were two maids, who doubled as waitresses since the house wasn't big enough for two full time maids. Neither of the maids were vampires. I wasn't sure if the maids would know anything about where groceries were purchased. Surprisingly, there was no butler. So much for cliché endings.

Frederick would have a half-dozen guards on duty when they were expecting people and three on the off shifts. There were a total of sixteen guards currently employed at the residence, six of them vampires. The old miser must have been pretty security conscious to pay for that many. I guess all vampires are security conscious, but some people find themselves spending their lives fearing things that have a pretty low probability of happening, like some drug turning a bunch of your guests and staff into bloodthirsty animals.

It was just our luck that this would happen when there were a bunch of guests with a lot of local clout. We started going down the list of guests. Sylvia Davidson was an obese woman who was the *de facto* head of the town's empath community. Sylvia had put in a brief appearance for local politics sake, and left early. She was gone before the vampire droppings hit the fan, so to speak.

Christopher Lee was a human who hid the extent of the contortionist abilities he got from having Ehlers Danlos syndrome. Christopher was a prime figure in the local dance community, which made him a socialite in the human high society crowd. Christopher can handle himself in a fight, and made it safely to the storm shelter. I knew him from being part of the same martial arts club, but liked him less and less as he become more of a society player.

Roger & Felicia Harris were there that night. They were elders in the werewolf pack. They had gotten some minor injuries, but nothing of great concern for a werewolf, even a very old one. I only knew them by sight, but Gary had met them briefly a few times.

Mitch Walker was a werewolf from Australia, who was the manager of the largest sporting goods store in town. Neither Gary nor I knew how he came to be living in Huntsville.

Cindy Rory was a female vampire astrophysicist, who was working for one the aerospace companies that does a lot of work for NASA. She had come in third in the world Vampkido competition. She is also head coach for Huntsville's Vampkido club. Vampkido is the vampire martial art form. I'm good at Vampkido, but not at Cindy's level. I would rather keep Cindy well chained until she had regained full control of herself. Another vampire present was William Burns, a senior administrator with NASA special projects.

Klaus Schuster was an ogre, who was the owner of a logging company. He is the single biggest employer of ogres in town. This makes him one of the most influential ogres in town, although ogres tend to be solitary and don't have any central governing body for their race.

The guest list rounded out with Milese Wendt, the guest of honor. Milese had invited three of her friends, all young vampires.

Gary and I discussed this list, and how to prioritize it. The first priority had to be finding out more about where the blood came from so we can get that drug off the streets. Going through statements from everyone else would come next. It was possible that no one present would be charged with anything, even killing the cook's assistant, due to being given drugs without their knowledge. However, dangerous situations tend to bring out the worst in people, so it was possible someone had done something they shouldn't in hope that the chaos would hide it.

Since the people to talk to about the source of the blood were Frederick's staff members, who lived in his mansion, we headed back over there. Along the way, Gary talked about having a friend custom machine a replacement part for the Indian motorcycle he was restoring. You bump into these people who are all preoccupied with their hobbies, sports, video games, whatever. I never completely understand such people, since I'm the sort who has to know what is going on in the world, plan for how I would handle potential situations, and work towards goals. However, who is to say what is best? The geeks living on a dime and involved in their video games may be happier with their lives than I am.

We got to the mansion and found Dr. Bowie just finishing up checking on the drugged vampires. He had been keeping long hours to take blood samples every few hours to map out how the drug is metabolized by the body. Today, he walked like he was going to topple over any step, that is to say even more than usual.

"How are they doing, Doc?" I asked.

"I've never seen a drug with such severe withdrawal from a first, single dose," he said. "Some of them are catatonic. None of them would pass for mentally stable. You had best talk to the others today, and the vampires tomorrow. Even if you get one to talk, you might get nothing but delusions."

The Doc was interrupted by one of his nurses bringing him something to look at which immediately took all of his attention. He didn't notice when we walked out of the room to go question the maids.

We found both maids in the rec room playing pool. Both looked human. It wasn't noticeable when they were working, but seeing them together outside work it was obvious that Kelly and Carrie were a couple. When working, they had blank facial expressions and smooth movements that reflected great practice at moving around without being noticed. Now, they were dressed in biker babe outfits, tight jeans and halter-tops, and had attitude to spare as they bantered across the pool table.

The girls knew Gary from a motorcycle club that was a group of supernaturals, and humans who were in the know. Both girls apparently enjoyed Gary's company.

Carrie said, "Hey Gary. Still burning rubber and breaking hearts?"

Kelly asked, "Did you come to get your butt kicked in a game of pool?"

"Sorry girls. I'm here on official police business. Gotta look into this drugged blood thing," Gary replied. I swear his chest puffed up to show the girls how important he was.

"Right. You're probably just carrying spare ammo and tampons for the detective there," Carrie replied sarcastically. I decided I liked her.

"Actually, vampires can't tell the blood is drugged. Werewolves can smell it a mile away." Gary was obviously used to this type of banter.

Kelly said, "Hear that Carrie? We finally found a use for one of Gary's body parts... his nose."

Carrie said, "He makes a good door stop or hat rack. Lousy paper weight though. The papers blow away every time he lifts his beer mug."

"Ladies, we need to find out if you know anything about where the latest batch of blood had been purchased." I was actually enjoying the banter at Gary's expense, but I didn't want it eating into my weekend any more than necessary.

"The cook got it someplace new" Carrie said.

"She seemed unsure about the source," Kelly said.

"but Frederick pushes her to keep the food bill down. The discount egg incident last year with salmonella was horrible. There was a run on toilet paper." Carrie said.

"She didn't give his name," Kelly said.

"or describe him," Carrie said.

"other than referring to him as a weasel," Kelly said.

"The blood salesman that is. She has other names for Frederick." Carrie said.

I changed my mind. They must be empaths to finish each other's sentences like that. It could be romantic having a lover who could sense your emotions, needs, and wants. Who can hear your every thought... on second thought, I just realized why empaths are usually single parents.

We also talked to the non-vampire guards, but didn't find out anything new.

We went to talk to some of the vampires. The doc still had them restrained. The first one we visited was completely catatonic, just staring off into space. We couldn't get any reaction from him. The second one looked at us and said "Hi", but she tried to bite us with an animalistic savagery. One more was clearly delusional. He seemed to be reliving some event he had experienced in the Civil War.

We gave up and called it a day. Gary was quiet as I took him back to his place. I wondered if the verbal barbs from the two maids had hurt him more than he let on. Or he might be getting a dose of reality at seeing what one being can do to another. Somehow drugs seem like more of a violation of a person's being than simply murdering them. I had already seen way too much reality in my life.

It makes me grumpy and cynical. Sometimes I wondered if I made a wrong turn somewhere when I set out to help fix the world's problems.

The year was 1862. I had decided I needed a slower pace of life for a while, so I took on a new identity as a teenager and got a degree in horticulture. My name at the time was Susan Boese. I had been working for the past ten years as a horticulture professor at Mississippi State University. I was crossbreeding strains of cotton plants to make new breeds that were more disease resistant. We were making progress on selectively breeding strains more resistant to bacterial diseases, but there were plenty more things for cotton farmers to worry about. The biggest problem for cotton farmers was boll weevils, a species of beetle that can devastate a cotton crop.

The agricultural researchers at the university had many interactions with local farmers. We often visited fields to look at the health of the crops, and could sometimes recommend improvements. In the course of this time I got to know the slaves who tended our test crop fields rather well. The services of these slaves were purchased from Jonah Douglas, the owner of the cotton plantation that was adjacent to the university fields. During the war, Jonah was off acting as a captain in the Confederate Army. His wife Wilma was in charge of the plantation while he was gone. However, the plantation was being run by the head hand, an elderly servant named Jerry. It wasn't clear if Wilma did anything other than hold tea parties for the other rich women in town.

My favorite of the slaves was Angie. She was sharp as a tack. She understood the implications immediately when we showed her some tidbit of agricultural science. In any other class in society she would end up running the company. It absolutely broke my heart to see her relegated to nothing but manual labor in the harsh sun.

Angie was married to John, a tall slave who handled enormous Percheron draft horses for the plantation owner. John wasn't a genius, but he loved the draft horses and had the low key but stern temperament needed to handle them well. John and Angie loved one another very much, but were smart enough not to show it. Such attachments could be used to punish a slave by harming or selling their spouse. The plantation owner's treatment of his slaves was probably average for the day. He kept the slaves healthy enough to work, and made sure there were occasional whippings to keep slaves from getting out of line.

The great sadness in their lives was not that Angie and John were slaves, but that Angie could not have children. Like many slave women, she had gotten pregnant at the age of fourteen. There were medical complications of some sort, but she carried the baby to term. It was stillborn breech after a twenty-seven hour marathon labor session. Something in that bad delivery must have damaged Angie's internal organs. Angie was never able to get pregnant again. Several of the white farm hands had taken Angie to bed, just to make sure that it was she that was barren and not John. The term "rape" didn't apply to slaves. Their owner offered slaves their freedom if they produced fifteen children, which was a common practice at the time. Thus Angie being barren destroyed their only reasonable hope of being free. The Civil War was raging and the slaves knew it was about slavery. However the common rumor of the day, at least in the South, was that the purpose of the war was to turn the rest of the union into slave states so that slaves would have no where to run.

Angie was my friend, and I had already decided I wanted to see the North win and slavery abolished. However, these were dangerous opinions in the Deep South during the Civil War. I kept my opinions to myself. There is a massive difference between holding an opinion and taking up arms to fight for that opinion. It wasn't a decision I would take lightly.

One day, I was out inspecting a section of cotton field that had been fertilized by burying fish with the seeds. Angie was paring dead leaves from the cotton plants under my direction. We saw four soldiers slowly coming down the road. Two were riding, and two were in a horse drawn wagon. The wagon carried a box that could only be a simple coffin. Tied to the back of the cart was the black mare that was Jonah's favorite horse. A riderless horse was a common symbol of someone's passing. We knew immediately that Jonah was dead.

A few days later, there was a meeting of all of the agricultural researchers at the university to discuss the Douglas plantation. Wilma Douglas had grown up as a rich girl in Charleston, leaving her with few skills other than throwing parties and spending money. She was closing the plantation so that she could return to Charleston. The male slaves were being sold to a coal mine that had been the death of many slaves. The female slaves were being sold to a plantation near Tuscaloosa, which had an owner who was known to be very brutal with his slaves. This meant that we could no longer buy the services of slaves from that particular plantation to maintain the test crop fields. At least until new labor could be hired or contracted, the students and professors would have to do more work in the fields.

I left that meeting with my head spinning. My heart ached for Angie and John. They had done nothing to deserve this. Something had to be done, and soon. A couple hours later, an immense sense of calm came over me as I realized I had chosen my fate. I set about making plans with grim determination.

That evening I went home, changed into dark clothing and came back to my office on campus. I waited until well after dark then slipped out of the greenhouse at the back of the agriculture building into the test crop fields. I made my way through the fields to the Douglas plantation.

None of the slaves were moving around the grounds, and there were two men I had never seen before guarding the slave quarters out back. The two were standing together in front of the building talking about news and rumors from the front lines. I watched them from the shadows at the end of the building. I must have watched them for an hour. I thought I was going to have to kill both in the yard when they decided one should walk around the slave quarters building. He came towards the end of the building where I was hiding. I silently and efficiently broke his neck, then drank what blood I could as his heart gave its last couple beats. I had been getting blood from a vampire in the campus medical office, and hadn't drunk live for a couple years. It invigorated me. When the second guard came to investigate where his companion went, I held my hand over his mouth and drank my fill before killing him.

I checked a couple married slave rooms that were empty before slipped into the meeting room at the center of the slave barracks, where they ate and held church services. All of the slaves were in that one room. I had thought about taking just Angie and John, but sighed as that decision was obviously made for me. I quickly told them where they were being sold, but they already knew. I told them I had never tried to help a slave run before, but I had an idea how to get them to the North. One very elderly woman looked like she wouldn't survive the five-mile walk to the university. She told the rest to go without her. I told them they had five minutes to grab any food in the building, shoes if they had them, and one personal item. After that I was leaving with or without them.

While they were getting their things, I broke two branches off of a tree, and tossed the guard's bodies under a tarp in a nearby wagon. Angie and John were the first to get there. I hoped it was dark enough that they hadn't noticed how easily I tossed those bodies around. I didn't have time to disguise how the men had died.

Within minutes all of them joined us. I handed the branches to John and one of the other men named Ted. I gave them instructions to walk at the end of the line and wipe away our tracks. I told the rest to follow me single file so we didn't leave too much of a trail to follow. I headed out at a fast but quiet walk with the whole train of twenty former slaves following me. I swear I didn't breath until we made it to the line of trees that separated the plantation from the university fields.

We followed the tree line for a way, then cut north across the university fields. The northern most section of the field had recently been covered in a thick layer of manure. This was part of an experiment to grow rhubarb, which didn't normally grow this far south. I told all of them to step in as much manure as possible. Depending upon how long it took for people to notice the slaves were gone, we had from one to four hours before bloodhounds would be on the trail. The fresh manure was my best idea for throwing them off the scent.

I led the group across the manure field, into the greenhouse, and down into the steam tunnels that ran underground between the university buildings. A few years earlier, Mississippi State University had put in central heat in the form of a large boiler that supplied steam to the whole campus. They had built a series of tunnels to run the pipes from the boiler to each of the buildings on campus. The two maintenance men who usually took care of the boiler and used the tunnels on rainy days had been drafted for the war effort.

I spent the next couple hours raking up the trail of manure from the field to the greenhouse, and washing the greenhouse floor with bleach. Luck was with us as it took longer than expected for them to discover the missing slaves, and longer yet for the Douglas woman to argue with the new owners about whose responsibility it was to get the slaves back. I didn't hear the baying of the bloodhounds until an hour after dawn.

An hour before dawn, I went down into the steam tunnels to talk with my charges. Those steam tunnels were dank places at the best of times, and now had a liberal dose of manure added to the aroma. I hoped that would keep the female staff out of the tunnels and most of the male staff had been drafted. I descended into the tunnel with single candle. There were twenty scared people huddled together in the pitch black of the dank, smelly tunnel. Four of them were children, but none too small to walk on their own feet and stay quiet when they had to.

I addressed the group, "Hi. My name is Susan. Some of you know me, and others may have seen me working in the university fields." They were silent, so I went on. "You stopped being slaves the minute you walked away from the plantation, but your life is still very much in danger. I cleaned up the manure in the yard and cleaned the greenhouse with bleach. I'm hoping the bleach and manure smells can keep the bloodhounds from finding you. My idea is for you to hide here for a few days, until they have stopped searching with the hounds.

After that, I'll come with you and we will try to sneak past the soldiers and go north, maybe to Chicago. Any questions."

"What will we eat?" This came from Ted.

"I'm going to go get you food now. Along the way, I'll buy food if I can, or we'll steal it," I said.

"What if the bloodhounds find us here?" asked Angie.

"If that happens you run. Go to the end of this tunnel; take the last turn to the left, then up the stairs. You will come out of the arts building on the north side of campus, as far from the Douglas plantation as possible. After that you stay in the trees, and go north. If no one is following you, go as quietly and hidden as possible, preferably hiding in the day and walking at night. If you are being followed by hounds, you run as fast as you can. As scary as it is, the best way to get away from hounds would be to split up separately or in groups of two. They certainly won't have enough hounds to follow ten different trails, so some of you would get away even if others don't."

"Once we get to Chicago, who will feed us?" Ted again. I sensed a theme developing here.

"You will have to get jobs to earn enough money to pay for food and a place to stay. It's much colder in the winter up north so you can't sleep outside. For a while, you might get some charity help from churches or former runaway slaves," I replied.

"Will we be in Chicago for church this Sunday?" This came from Angie, who was smart enough to think about logistics, but had too little education to have any idea how far away Chicago was.

I said, "You might wait here three days, then it is two more days to Sunday. I don't think we can even get to Union territory by Sunday. If we have to walk the whole way, it could take two or three weeks to get to Chicago. I'll be honest with you. There are two really dangerous parts here. The first one is getting away from the bloodhounds that plantations send out after runaway slaves. The second is getting past the battle lines in the war. And you are in danger anywhere in the Confederate States."

I left them the candle and headed back to my small cottage just off campus. I had two messenger bags on long straps. I filled them with food, slung them over my shoulder, then put my most billowy dress on over them to hide the load. I stuffed every bit of money I had and every sharp knife in the house into my corset. I didn't own a gun, and wouldn't want the potential for noise to attract attention. I ate well and packed a very large lunch basket, then headed back to the university.

I took the food and a pail of water down to the tunnels. I handed all of the knives except one to them. Angie took a knife with a grim look of determination on her face, and the other adults followed suit.

I spent the rest of the day trying to go about my normal routine so no one would notice anything unusual about me. I was a nervous wreck. I had fought for my own life many times, but had never been responsible for other people. I flinched every time a dog barked. I listened in a cold sweat when people outside my office door gossiped about news of escaped slaves. The bloodhounds were walked all the way around the field of fresh manure, but didn't find where we left the field. The deputies with the hounds decided the most likely scenario was that the escapees would go north through a wooded area that bordered the field, and avoid people and buildings. They led the dogs north, and I let out a sigh so big that it could have dropped me all of the way into a coma.

The next three days were nerve wracking. The bloodhounds came back in a second attempt to pick up the trail. They even circled the university. If we had left, they would have picked up the trail where we left the grounds. Every day, I went shopping for food at multiple stores in Starkville, to hide the fact that I was buying way too much food for one person. I bought some things that could be eaten on the road like dried meat and hard tack. I also picked up some hot water bottles that could be used to carry water without implying you were traveling. No canteens were available, since all such items went to the war effort.

At the end of the third day, it was time for us to leave. We crept out late at night. I was on edge until we got well into the woods. It's nearly impossible to keep that many people silent and invisible.

My plan was to follow the Tombigbee River north. I wanted to keep the group in the woods overlooking the river, since there would be too many people along the banks. This was easier said than done. We were intentionally avoiding following roads. A few times we followed game trails. Sometimes we got too far from the river and had to go back towards it to keep from getting completely lost. We bumped into a number of farms and small villages that had to be detoured. All of this was done stumbling along in the dark with moonlight at best to see by.

During the day, we would find a spot that was reasonably well hidden in a gully or tall brush. We would eat then sleep as best as we could. All of us were covered with bug bites, scratches and occasionally leeches or ticks. I slept what little a vampire needs, and spent the rest of the time keeping an ear out for trouble. John realized what I was doing and took the watch while I slept.

Around early evening, the members of the group started to wake. This was the most dangerous time for us since people wanted to talk and children wanted to play, but nearby residents would still be awake and outdoors. It was particularly difficult keeping the youngest member of the group quiet, a five-year old boy named Tommy. This task was taken on by Molly, a twelve-year old girl who was just starting to develop breasts. Molly was a naturally nurturing mother type. She gave the younger children tasks to do, and invented games to occupy them. I realized how clever Molly must be to invent those games. Molly understood what was going on and how much danger we were in. However, she kept a positive outlook and focused on taking care of Tommy. I really liked Molly and hoped she would be able to get a basic education as a free citizen.

Our progress was slower than I had hoped. After three days, we ran out of food. I left the group and went into a nearby town to buy what I could. The town's people were concerned with war news, and not paying a lot of attention to a stranger passing through. I bought some big bags of supplies and headed back carrying a bit more weight than a human woman my size could have carried. I made my way back to the group's hiding spot by a round about path, hoping to throw off anyone that might have seen me. While I was gone, a couple of the women had picked blackberries from a nearby berry patch. That night we had a feast of griddlecakes and blackberries. I don't really like blackberries, but they tasted wonderful that day.

It took another three days to reach the front lines, which at this point in the war were somewhere near the Tennessee Kentucky border. We reached the front just before dawn one morning, as we were getting ready to hide during the daylight. From high up on a mountain, we looked down at both armies arrayed in the valley below. It looked like we would encounter fewer soldiers if we followed the ridge a bit further west, then head north. It felt like a storm was coming. Rain would make the perfect cover to cross the lines into Union territory.

Regardless of how the crossing would go, we were out of food again. I left the group in a gully behind the ridge from the arrayed armies and went looking for some food to buy. A couple miles away, I found a mobile town of civilians who were following the army. There were merchants selling various wares to individuals or to army buyers. There were moonshiners and prostitutes to comfort the soldiers, and a number of wives, girlfriends and families of soldiers. New people were constantly coming and going from this portable community of tents and wagons, so I didn't attract any attention. I bought a bunch of food claiming that I was going to prepare a meal for my fiancé's squad, and got out. My cash money was running low, although at this point in my life I already had some wealth stashed a couple places around the country.

As I approached the group's hiding spot, I realized the worst had happened. Confederate Army soldiers had found them. The group had fought back, but the knives I had given them were no match for soldiers with rifles and bayonets. Ted and John were dead. A few more looked like they would be dead soon. Angie had blood oozing out of a wound on her right arm, but looked like she would live.

Worst of all was what the soldiers had done after winning the short skirmish. The former slaves were put on their knees and made to watch as one soldier after another brutally raped little twelve-year old Molly. Rape has been a weapon of war as long as the history of mankind. It even still occurs today in some parts of the world. If you want to know which side are the good guys in a war, look for the one that does not employ rape and torture as strategic tools. Often there are no good guys in wars. Even in the best of circumstances, sociopathic killers are often drawn to military service in the chaos of war. This group of soldiers apparently had such a leader, who had gathered a group of like-minded individuals.

I approached as Molly's defilement was ending. I dropped the supplies and walked as quietly as I could towards the backs of the soldiers, so the escapees could see me, but the soldiers wouldn't as long as their focus was on the group. I'm no wilderness expert, so I tried to walk quietly by stepping only when someone in the group was talking or making noise. I motioned to them, and Angie realized what I wanted. Angie started making noise, offering herself in exchange for the groups freedom. She knew this wouldn't happen, but realized I needed her to keep the soldiers attention. A few of the others caught on and started arguing over who would be self sacrificing.

I slowly walked forward, in plain sight of the soldiers had they turned around to look. I was already angry, but had enough battle experience to know my best chance lay in controlling those emotions. I calculated my odds and they weren't good. With everyone empty handed, the odds would be on my martial arts skills being able to take eight draftee soldiers. My odds weren't good facing eight armed soldiers. I had some ideas about who to kill first, and where to stand so that some soldiers would act as shield if ones on the other side of the group fired. It was a desperate gamble at best, but things could only get worse from here if I didn't fight them.

When I was about eight feet from the group of soldiers, the leader of the group decided he had had enough of the escapees' pleas and Molly's whimpering. He pulled out his pistol, put it to Molly's head, and pulled the trigger. That was the point when I lost all self-control. My fangs came out of their on volition, and I charged in. At that point I was in a complete rage.

The first two fell to the ground with broken necks before they even realized they were under attack. The next one was gutted by my knife as a couple of his not so bright buddies fired towards me and into his back. Next came the one I had pegged as the squad leader. His revolver put a bullet in my shoulder before I took the gun from him. My knife removed his manhood and I left him twisting on the ground in agony to contemplate the error of his ways while he bled out for the next few minutes.

The next three made one mistake that gave me a chance to get out of the situation alive. All three came at me in ranks so that all three bayonets would reach my chest at the same time. My forearm block knocked all three bayonets aside at once. I stepped closer to them so they bayonets would no longer be useful. I grabbed the one closest to me by his hair, pulled his head back, then ripped his trachea and jugular vein out with my fangs. The other two suddenly realized what monster they had encountered and started fighting to save their lives instead of to end mine. They failed on both counts.

After dealing with those two, my battle reflexes had me immediately getting to my feet and looking around for additional opponents. I was too late. The last man was twice my weight. He hit me with a flying tackle just as I started to look around. Vampires are strong, but that doesn't change balance and inertia. I landed on the ground with him on top of me, and felt a few of my ribs crack as we landed. One more use of my fangs and knife, then the battle was over.

I stood up brushing intestines off my clothes and wiping the blood off my chin. From their expressions, it was clear that my charges were now more afraid of me than they had been of the soldiers. It didn't help that I was still angry about Molly's death. I would have killed a few more soldiers to work off that anger if any had been in sight.

We didn't have the luxury of lamenting over the dead. We had no way to bury or burn the bodies, so the group settled for arranging John, Ted, and Molly on their backs with some wild flowers. Another woman died of her wounds before we could start walking, and was placed by the first three. It started to rain as Angie was saying a few words over the dead. The rain was our best chance of slipping past the front lines and into Union territory.

The group headed out single file with Angie in the lead. I brought up the rear to watch for attacks from behind. After a couple hours of slogging through the mud, we must have passed the front lines without know exactly where the line had come. We came upon a small army encampment with a Union flag flying. There were both black and white soldiers in the encampment. The group of former slaves was greeted warmly by a group of black soldiers. They apparently had a mechanism in place for getting freed slaves integrated into free society in the North. As soon as it was clear they would be fine, I slipped back out of the camp.

I was still livid about how Molly had been treated. After that, I demonstrated why one of the most fearsome enemies you could ever have is a vampire with a vendetta. I spent the next year and a half in confederate territory. I slipped through the shadows and soldiers on watch disappeared, never to be heard from again. Many of them were probably labeled as deserters. I posed as a helpless woman with a broken down wagon blocking the road and supply shipments ran late or never arrived. I rigged a fuse in the dead of night and gunpowder stores mysteriously exploded. Slaves were freed in droves as slave masters mysteriously dropped dead. Although violence is seldom in the best interest of society, I have to say that a rampage for a good cause can be very cathartic. Those events in the Civil War are what set me on a path of fighting societies problems, if not by planting daisies. That path eventually led to my present position as a police detective.

Chapter 5

On Sunday morning, I decided it was time to talk with some of the vampires who had been at the party. I had an idea and called Liz Macey.

I arrived at the mansion around one. Gary pulled in right behind me on the occasionally misfiring Indian motorcycle. The weekend hours didn't bother him since he was never a regular hours person anyway and needed the money to get the motorcycle working better for an upcoming antique bike meet.

Liz Macey arrived at the mansion driving a yellow VW Beetle that Mike had bought for her. It was the kind of cutesy car that no cop would be caught dead driving. Liz is pretty young and not the most experienced empath in town. However, she has a bit of experience doing interrogations and connections to the law enforcement community via Mike.

At the mansion, we used the dining room as an interrogation room. At the precinct we use one of the larger interrogation rooms that was a repurposed conference room. Cops don't really get off on big meetings anyway. I sit across the table from the suspect being interviewed, and Liz sits at the back wall of the room, where I can see her but the person I'm talking to can't. The suspect is told Liz is there to take notes, but she was really there to read his emotions. She has been learning a bit of American Sign Language, so she can let me know truth, lie, or other emotions she picks up.

My first priority was interviewing Teresa Wendt. The doc said he had removed her restraints and asked her to stay in her room at the far end of the servants' floor of the mansion. We went to Teresa's room to get her. Teresa's room was basically a studio apartment. She had a private bath and one big room containing a bed, kitchen, and sitting area. Her hobbies must have been watching TV and knitting judging from the large flat screen and stacks of storage boxes full of yarn. She still looked agitated.

We escorted her to the dining room. I was hoping a room with fewer distractions would help her focus on answering questions.

"How are you feeling?" I asked.

"My daughter, she looks terrible. Shelly dead. Could have been me." Teresa was obviously not fully back to health.

Liz shook her head, and signed that she wanted to talk to me out of the room.

"Christine, her head is a mess," Liz said. "Her thoughts and emotions are a turmoil. All you will get is random odds and ends."

"Can you see what I need to know in her mind?" I asked.

"It doesn't work that way… but I could calm her down enough to get some lucid answers," she replied.

"That sounds good."

"You realize that you will feel the same thing," she went on. "You will have to focus to keep yourself on task."

"OK, let's go," I said.

We went back into the dining room and sat down. Liz took a deep breath and closed her eyes for a second. Teresa visibly calmed down. I felt an immense calm come over myself. It was like the best afterglow I had ever experienced. I suddenly noticed how comfortable the dining room chairs were, then started planning a vacation in the Caribbean. Snap out of it Christine, or whatever my name is this decade. I pulled myself back to the task at hand.

"How are you feeling?" I asked.

"Terrible," she said. "I'm sad at seeing a friend die. I'm fighting cravings for more of that blood. And I feel immensely violated that someone drugged the blood."

"What do you remember about the night of the party?" I asked.

"Party? Is it someone's birthday?" she asked.

Liz made the sign for shock.

I tried a different tactic. "Where did you buy the blood?"

She thought a second then said, "He came up to me at the farmer's market. A weasely man. His name was Peter something. Mulberry. Mullins. Something like that. I didn't like him, but the price was low. Frederick always pushes me to keep grocery cost down, and still prepare good food. I knew something felt wrong, but the low price allowed me to make the artichoke dip I wanted to do."

"Could it be Peter Mulgrew?" I asked.

"Yes, that's it. Peter Mulgrew"

Liz made the sign for truth. I knew she had some ability to tell the difference between someone remembering correctly and someone jumping on a story that sounds plausible. This was the first good news I had gotten. At least, I'm only chasing down one scumbag.

"Can you describe him?" I asked.

She replied, "Short. Dark hair, kind of oily. Sharp nose."

"Do you know anyone who would want to harm Frederick?"

"No one who did business with him loved him because he was so cheap," she replied. "But I can't see that being important enough to drug people."

I asked, "What about the other people at the party?"

"I know most of them. None have enemies that I am aware of."

"Why does Frederick have so much security?" I asked.

"I really don't know," she said. "I've been with him thirty years and never found out. I've heard someone ask, and he just said it helped him sleep at day."

"Was there something that seemed to set off the chaos?" I asked.

"Chaos? Is that a new band?" she asked.

Liz signed that she was gone.

I told Teresa we were done asking her questions. I felt when Liz dropped the calming empathic projections. Teresa went back to ranting quietly under her breath.

The doc soon came in to check on her, and have a nurse escort her back to her room. He told us the drug was out of their systems, but it could take a few more days to get over some of the mental shock, and probably weeks to get over the addiction cravings. He pointed out that drugs with this type of designed addiction had been hitting the streets for a couple years, although at high price and low quantity. After it was out of their system, the symptoms would look like any other case of drug withdrawal. He said this was odd because vampires aren't as susceptible to this class of narcotics as humans. His conclusion was that it was likely this drug was engineered specifically for vampires. I already expected that from Paul's chemical analysis, but it's nice to see consistent facts.

As best as I could understand his description, the drug filled the body with endorphins and testosterone. The endorphins make it addictive, and the testosterone gives aggressive tendencies, possibly strong enough to override cognitive abilities. Your body naturally generates endorphins when you are afraid or aroused. That is why men like movies with deadly, sexy heroines, and why women like dating bad boys. The fear endorphins give an extra kick to the attraction endorphins. In fact, a vampire's pheromones are so effective because they include a compound that triggers the body's mechanism to generate endorphins. However, too many endorphins are a big problem.

The doc said he would give her extra non-tainted blood so that normal blood need wouldn't complicate the situation. He lamented that the supply from the local blood bank was very low at the moment. That didn't bode well for me, either.

We interviewed the vampire guards. Gary escorted each one in. Liz and I discussed their answers and mental state while waiting for Gary to bring the next one. One of them was still too unstable, and Gary had to restrain him. All those interviews revealed were a few more small details about the events at the party. The drugged blood had not been delivered to the house, so none of them had seen anything that could help us find the drug dealers. They did give us some indication that the drugged vampires tried to fight the effects of the drug, although in the end they all failed.

I sent Liz home, then went with Gary to escort the last guard to his room. After closing his door, Gary asked what we would do next. I paused in the hallway for a few seconds to think about that.

As we stood in the hallway, we started hearing sounds. They were coming from behind the door across the hall. For a couple seconds I thought someone might be injured. Then I realized it was the room belonging to Kelly and Carrie, the lesbian maids. They were obviously having an intense romp in bed. We listened to the loud moans and little screams a bit longer than we should have before it occurred to us that we should be on our way and give them their privacy.

This round of questioning hadn't gotten us anything very useful. One of my techniques for pondering over cases is to write what I know on a whiteboard and look it over. I know the cop shows do this in a crowded precinct, but I prefer using my apartment living room where I can sip a glass of wine while I look it over. I explained what I wanted to do and asked Gary to follow me back to my apartment.

As I drove home, I got a call. It was from Melinda, one of my general contacts who I had called earlier. Melinda is a short, dumpy girl who works one of the ticket counters at the Huntsville airport. She also helps maintain their computer systems, so she has access to more data than the average ticket agent. Melinda is a human, but she had worked for Frederick earlier in her life and thus knew many of the people in the supernatural community, at least by name and reputation.

Melinda told me she had identified two trends in the recent and upcoming incoming flights. One was more than a usual number of passengers coming in from Columbia. The other was a lot of upcoming flights for people who are vampires.

I had expected there would be many vampires coming to town, but I was impressed that Melinda picked up on it. The only way to find that information was scanning passenger manifests by eye. I wondered if Mike Brown had taught her some of his mental tricks, like speed-reading.

The arrivals originating in Columbia were more concerning. I didn't think Columbia had a big aerospace industry, which is the primary reason that people come to Huntsville. One possible explanation was that the drug cartels were using Huntsville as their test market. If that were the case, the good side would be that the drugged blood problem wasn't a nationwide or worldwide problem. The bad side would be some heavy hitting drug cartel enforcers in town.

As I drove, I checked out Gary on his motorcycle in the rearview mirror. Sometimes those happy go lucky guys are great in bed. They are the ones who are completely focused on the moment, not obsessed with life, money, etc.

We got back to my apartment building. Gary gave me a sidelong glance as we rode the elevator up. He was probably trying to figure out if I was wanted to sleep with him. I didn't give any indication. I hadn't decided yet.

Once in the apartment, Gary checked out the décor for a few seconds then settled onto the comfortable couch. I pulled out the whiteboard, then put out a bowl of crackers and poured sodas for us. For the next hour, we laid out the case on the whiteboard. I wrote everything on the board as both of us contributed details. I let Gary get a good look at the shape of my ass as I bent over to write the last item on the bottom of the board.

I set the first whiteboard in front of the TV and put a second one on the easel. Then we threw out some guesses as to what was going on and who was behind it. The last part was most difficult. It was coming up with plans for how to chase down our drug dealers. We noted cooperating with the team already working on the local drug ring, but also that they didn't know what they are getting themselves into.

I poured us glasses of wine to drink as we pondered this. I sat on the opposite end of the couch from Gary. I put one knee up on the couch so that he could almost see up my skirt.

"What do you think?" I asked him. From the pause before he answer, it was clear he had forgotten about drug dealers for a second.

"I think it's in everyone's best interest to put a stop to this, even if it means going a bit outside the normal range of police activities." he finally replied.

"Believe me, I know how to run outside the law when I must," I replied.

"You might have to get those designer clothes dirty," he said. I knew he was goading me because he's seen how I fight at our martial arts club.

I leaned towards him, letting him see down my blouse, then poked a finger into his chest as I said, "I know how to get down and dirty." I left my finger poking into his chest.

He pulled my hand from his chest with his left hand. Then he put his right hand on the back of my neck and pulled my mouth to his in a rough kiss.

I kissed him for a minute then pulled back and said "You think you're man enough to take me?" At this point my skirt was hiked up and I was straddling his lap.

He shoved me backwards onto the coffee table. All four table legs broke as I landed on my back on the stylish piece of furniture with my legs still spread. He ripped my panties to pieces and off of me in a single movement. Within seconds he was pounding deep inside of me, right there on the broken coffee table.

I goaded him on, by saying, "Is that the best you can do? Come on. Show me how hard you can fuck." He redoubled his efforts, pounding me so hard the other residents in the building might have thought it was an earthquake. I was loving it.

I let him pound me for a couple minutes then decided it was my turn to be in charge. I put my left leg straight up in the air, then put my foot on his throat. I shoved him backwards with my foot. He landed on the floor on his back. I was on top of him in an instant. I pulled his hands over his head, slipped a pair of handcuffs from under the couch, and cuffed his hands to the leg of the couch. I had left the cuffs there for just such occasions.

I ripped his shirt open, then pulled off my top and bra in a single motion. I slid myself down onto his erection, but not all the way. I wiggled my hips left and right, teasing him as only half of his length was inside him. He tried to shove his hips up to enter me all the way, but I wouldn't let him. I wiggled a bit more then slammed my whole body down to get full penetration. I wiggled and slammed down onto him a few more times.

Then I leaned forward, feeling him no longer inside him as I did. I dangled my shapely bare breasts with hard nipples over his face, just a little too far away for him to suck on them. I teased him asking if he wanted my tits. His tongue shot out, just licking the tip of my nipple.

I goaded him some more saying, "Looks like the big bad werewolf is getting trained like a lap dog."

He shoved his head forward trying to clamp his mouth onto my nipple, but I pulled it just out of range. He screamed and pulled his arms forward, first ripping the leg off the couch, then breaking apart the handcuff chain. It was a pair of sex cuffs that had a release he could have pressed, but what was the fun in that.

He grabbed me and threw me onto the couch so hard that the couch flipped over backwards. He was on top of me in an instant. We had a most erotic wrestling match with each of us trying to simultaneously grope the others private parts and to physically control the other one. A lamp and an end table met their demise in the process. It ended up with me bent over the broken couch and him roughly pounding his erection inside of me from behind. He was saying, "Now you're my bitch."

I was having a great time. I have sex with humans, but they never have the strength and endurance to arouse me like this. I threw all decorum to the wind and screamed as my orgasm shuddered through my whole body. A few seconds later I felt him get even larger and explode inside me.

We were panting and sweat covered. We sat on the back of the couch, which was now on the floor. Both of us just reveled in the experience, still checking out the other's naked, sweaty body.

After a while he said, "Sorry about the furniture."

"Don't worry about it," I said. "I was looking for an excuse to remodel anyway."

I grabbed a bag of cookies out of the cupboard and we wolfed them down, sloppily getting crumbs all over his chest and my breasts.

"Let's take a shower then go get dinner," I said.

We washed each other off in my oversized shower then had sex again on the bathroom counter. Dinner was a leisurely meal of friendly small talk at a good Chinese buffet. I wore a t-shirt and jeans hoping that it would put him more at ease. I left my hair down and a bit mussed up. I let my guard down and was very relaxed and open with him as we chatted. I hadn't talked with anyone like that since World War II. We went back to my place then had a long, slow, tender love making in my bed.

Chapter 6

On Monday morning I slipped quietly out of bed, although I suspected Gary could sleep through a hurricane. I slipped on workout clothes, and gently shut the bedroom door behind me. I got a bagel and drank from a bottle of raspberry flavored water. I drank half of the bottle then threw the rest into a pitcher to make a fresh batch of ice tea.

I started cleaning the living room, bagging up all except the couch. I left the couch on it's back and swung it around so that you could see the TV from it. As I cleaned up the debris that had been my living room, I thought about how to remodel the room. Mid century modern was a possibility, as was traditional Japanese or perhaps Tibetan. I made a mental note to look into couches in various styles. One of my requirements for a living room is to always have a piece of furniture suitable for having sex, although off the top of my head I couldn't think of a piece of furniture I hadn't had sex on.

I called in to work and told them that I was taking the day off because I had worked all weekend. I also said that they should call me if there are any developments on the drug sales organization case.

I did a whole series of exercises on the now mostly empty living room floor. My years have taught me that you have to be flexible. That is to say not too set in your ways, although being flexible in bed has it's advantages also. My floor exercises are a combination of martial arts movements and gymnastics.

After the exercise routine, I took a shower and changed. I decided to put on casual clothes. I put on a red pleated skirt with the hem just above my knees and a Mexican peasant blouse. Pumps with two inch heels and my hair back finished off the look.

I settled in on the computer in the spare bedroom. I went to a web site which was an email service acting as the front end to a hidden web that caters to the supernatural community. I contacted a number of friends, family and acquaintances, including one at the ATF. I explained what we are seeing with the drugged blood, and asked if anyone else had seen something similar or had additional relevant information. After that, I spent some time looking at pictures of stylish futons available for sale online.

I was beginning to wonder if I should put a toe tag on Gary and go to lunch alone when he showed up. He was in jeans, but no shirt. He still had a broken handcuff on one wrist. I looked in my lost and found pile and got him a red plaid flannel shirt. Muscular men in flannel shirts never go out of style.

We were just walking out the door to go to lunch when my phone rang. It was Mark Blout. He said that there had been a massacre at a frat house at Alabama A&M University and they thought it was drug related. I told him I'd be right there. Lunch was burgers from a drive through.

The fraternity house was a large, older two-story home. Alabama A&M is not Harvard. There are no marble pillared, mahogany walled fraternity houses here. The frat house had mismatched construction barriers with hand written signs saying "Do Not Enter" at the entrances. The person who reported the incident was a young man coming to give a friend a ride to an afternoon class. He was explaining to one of Mark Blout's detectives that everyone on campus knew the guys living there were sleeping off hangovers when they put the construction barriers out after a party.

Gary and I put on rubber gloves in accordance with procedure for avoiding contaminating the crime scene with our fingerprints. However, I was guessing there were a million fingerprints from hundreds of people in the house so it was probably a useless nod to protocol in this case.

We walked through the house. In the large living room two detectives discussing how a pile of plastic Halloween vampire teeth could have planted a bad suggestion when their judgment was clouded by drugs. I pointed out the stack of Wesley Snipes vampire movie DVDs to the detectives. I knew it was the wrong track, but it was easiest to let the other detectives do the work of creating a cover story for me.

The incident must have happened late when many of the guests had left because there were only seventeen bodies, a pretty lame party turnout for a frat house full of football players. Only three of them were female, probably those planning on spending the night. Every body was gashed and bloody in some manner. There was also damage to furniture, walls, and ceilings.

"This isn't from Halloween vampire teeth is it?" Gary asked, whispering so only I could hear.

"Not a chance. Those plastic teeth can't rip open someone's throat near so neatly. Also there are random, clumsy stab wounds as well as ones that hit the carotid artery perfectly. That's a technique for disguising the real attack as the work of a maniac," I whispered back.

I pointed up and said to Gary, "See the indentation of a body in the twelve-foot ceiling of the entryway. Even an A&M football player would be hard pressed to throw someone that high that hard. Besides, they wouldn't have mopped the field with Tennessee last week if the whole team were on drugs."

"How many vampires would it take to do this?" Gary asked.

"One could do all the killing but it takes two to work in from the exits and prevent someone from getting out and raising the alarm," I replied.

I looked at my cell phone. Zero bars. Whoever did this had enough presence of mind, at least at the beginning, to place a cell phone jammer and cover the exits.

"Go through the house. Don't disturb anything. Sniff for the drugged blood. Also look for any of the dead that might be non-human," I told Gary.

I did the same. All appeared human, although neither of us could tell a dead human from a dead empath. For that matter, some of the football players were big enough to be ogres. I was betting that anyone with enough forethought for a cell phone jammer would have remembered to pick up gloves at a drug store. Without any witnesses, we wouldn't be able to do much. An unsolved mass murder in a state full of gun loving rednecks creates new problems. We could expect a rise in violent crimes of passion as more people decide to carry their weapons.

Gary reported back that he had caught only the slightest whiff of tainted blood, and didn't see any non-humans. He suggested that such a slight smell could be odor from someone's breath clinging to carpet or curtains. I asked Mark Blout if his detectives had found out anything from people who had left the party before this occurred. I knew it was too soon to have found those people, but asking was a gentle way of suggesting what his next investigation step should be.

I took one last look around before walking out. Sadness tugged at my heart. I have a soft spot for muscular black men.

The year was 1943. At the time I was going by the name Betty Winston. I had been working as a nurse for the last five years. When WWII started, I enlisted in the Army as a nurse. I was sent to an accelerated boot camp for people who already had needed skills. After a very brief boot camp introducing us to Army life, we were uniformed and had just enough experience to know who to salute. My boot camp class was soon assigned orders and we were sent to various commands around the country and abroad. I was sent to a temporary base in Virginia, which everyone presumed was a staging area for sending people to Europe.

We were assigned temporary jobs on the base until our orders came in. I inventoried medical supplies, and took notes for physicians on their rounds. A couple days later my commanding officer called my name at morning muster, handed me a manila envelope with my orders and told me I had to be packed and on a bus in one hour. I was part of a group of Army personnel being transferred from the East coast to the Pacific theatre.

The Army bus was clearly a well experienced school bus with a layer of olive drab paint hastily applied. A few hours later, the bus trundled onto a pier at the Washington Naval Shipyard. We disembarked and hauled our bags onto the New Haven, a cruiser that had just been built and launched. It was smaller than a battleship or a carrier, but still one of the larger ships in sight. I counted that as a stroke of good luck.

The ship wasn't designed for female personnel. Although I was given the rank of corporal, I was assigned to share a junior officer's stateroom with three other women. The stateroom was the size of a pantry closet with four bunks that had one side hinged to the wall and a chain anchored to the ceiling on the other side. A sign had been posted on the officer's showers stating times of day for male and female use.

Joan was the senior woman on board. She was an Army captain who was a supply officer, and seemed to have no sense of humor. Jane was a yeoman sergeant, another type of paperwork clerk. A yeoman sergeant was indistinguishable from a supply officer to me, although I never mentioned that fact. Elizabeth was a private corpsman, a step further down the medical pecking order from myself.

Each of us was assigned a daily rotation of work in our perspective fields. However, there wasn't enough work to do while underway, even for the ships complement without the extra help, so we ended up frequently playing cards along with the medical officer, or on a bunk in our quarters. I got along quite well with Elizabeth and we soon became close friends. She was very young. She had graduated high school just a few months ago. Her high school sweetheart, a man named Jim who sounded nice, had proposed to her ten minutes before being shipped out in the Army. He hadn't had time to get a ring but had pulled a button off of his dress uniform, which she wore on a thin chain around her neck. The next day, Elizabeth had enlisted in the Army in hopes of being on the same base with Jim, but he had been deployed to the front lines in Europe before she got out of boot camp.

The ship was going to Hawaii by sailing around Africa. This was a longer route, but there was some sort of mission to patrol that route along the way. They had six lookouts scanning the water for German U-boat periscopes during all daylight hours, and all external lighting blacked out at night. The captain, a Naval academy graduate named William, was rather young for such a large command. He had spent a year commanding a frigate, which limped back into port with casualties after exchanging blows with a U-boat. William ran a number of types of drills, which he timed with a stopwatch to see how long it took before all stations were manned for the particular incident that had been simulated. These were usually at reasonable times between meals, but once we were scrambled as people were climbing out of bed and I arrived at my station with my bust squeezing out of Elizabeth's uniform shirt. We arrived in Sydney, Australia after a few weeks. We had become so accustomed to shipboard life that our civilian life seemed like a memory of a dream. It isn't wise for vampires to dwell on the past, so I had engrossed myself in the current environment, studiously avoiding making comparisons to my time on a merchant sailing ship a hundred years earlier.

In Sydney, U.S. sailors and soldiers had set up a small tent village at one side of the harbor. An hour after our ship came in, a destroyer pulled in coming from Hawaii. It had encountered a German pocket battleship a few hours earlier and was listing badly to port with many of the crew injured. Elizabeth and I had no more than thrown our bags on a bunk when we found ourselves still in dress uniform and assisting the doctors in surgery.

I had seen people die before, and killed quite a few myself. Heavy weaponry had brought a whole new realm of bodily mutilation to the art of war. The doctors triaged the incoming casualties. A few of the worst were sent to a tent between the surgery tent and the morgue tent. One of the doctors told me to make them comfortable. It took me a few seconds to realize that these were men who could not be saved, and there wasn't enough medical staff to even make an attempt. Attempting to save one of these sailors would occupy so much of the medical staff that five more would die waiting for surgery. Perhaps a few could have been saved in a modern hospital with a team of trauma surgeons, but not then and there.

Most of the dying were already unconscious or mostly so. Only one was pretty lucid, a very young sailor named Reggie. He looked like he was only a few months out of high school.

"Am I dying?" Reggie asked.

"You need to sleep now," I said.

"Damn. I'm no doctor, but I'm pretty sure I won't wake up if I go to sleep," he said. He was right.

He went on, "I can't die. I've never kissed a girl. Here I was all noble and walked away when some the guys got hookers. I guess the joke's on me." He was panting heavily. Only his concern about having never kissed a girl was distracting him from the pain.

I leaned down and gave him a long, soft kiss. Then I leaned closer and bit his neck. I'm not sure if he realized what I was doing. I drank deeply, in need of a drink myself, and injected my venom into his blood. He died a few minutes later with a serene look of sexual ecstasy on his face. I slapped another bandage over the puncture marks on his neck. When the morgue boys came to get the dead, they looked at the expression on Reggie's face then questioningly at me. I kept an aloof professional air, and pointedly ignored them.

A couple weeks later, Elizabeth and I were shipped out. We couldn't go on the New Haven because it had been assigned to hunt for the German pocket battleship patrolling the South Seas. We were put on a civilian ship, the Honolulu Star. It was a rusty tramp freighter, but the captain and a number of the crew were former U.S. Navy sailors who were happy to be helping out the war effort in their own modest way, and would therefore look after us. Elizabeth and I were sent along with six stable patients. Michael, Jesse, and Jerome would soon recover fully and go back on active duty. On the other end of the spectrum were Jeb, James, and Mark who would be discharged and sent home due to the severity of their injuries.

We had no duties on the Honolulu Star other than taking care of our patients. Since the patients were stable, that consisted of nothing more than changing some bandages and keeping an eye out for infections. We ended up spending most of our time as the recreation committee for the patients. Elizabeth had the presence of mind to pick up a couple decks of cards in Sydney. Our card playing experience came to the rescue.

At the reasonably mature age of a hundred and sixty something I had gained a fair amount of experience guessing at the personality traits of various types of people from a minimal amount of interaction. Our card playing sessions were a chance to find out more about the deeper psychology of our patients.

Jeb was a good old southern boy from Georgia. He was missing an arm, but it didn't seem to bother him. He often talked about farming, and about all the people who have had farming accidents. He talked like he knew everything about agriculture, but I knew from my previous career in that field that he got some things wrong. I didn't see any value in correcting him, and it was best that he didn't have anything shaking his ego and positive attitude while he was convalescing. He enjoyed playing cards, but didn't do very well because he never took it seriously. He was one of those people who consider life to be one big game. Perhaps he was happier for having faced the horrors of war and knowing that he will never see them again and that the worst time of his life was past.

James had been a philosophy major in college before entering the Navy. He was on crutches, but would one day be able to walk with a cane. He was a deep thinker, who took a long time to choose which card to play. He would sometimes win card games, not because of mathematical ability but because of an ability to think out the likely future sequence of moves quite a few steps ahead. Although not an emotional person, he was looking steadily towards the future as he considered what job he wanted, and where he wanted to go back to college.

Mark would go home with no outward sign of his injuries. However, his injuries were more profound, he would need to watch his diet for the rest of his life, and would not be able to have children. His worst wounds were psychological. He would brood, stare off into space, wake up in the middle of the night screaming, or go into a rage, throwing cards across the room. He couldn't focus and would get confused and throw away cards that blew a winning hand. We could only hope that he would be wise enough to get psychiatric help from the VA before he ended up throwing away jobs and relationships the same way.

Michael had a simple broken leg from falling off of a bosons chair while he was painting a destroyer. He was mostly embarrassed that his big war injury was from being a klutz. He was anxious to get back to a ship and into battle so that he could have a chance to do something truly heroic. He would be a great military man if he didn't get reckless and get himself killed. Of course the ones who played it safe got killed in wartime as well. He played cards a bit reckless, either winning big or losing big.

Jesse was a large black man, who was a junior Marine Corps officer. He had gotten shot but would recover fully. He was driven, always trying to win the card game, and observant enough to read the personalities of the other players. He was also smart enough to catch that I had more knowledge and wisdom than someone of the age I appeared to be. He probably figured that was because there was more in my past than I was letting on. I really liked him, but had to be careful what I said around him. He made me excited and scared at the same time, which was something new since vampires have little to be afraid of and at most would fake fear when a human would be afraid.

Jerome was angry. He would also recover fully and go back to full duty. He had been engaged when he went into the Army, but his fiancé broke it off when she fell in love with someone else. He was cynical about life, the military, the war, people and everything else. He was Jesse's big rival in the card game because he took everything seriously. He was one of those people who could focus his anger to do whatever it took to accomplish a task. He would probably be promoted up the ranks for doing a great job, but be the sergeant who all of the men hate.

The third night out there was a massive explosion sometime after midnight. It rang through the steel hull of the ship so loudly that we were temporarily deaf. Elizabeth and I pulled on most of our clothes as quickly as possible then went to help our patients. The passageway was already filling with smoke as we left our small stateroom. It also seemed like the walls were starting to tilt slightly.

We got to the crew quarter room with all of our patients. We all knew the ship was under attack, but it was Michael who had enough experience on ships to judge how fast the ship was listing to starboard and realize that it would sink before they could make repairs. We headed immediately towards the top deck with its row of lifeboats. As we were leaving the crew quarters, there was another smaller explosion and the ship lurched further to starboard. This threw us against the wall, and a heavy steel door slammed into Jesse's leg opening a large gash. We didn't have time to get to the medical supply closet, so I ripped off a section of my slip and quickly bound Jesse's leg. At any other time, the men would have enjoyed seeing me pull up my skirt and ripping my slip but billows of thick, black smoke were starting to fill the ship.

We made it up to the main deck with all of us coughing and crying from the smoke. The ships crew members were busy doing damage control and the captain hadn't ordered abandon ship yet, so our group of nurses and patients were the only ones trying to ready the life boats. I threw caution aside and used all of my strength to flip the lifeboats upright. Only Jesse seemed to notice me moving heavy boats that would have been difficult for a much larger man.

The deck tilted more, and the lifeboats started to slide towards the ever-closer waves. For the first time, I noticed that it was raining and there were large, angry waves. We held the lifeboats steady for a couple minutes as we tried to decide what was the right time to abandon ship. We were hoping the captain and crew would take charge. We didn't have that luxury. The ship rolled further, and the heavy lifeboats were sliding into the water with or without us. We jumped into the boats as best as we could as they careened towards the water. Jesse, I, and Michael were in one boat. Mark, Jerome, Elizabeth, and James were in the second boat. Jeb slipped on the deck and was pulled along with his one hand grabbing the gunnel of the boat the others were in. I saw Elizabeth trying to help him on board as the lifeboats slid off the deck and plunged into the water.

We hit the water hard and one corner of the boat plunged under water for a few seconds causing an alarming amount of water to fill the boat before it bobbed back up and righted itself. I thought we were safe, but Michael knew better. He yelled at Jesse and I to grab the oars and row away from the ship while he bailed water from the bottom of the boat with a bucket that had been tied to the seat for that purpose.

As I rowed, I could see that the other lifeboat was not attempting to get away. Jeb had lost his grip when they hit the water, and Elizabeth was pulled in after him. They were searching the choppy, inky water and calling the names of their missing members. I thought about going back for them, but the fear in Michaels voice made it clear that we were still in danger also. Nor was I certain there was anything I could do.

It seemed like only seconds before the old freighter slipped diagonally into the water with the bow and starboard side going in first. This caused the aft end and propellers to briefly rise out of the water. The two large propellers were still spinning. As the propellers went back into the water, they pulled in everything in front of them. I had to close my eyes as I heard the crunch of the other lifeboat caught in a propeller and the screams of my dying friends. The undertow from the sinking ship pulled us back towards where it had been, but we were just far enough away that it couldn't capsize our little boat. Seconds later, the world went quiet. We were the only survivors in a small boat on an open ocean with only a little bit of debris in the water to mark the grave of our friends and shipmates.

The weather was getting rougher, so we had to keep rowing to keep the bow of our lifeboat pointed into the waves. I caught one glimpse of a shark fin in the water, and tried to block out the image of our friends' bodies as fish food.

We rowed through the night, and finally fell asleep when the sea calmed near morning. I had dreams of a beautiful tropical island with large waves rolling onto the sandy beach. Then I woke and realized that I really was hearing waves breaking on a shoreline. I woke the other two, so we could survey the situation. We were being pushed towards a small island with a small mountain in the middle. The mountain was completely covered with vegetation, so I was guessing the volcano was long since extinct. There was indeed a sandy beach, but also a concerning number of jagged rocks between us and the beach. Jesse and I started rowing again with Michael giving us directions. We rowed past one rock, and a large wave lifted us over a second rock. We rowed furiously to avoid the third rock, but a large, breaking wave shoved the boat onto it. The hull of the little lifeboat splintered like a balsa wood toy. We kept rowing the rest of the fifty yards to the beach. However, it was clear the remainder of the boat only came along with us because it was made of wood that floated, rather than because it maintained any shape of a boat. Welcome to paradise.

I half carried Jesse and Michael up the beach to the shade of the jungle. We all collapsed under the trees and slept a couple hours. When we woke our clothes had been dried by the warm south Pacific air, but were plastered to our body and caked with salt.

The reality of shipwrecks is that life is not like Gilligan's Island. We had all gotten a host of cuts and scrapes from getting off the ship and having the lifeboat hit the rocks. These scrapes had all been filled with stinging seawater and all of the silt, plankton and bacteria that comes with it. Being a vampire, I have a pretty good resistance to infections, which might come with the blood we drink. Both Jesse and Michael were running fevers from the infections.

I did what little I could to comfort them, then set out to find help. It must have been late morning when I left them, choosing a direction to walk up the beach at random. By dusk I had walked all the way around the island back to my patients and hadn't seen any sign of human habitation. The best I had done was to pick up a ripped section of fishing net that had washed up on the beach. Worse yet, I hadn't found a source of fresh water. I had found a couple of tiny streambeds, which must have had water only when it rained.

Jesse was a bit better. He was sitting up, looking around, and hungry. Michael was much worse. He was burning up with a high fever and delirious. I was hungry too. I made a mental note to memorize some of the edible flora and fauna in every region I went to, and have done so for the rest of my life. Jesse and I huddled together, both lost in our own thoughts mostly of what we would like to be eating just then.

The next day was devoted to finding food, and water if possible. The tropical jungle had plenty of lizards and birds, but no larger animals. No shortage of insects either. Fortunately, it was the right time of year for wild fruits to be ripe. I recognized coconuts, but only found a few that had fallen on the ground and wasn't sure how to climb the tree or recognize if they were ripe. I found a couple types of wild fruit, which I didn't recognize. I took a bite to make sure they didn't make me sick and they tasted wonderful. I would later learn that these were papaya and mango, which hadn't yet become available in much of the mainland U.S.

I followed the two small streambeds inland until the ground got steep. One had a small pool that had a bit of water left in the bottom from the last rain. I decided that the best place to live on the island would be not too far from that pool. I scouted about fifty yards in all directions from the pool but didn't find any signs of previous inhabitants. I also found a fish, a crab and large conch (like an eight inch snail) in a tidal pool.

I brought my groceries back to Jesse and Michael. Jesse was looking pretty good, if hungry. He had fashioned hats for us out of palm fronds.

Michael was apparently comatose. Without an IV or antibiotics I didn't expect Michael to live long. Michael died two days later and we buried him there on the beach with only a few stones and a palm frond hat to mark his grave. I found a pocketknife in Michael's pocket and took it with a combination of thankfulness for the much needed tool and guilt for taking it from a dead friend.

Jesse and I setup housekeeping about forty yards downwind from the fresh water pool. Jesse was still limping, so I did most of the food gathering. Jesse built us a lean-to shelter and laid out areas for food preparation, garbage disposal, and personal hygiene. He also setup a calendar scraped into a piece of wood.

Jesse and I soon became lovers. I was attracted to him anyway, and he wasn't one to turn down a great lay. With long hours with nothing to do, we had lovely long lovemaking, experimentation, and excited vigorous sex. Sometimes we went days without any clothes on in the warm tropical air. We also had an infinite amount of time to talk to one another, and soon had fallen deeply in love, as well as in lust.

Jesse was still an officer and regretted being involuntarily taken out of his career and the war. He blazed a path half way up the small mountain from our dwelling and set up several observation posts where he could look out over the ocean in all directions. He started making logs of ships he saw in the distance. None ever came near our island. I wasn't sure there was any point in doing this, but I didn't say anything because his mental stamina would be better if he had a purpose in life.

After a couple weeks on the island, I began to become weak. I had been living as a human amongst humans. In all of the traumatic events in my life, I had temporarily forgotten that I am a vampire and occasionally need human blood to survive. I was very apprehensive about discussing this with Jesse. If he didn't accept it willingly, the only way for me to survive would be for Jesse to become my caged pet, or worse yet I could let him go free just to know the fear of a prey animal that knows it is being hunted. I didn't think I could bring myself to abstain from drinking blood as long as would necessary for me to die of severe anemia. I started thinking about the best way to explain it to him.

A few days later, Jesse was in a good mood as we lazed near the fire after a sensual lovemaking. I decided there wouldn't be a better time.

"Jesse?" I asked to get his attention.

"Yes?" he asked in return.

"You know how everyone has a past? How you never really know someone completely because there are parts of their life that you weren't there for?" I asked.

"It's OK," he said. "I wasn't a virgin walking onto this island and didn't expect you to be either."

"No. It's not that. It's just that…" I was having a hard time finding the best words.

"Are you trying to tell me you are engaged? Married?" he asked. He was so gentle and understanding that it was making this all the harder.

"No. Nothing like that. It's. Well. I'm a monster." I said. Maybe if I get his imagination thinking of the worse case scenario, the reality won't seem that bad to him.

"Is it that time of the month?" he asked.

I laughed. Did I mention I also fell in love with his sense of humor?

I went on, "No. You know how there are silly Hollywood films about monsters. How they might live a long time, but need to prey on humans? It would be silly to think of a person turning into a bat or melting in sunlight. However, it's not that hard to believe that some people eat good food and vitamins and liver longer. It wouldn't be that much of a stretch if some people could live a lot longer if they had a very special vitamin, like human blood."

Jesse laughed and said, "Woman, I told you eating raw fish wasn't good. Don't go completely nuts on me. You might have had a weird dream, but you are not a vampire."

I leaned closer to him, as though I was going to kiss him, then flicked out my fangs. He fainted dead away. He hit his head on palm

211

tree with a hollow clunk sound as he slumped backwards. I hadn't planned for that.

His brain did what it must to deal with difficult concepts by knocking him out then into a dream state. He started to snore and woke up again forty minutes later. He stared at me. I stayed on the other side of the fire, watching him but not saying anything.

He started to speak several times, then eventually got out, "You said you lived longer. How old are you?"

"One hundred and sixty nine," I said slowly.

"How long will you live?"

"Perhaps a thousand years, or a bit less."

"Any other special abilities?" he asked.

"Diseases don't hurt us as easily. We tend to be good looking to attract humans with sex appeal. We give of human scents associated with sexual attraction. My fangs emit venom that gives any human I bite a feeling of sexual ecstasy. And I'm faster and stronger than a human. Although I'm overdue to feed, so I'm probably only twice as strong as you right now," I replied.

"When we put up the larger cottage, you let me take most of the load. Are you saying that you could have lifted those walls easily?" he asked.

I stood up and slowly walked around the fire to him. I slowly squatted down and grabbed his ankle gently but firmly with one hand. I slowly stood up and lifted his entire body off the ground.

While holding him upside down off the ground I said, "See, I'm weak right now. You weigh twice as much as me and I'm straining to lift you. At full strength, I could throw you thirty yards." I gently put him down and returned to my place at the other side of the fire.

He asked, "What have you done all these years?"

"We integrate into human civilization. Every ten to thirty years we take a new identity and move to a new location. Depending upon the vampire, they may explore many different careers or become the master of a single field or hobby spread across several lifetimes. I have a half-dozen degrees, along with experience as a sailor, martial artist, barmaid and a couple dozen other things.

"Are you going to kill me?" he asked.

"No… but I have to drink some of your blood every few weeks if I want to stay alive. It won't hurt you any more than giving blood at the Red Cross, and will be a lot more fun," I replied. He thought a long time about that.

"If I participate willingly, will you give me something in return?" he asked. Being a person who tries to make every situation work to the mutual advantage of both parties would make him a great business leader. It was perhaps an odd trait for a military leader.

"What do you want?" I asked, taking mental inventory of the funds I have squirreled away in a number of countries.

"Teach me anything I ask, as best as you can," he replied. No wonder I liked him. He was wise enough to know that knowledge is more important than money or having a henchman.

"Deal. What would you like to learn?"

"Starting tomorrow, spend some time every day teaching me martial arts and answer other questions in the evenings," he said. Then he went on, "Tonight I want you to tell me about vampires, their culture and your whole life, not just your current cover story."

I talked clear through the night. There are so many times that I would like to have conversations with my friends and have to stop myself before I let slip something I shouldn't know in my current identity. It was cathartic to tell anything I wanted to about myself, my life, my views on supernatural culture, and anything else. I talked until I was hoarse and enjoyed it all. It also endeared me all the more to him that getting to know me better was at the top of his wish list.

As the dawn sky began to lighten, we made love and he offered his neck to me.

The next few months settled into a wonderful routine. Jesse checked his lookout posts and logged the air and ship traffic four times each day, at dawn, noon, afternoon, and dusk. While he did that, I picked, and caught food. We managed to keep from starving although the variety was a bit lacking. We had coconut milk to drink any time there wasn't fresh water left over from the last rain. It worked out great then, but to this day I can't stand coconut milk.

We had a late morning martial arts lesson. The afternoon was for napping, being lazy and sometimes sex. Late afternoon was spent on survival activities, like drying fish for lean days and walking the beach to find anything useful that had washed up. The evening was for exercise and martial arts drills. We spent the nights talking and enjoying each other's company. I've never been as close to another vampire as I was to Jesse.

Our little stint in paradise had to end eventually. We had both agreed that long-term relationships weren't a good idea for a vampire and a human, so we would go our own ways without remorse when the time came. That time came when we had been on the island for three months and twelve days. That afternoon, Jesse headed up to his observation post while I headed to the beach to check the tidal pools. Just as I was about to step on to the beach, I saw the incoming ship, which was still a few miles away. I rushed back to our cottage and pulled on my slightly tattered uniform skirt and top. I had been wearing only my bra and panties as a makeshift bikini. My shoes had been lost in the shipwreck.

Fortunately, the ship was U.S. Navy. We met them on the beach. They were coming to put an observation post in place. This island was to be a command post for observation posts on a number of surrounding islands. The officer who was supposed to be in charge of the command post had come down with malaria the day before they arrived. The obvious solution was to put Jesse in charge of the command post, and he was given a field promotion one rank higher. They spent a few days on the island, during which Jesse was trained on the duties expected of him, and we trained the people who would man the series of observation posts on how to survive on these islands.

When the ship left Jesse and two enlisted men on the island, I was on the ship. I stayed on shipboard as they dropped observers off at four other islands. Then the ship returned to Perl Harbor and I was sent on to my next duty station. I never saw Jesse again, but years later I heard that he had become one of the first black flag officers. To this day, I have a soft spot for muscular black men.

Chapter 7

We got our break in the A&M case on Tuesday when police canvasing the surrounding buildings were told of an argument outside the fateful frat flat. It was between a man matching Benny Marsden's description and a student named Drayon Digs. They found Drayon Digs in his dorm room, but he was still a bit strung out for questioning. He spent the night in jail on a possession charge while we waited for his mind to clear a bit.

Mark Blout questioned Drayon. I listened from the observation room.

Mark started, "We have a witness who says you were arguing with a man last night around ten. About what time would you say that was?"

"It was more like ten thirty," he said. Then he realized he was being cooperative and said, "But I don't see as it's any of your business."

"We have you on a drug possession charge. If you don't start pointing fingers at someone else, you're not going to finish the semester at A&M," Mark pointed out.

"Look. I don't know the guy. I only met him a couple times. His name is Jeff Pine," Drayon said.

Pine. I forgot about Chris Pine. Everyone forgets about Chris Pine. This must be another one of Benny Marsden's Trekkie aliases.

Mark asked, "What were you arguing about?"

"He would only sell me half as much as I wanted because that was all the cash I had. I told him I was good for the rest."

"What did he say to that?"

"He just said No in a snotty arrogant voice. I pushed him a little... to scare him a bit. He wouldn't budge and said that someone named Bacon would kill him if he didn't bring back cash," Drayon replied.

Mark asked, "Could he have said Bakwin?"

"Yeah. That's the name. Sophia Bakwin."

Mark kept questioning him for a while, but he already had what he wanted. Our small time pusher had slipped up and implicated the local drug boss by name.

The next hour was a mad scramble of planning. Their team had been setting up a raid on Bakwin's place for some time and now they had enough evidence for the warrant and to charge her. I sat in on the whole thing since I had offered to participate in the raid. I offered to have Gary along as well, but Mark wouldn't hear of it, and I didn't think it was wise to push it. The raid was planned for that evening when the team knew she would be most likely to be in the bar she owned. They wanted to bring her in before she had time to run or destroy evidence.

Sophia's nightclub was named "Slippery When Wet", but locals just called it "Slip". The club was at the back of a mostly abandoned strip mall. The seedy motel next door probably stayed in business because of the prostitutes who worked the club. We later learned that Sophia was getting a cut from the prostitutes, the motel, and the illegal card games in the back room, as well as overcharging the customers once they had a couple drinks.

Mark laid out the floor plan. The club has a front entrance and a side door for staff and taking out the trash. I pointed out that this style of two-sided strip mall often has a service corridor for accessing utilities and as a back way into all the units. Mark didn't want to look foolish so he said, "That's right Christine and you are covering the service corridor."

We went over a hand drawn depiction of the inside of the club. It had a bar to the left and stage at the back of the room from the door.

The bar tender was dishonest, but not prone to engaging in physical confrontations. There were several bouncers who might be working on a given night. Most of the bouncers were former college football players who had washed out of school after addictions killed their grades, or they had been kicked out for cheating.

An undercover officer had paced off the size of the club from the inside and outside. A full half of the unit had to be behind the stage. That was way too much space to simply hold a kitchen, storeroom, office, and dressing room. We knew the prostitutes used the motel next door, so the logical conclusion was some other illegal activity such as gambling or drug distribution. It wasn't likely that Sophia was dumb enough to sit with her entire storehouse of drugs ten feet away waiting to implicate her, but we were hoping to find enough there to strengthen the charges against her. A number of officers were assigned to charge through the main room and into that back area before any evidence could be destroyed.

One of the detectives gave us short notes on the club employees, and a more detailed description of Sophia Bakwin. She was a busty woman with red hair. Most people would call her beautiful if a few pounds overweight. However her personality was sociopathic and bipolar. She was prone to radical mood swings between the sexy seductress and the ruthless killer. She was always carrying a pistol or two and possibly a knife. A number of suspicious deaths around her suggested that she was adept at using poisons also.

That night was cloudy and windy. It felt like we would have rain before the night was out. The strip mall was run down. It looked like the owners had stopped maintaining it in hopes they could sell the land to someone who would tear down the building. The club was on the east side, where it was not visible from Memorial Parkway. Also on this side of the building were a run down gym, an electrical supply store, and a sewing machine repair shop.

Only the club was open. The sign for "Slippery When Wet" depicted a busty woman standing with a pool cue held between her spread legs. Her pose suggested she might be pressing the cue into her crotch, but you couldn't be certain. The sign was lit, but not very prominent. There were a dozen cars parked outside the club, all of which were older and in need of paint or washing.

I was dressed in navy blue pants and a police issue dark jacket with the lapel folded inward to cover the badge until I was at the door. I had a form fitting Kevlar vest underneath the jacket. I parked in the next lot over and watched the time. We had planned the timing of the operation. The side and back entrances would be covered just before the first officers approached the front.

At the appointed time, I headed for the side door that would lead to the service corridor. The door was locked as expected, but it was an older lock. I pulled out an autopick, a gun-like tool that was not available to the average locksmith. The tool laser scanned the shape of the keyhole, loaded the correct lock pick, then opened the lock. The whole processes took about five seconds. I wasn't opposed to using a few gadgets from the supernatural community.

I slipped in the door, pulled out my Beretta, then flipped my lapel right side out so my badge was showing. The corridor was dimly lit by bare light bulbs in ceiling fixtures. Half of the bulbs were burnt out, so there were patches of light every forty feet. The corridor wasn't meant to be seen by the public. It had a bare concrete floor. Pipes and electrical conduit ran along the walls. There was a door into each business. The doors had rust showing through the paint, probably because they hadn't been repainted since the structure was built.

A woman who could only be Sophia slipped through the door from the club with a pistol already leveled at what was in front of her. It looked like one of the illegal fleche pistols that Russian mafia had been selling on the black market. Fleche pistols shoot a modified shotgun shell, intermediate in size between a 20 gage and a 410. That was probably to keep the owners of these guns dependent on the Russians for ammo. It was loaded with slivers of metal that did more damage than shot pellets. The spread was larger than an equivalent shotgun spread because of the poor aerodynamics of the slivers of metal. Even a shot to the center of my bullet proof vest was likely to send a few slivers to my jugular vein or eye sockets, which could kill me.

"Put the gun down slowly and you will walk out of this building alive," I said in my authority-you-shouldn't-mess-with voice.

"Even if you shoot me, I can still pull the trigger and kill you as well," she said.

Under different circumstances, I would have killed an armed suspect before they were through the door, but I needed information from her. She was smart enough to understand the consequences of killing a cop. We were at an impasse.

We stared at each other for a few seconds, then she said, "So the police have a pet vampire. I have a whole shipment of blood. Selling it to your friends could be a million dollar payday."

She was smart enough to know it was more likely that I was manipulating the police, but made the pet remark to goad me. After two hundred years of dealing with people, it would take a lot more than that to make me angry. It took some training and a shrewd eye to recognize the slightly different shaped cheekbones that hide a vampires venom glands and fang retraction muscles. Sophia was obviously tapped into a source of information about the supernatural community.

"I know about your blood. I wouldn't feed it to my vampire cat," I replied. There aren't any vampire cats, but I wanted to raise some doubt in her mind as to how much she knew about the vampire community.

I went on, "You realize that turning vampires into blood thirsty animals won't improve you life expectancy."

"After a few doses they learn to control it a bit and act like any other junkie. Most will spend their life fortunes, and a few will work for their fix as hired muscle," she replied.

So that's her game. A bunch of vampire enforcers working for the drug cartels could be a big problem. It won't work as well as they expect. Vampires are independent hunters, not herd animals, or pack hunters like werewolves. Nonetheless, any vampire mob muscle becomes a big problem for the police.

Sophia had an idea. "Hey cut me a deal and I'll give you the scoop on some cartel big wigs coming to town. But you have to rough me up a bit, so that they think you beat it out of me." She could do the math. Getting out of prison time was good, but the cartel thinking she informed would get her killed even in prison.

"Your tip would have to pan out before we cut the deal," I said.

"There is a cartel boss called Mr. D coming to Huntsville soon. This is where they are test marketing Apocalypse," she said.

I negotiated more. "Do you want time off the prison sentence for giving us the details of his arrival? Or do you want to walk free in the witness protection program for testifying against the cartel?"

"I forgot about witness protection," she said. "Yes. I would testify to walk free."

I could tell from the change in the tone of her voice that she was lying. Also, people tend to stop using contractions or slang when they are lying and trying to cover it up. Most likely she was planning on stringing the police along a bit before making some other move, but what? I would watch for that, but getting the gun away from her was my immediate concern.

It felt like she was stalling for time as she went on. "The cartel bosses meet here in two days. They try to act civilized by choosing a swank location. It's a lodge in Scottsboro. That's all I know."

"All right. Put the gun down and..." she shot at me in the middle of my sentence so that I would be slightly distracted. Fortunately, I had a fraction of a second warning when I saw the muscles of her arm tense up to fire. I pushed hard with my left foot, so I would land on my right shoulder. I fired as I was falling. Years of practice allowed me to rapid-fire two shots getting one clean shot through her heart even while I was in free fall on my way to the concrete. I wasn't good enough to shoot the gun out of her hand at that second, and I was smart enough to know it.

I stood up and contemplated her body. My hands swapped the clip in my Beretta for a full one without my giving them any thought. That could have gone better, but it could have gone a lot worse. The detective in me is always suspicious of coincidences. Having a drug cartel trying out a vampire drug in the same city where large numbers of vampires were already arriving was not a pretty thought.

I walked out of the building to find the rest of the raid was going well. The bar tender and one of Sophia's lieutenants were being taken in separate cars for questioning. Strippers and prostitutes were being loaded into large police van. Mark was miffed that we didn't take Sophia in for questioning, but he didn't give me too much hassle since a couple scratches from the fleche gun left blood running down my left arm and my left cheek. The scratches were well worth it to keep Mark off my back.

I told Mark about the cartel boss meeting. That certainly got his interest. Huntsville police don't have jurisdiction in Scottsboro, but this sort of thing was way beyond the capabilities of Scottsboro police so they would probably work together on it. Mark said that he would contact Scottsboro PD. I said I would try to use unofficial means to find the exact location of the meeting.

Chapter 8

The next morning I took my time with my morning workout and home chores. I got a couple pieces of furniture ordered for the new living room. I knew the person I had to see was not a morning person.

Gary called mid morning, and I arranged to pick him up in an hour or so. I didn't really need him along today. However, I would enjoy the company and he was anxious to hear about the raid the night before. I didn't invite him over to my place because I didn't want any romantic distractions before the day's work was done. About an hour later I grabbed my cooler with raspberry ice tea and headed for Gary's place.

Gary must have been watching out the window for me because he came out of the door as soon as I pulled into the driveway. He quizzed me constantly about the raid the night before as I drove over to the five points area.

I pulled into a little row of shops in five points. There are many places where shops are decorated to be quaint or quirky but you can tell it's really just business trying to establish an atmosphere that people will like. This was one of the rare places where you could tell the décor was sincere. The shops were certainly decorated in quirky multi-colored paint and furnishings, but somehow you could tell that it was just the personalities of the owners showing through and not for any commercial reason.

As we got out of the car, Gary was giving me a raised eyebrow look that asked what we were doing here. I grabbed his arm and pulled him close to emphasize the conversation.

"Gary, do you know Alice Stafford?" I asked.

"I can't say as I have had the pleasure," he replied.

"She is an empath who is one of the world's experts on all things travel related. You have to deal with her in a particular way. Don't go thinking you won't pay for it later if you make a deal of the high school cheerleader act I'm about to put on. And as for you, be cheerful and pleasant, and that's an order."

"Yes ma'am!" he said with a grin that I was tempted to slap off of his face.

The shop, called Wonder Travel, was a cacophony of color. The walls had originally had the typical posters of exotic locations, but had since been covered with memorabilia from around the world. Unusual items were on shelves and nails filling in every bit of wall space, often right on top of the travel posters. You would be hard pressed to find enough bare wall to determine the original wall color underneath the posters.

As we entered Alice squealed, "Christine!" and raced to embrace me.

"Wonderful Alice!" I said. We kissed on both cheeks and giggled like high school sophomores. I suspect that her bubbly personality is meant to put others in a good mood so that their emotions will be less oppressing to an empath.

"And who is this hunk of a man?" she asked.

Gary gave a deep bow and kissed her hand as he said, "Gary Halvorson at your service ma'am." Alice was obviously pleased with his archaic gesture.

We didn't have to go through the ritual of identifying ourselves as vampire and werewolf. Alice already knows me, and neither of us could hide our species from an empath no matter how we tried.

With Alice, pleasantries must come first. She served us a proper English high tea from a silver tea set. I asked her about her recent travels, and she regaled us with an account of the people and culture in Bhutan. Alice is partly of Icelandic descent and has the palest white complexion you've ever seen. I'm pretty sure the complexion isn't makeup, since I've seen her with some revealing outfits draped over her thin body. She can't be albino since some other part of her heritage gave her jet-black hair. She could be the perfect Hollywood vampire with a little blood red lipstick, but she keeps her lips a pale pink and uses various colors of shimmering eye shadow. She also has a passion for vintage clothing. Today she was in a long, flowing skirt that was awash in color, with a red top, black vest, and gold chain around her hips. Her outfit could have been used as a gypsy costume.

Once pleasantries were over, Alice used her friendly, sultry voice to say, "Now Christine. You didn't come to visit me with that artillery under your jacket just to have tea. What is todays business?"

"We have a bunch of very bad men from South America coming to town. You know, the drug lord types. We think they might be staying at a high-end lodge near Scottsboro. I was wondering if you knew anyone in the area who could help us find where they will be staying?" I asked.

"Honey, I know lots of people," she said in a Rosalind Russell impersonation.

Gary and I sipped tea and ate cucumber sandwiches as we listened to Alice make phone calls to concierges and desk managers at the best lodges. She gave an animated account of how she had a client with a terribly thick Spanish dialect who was adamant about finding where her boyfriend would be staying so that she could arrange for a surprise for him. With each telling the story become more elaborately embellished with romantic and culture details. After the fourth phone call, Alice wrote down a lodge name for us and told us that a group of South American businessmen would be arriving there this evening through tomorrow afternoon. Most were traveling in small groups.

We left Alice with a flurry of hugs and a few international travel pamphlets in tow.

I called to give Mark the information about the meeting site immediately after we walked out of Alice's shop. We stopped for lunch at a small sandwich shop a few blocks up. Both of us were quiet as we ate. The thought of a raid on a group of international drug lords and their bodyguards can be a bit sobering.

I took Gary back to my place. We spent an hour together, mostly in my bed. That was followed by a twenty-minute nap. Sex is always better when you have the luxury of falling asleep right afterward, and better yet if you were fully awake when you started.

I took Gary home, then went by the precinct. Mark already had a couple officers who were hunting buffs stationed on hills overlooking the lodge. They were wearing camouflage gilly suits and observing everyone arriving. The Scottsboro police had a detective undercover as a waiter in the lodge dining room. Frankly, I was impressed by both of them for putting so much together on such short notice.

Officially, this type of operation probably belongs to ATF, the Alcohol, Tobacco, and Firearm enforcement agency. I didn't know if ATF had been contacted, or if they would be able to respond quickly enough. I wasn't the lead detective on this one, so I decided I was better off not knowing the answers to those questions.

We spent the rest of the afternoon planning a raid on the lodge to be held the next evening. The plans were complicated by the fact that we didn't know if the group was meeting at the lodge or someplace else, or at what time they might leave. Thus we had to be ready to spring a trap on short notice in hopes of getting all of them at once.

The next day, most of the officers involved were antsy. Most had been told to come in after lunch so that they would be fresh for an evening raid, but who can sleep when you know you will soon face a group of international drug lords and their hired muscle? The afternoon hours crept by as officers cleaned up miscellaneous paperwork and checked the time every five minutes.

Mark was the only one not waiting anxiously. He was actively working to get additional officers. He got most of the other detectives reassigned for the evening. He got the entire S.W.A.T. team, which consisted of nineteen men and one woman. I was the only officer who knew that two of the men on the S.W.A.T. team were werewolves. I was able to pull those two aside for just a couple minutes to bring them up to date on the vampire drug connection. Mark also got about a dozen other officers borrowed from the police departments in surrounding towns. I don't have the connections to get men from other towns, so I was glad Mark was on point for this one.

After a couple hours of putzing around the office, I went to the firing range with a group of other officers. The time passes much easier when you can spend it puncturing targets with high velocity projectiles.

As three o'clock approached, everyone converged on the ready room. It was one of the few times that I saw people looking forward to the ready room. It was probably one of the few times that something significant would happen there. Everyone fell silent when Mark brought his first slide up on the screen. He spent quite a bit of time on the first few slides. These were aerial photographs, pictures from the ground, and blueprints of the building. He went over where various officers would be stationed and lines of sight. He outlined four slightly different sequences of events for the raid and gave everyone a piece of paper summarizing them. The four scenarios differed by whether our suspects were in their rooms, the lodge dining room, outdoors by the pool or lakeshore, or filing into vehicles. The meeting ended and we were all informed that we had fifteen minutes to get to our assigned vehicle. The fifteen minutes were spent grabbing bulletproof vests and extra clips and anything else we hoped not to need.

Since we didn't want to announce our arrival, we took unmarked cars. I had three other officers riding along in my car. The back seat of the T-Bird wasn't exactly spacious, but they didn't complain. I tried not to think about what a snag with an ammo belt could do to the baby blue leather upholstery. Recently the police department offered detectives an extra transportation stipend if we use

227

our own cars instead of the unmarked Crown Victorias we used to drive. It saved the department money, but didn't pay for your car unless you were driving affordable used cars. Nonetheless, the program was popular with the detectives because it gave you an excuse to buy a cool car.

I was in the group that would approach the lodge from the South end of the building. The parking lot was on the East side of the building. The pool was on the West side of the building, and the lakeshore was another hundred yards west of that. There were only four rooms with South views. Our observers had been watching those windows and determined only one was occupied and had the curtains open. They made their best guess as to the location of the occupant, to minimize the chance that we would be seen approaching the building.

The lodge was watched through the afternoon as guests engaged in various activities. Around 5:30 all of the guests had gone inside, presumably going to their rooms to prepare for dinner. We got the signal to move in. There were three other officers with me on the South approach, one of them the South side observer. We waited another minute until the observer said it was clear.

We approached the South side of the building. A patrolman I didn't know and myself went left, and the other two went right. When two people are coming around a blind corner, the best option is for one of them to get down on the ground and first peek around the corner near the ground. Since most people expect to shoot at the level of the chest of a standing person, looking low gives you an extra second to pull back if there should be someone around that corner with a gun pointed at you.

I motioned my impromptu partner to wait, while I sat down and looked. The only person around back was an employee in a white jacket, who was collecting damp towels from around the pool. We grabbed him from behind and clamped a hand over his mouth to keep him from accidentally alerting the guests. We pulled him into the building and put him in the employee's locker room as planned. That was about the last time that things went according to plan.

My group took the South stairwell, while others took the North stairs and elevator. Apparently one of the South American guests had seen the assault coming and all of them were ready. The first officers to peek into the second floor hallway were met with a hail of gunfire. The SWAT commander wisely ordered his men to shoot gas grenades into every window. It was much better to break up the resistance with gas than to face a well-organized group of professional killers.

We threw our gas grenades into the hall then backed down to a landing a half flight of stairs below. We kept guns trained on the door to the hallway, but no one came through. There was a loud sound as glass broke out of most of the windows. For a couple seconds I thought it was a sonic boom, but then I realized what the trapped men would be doing. I took a deep breath, then ran into the gas cloud.

The drug lords must have had a plan B established. They came crashing out of the second story windows, nearly simultaneously. All of them immediately headed for vehicles without wasting any time on shooting. Officers were shouting for them to halt, but were uniformly ignored. A couple of them were shooting at officers as they ran. I took a few shots at the legs of the fleeing gunmen, and saw one drop to one knee.

They must have rented every large SUV available at Huntsville's palatial two-baggage claim airport. The fleeing men had no qualms about smashing into any patrol car that got in the way. Most were familiar enough with car chases to hit the patrol cars in front of the front tire or behind the rear tire so that the patrol cars would rotate out of the way. The chase was on, and there was no way I was going to get back to my car soon enough to be part of it.

I took charge of the officers on the second floor. We searched every floor. None of the guests remained. We found a maid in an upstairs broom closet.

I heard repeated stories of the ensuing car chase told around the precinct for days afterwards. Many of the stories sounded more like a script from a Die Hard movie. The tally, after discounting some exaggerations, came to; three officers shot, one seriously, twenty three

Columbians arrested, one car load of Columbians killed when they drove off a steep embankment, and damage to a dozen police vehicles. Worst of all, one of the SUVs with four Columbians in it was still at large when night fell a few hours later.

Having done all I could at present, I headed back to the precinct. The shit was going to hit the fan there, and I wanted to slide through my part as quickly as possible. We soon had some senior ATF official getting all red faced about why his men weren't involved and in charge, and a number of FBI agents asking questions to find a reason they should have been involved. Mark Blout was in the thick of that mess. For once I was happy not to be the person in charge. By comparison, the two hours I spent filing a report about why I had discharged my weapon was a small inconvenience. I got out of the building as soon as I could. On the way out, I passed the front desk where a rather irate resort owner was shouting about his resort full of broken windows and a stench that would drive out a skunk breeder's convention.

Chapter 9

The next day the dust had settled a bit, and I was assigned to interrogation duty. Mark was nowhere to be seen. The gist I got from the chief was that we didn't have enough evidence to prosecute, so it was up to interrogation to see what could be shaken loose.

All of the interrogation rooms were full that day. We had quite a few prisoners and too little time to question them. Liz knew today would be interrogation day and was a couple blocks away at a lighting store when I called her. Mike probably gave her a heads up about the arrests, although I can only guess at how he found out. I'm sure the UN has a few tricks up its sleeves.

Juan Garcia was handcuffed to the table. We were in interrogation room three. The sergeant who assigns interrogation rooms knew that I prefer that odd shaped long room for the psychological effect of having a place for one of the interrogators behind the suspect's back. I'm good on my own and great with Liz helping, so they give a bit of preference to their best interrogator.

The door of the interrogation room opened right next to where the prisoner sat handcuffed to the table, so you had to walk near him to get to either chair. Liz had her hair done nice and a tight skirt. She walked in first and looked Juan in the eyes and had the slightest smile on her lips. She gave a little burst of empathic lust projection as she passed him to sit behind his back. Just before stepping into the room, I unbuttoned another button on my blouse. I let him get a little whiff of attraction pheromones as I walked by to sit in front of him. He seemed like the macho type, so we were hoping he would talk more if he was bragging to couple pretty women.

I sat at the table opposite to Juan Garcia. I looked through his file, while he tried to get a bit better look down the front of my shirt.

"So… what brings you to Alabama, Mr. Garcia?" I asked.

"No Hablo Ingles," he answered with a heavy accent. A slight shake of Liz's head indicated he was lying, as if I didn't know that already.

"Mr. Garcia, a man who charmed so many women while getting a degree in packaging from Brown University certainly speaks English," I said with a smile. I was guessing at the charming women part, but it was part of my strategy to play to his ego.

"Getting many women is not too difficult when you have a foreign accent and my good looks," he replied with an obviously inflated opinion of himself.

"And how many women have you been with on this trip?" I asked.

"All of them," he replied with a big grin. We might have overshot on the ego thing.

"And how many of them traded their body for pharmaceuticals delivered to this country courtesy of your packaging skills?" I asked.

"I don't know what you are talking about," he replied.

"Oh come on," I cajoled, "A man as brilliant as you are can certainly fool a few customs officials."

"They are pretty dumb," he responded.

"And yet, you are in jail, and in northern Alabama at that. You are pretty far from the Rio Grande," I replied.

"Border towns are the worst place to bring something into the country," he said. "However this doesn't matter since you have no evidence that I did anything." Liz gave a hand sign to indicate that he is unsure of that fact. This told me that there is physical evidence, even if it can't be connected to this guy.

"I don't need evidence, Mr. Garcia. Your bosses are going to give you up in order to save their own skin." From the look on his face, this didn't occur to him. I waited a few seconds to let him think about that.

"That new product line of yours is going to create some very powerful enemies," I pointed out, "Your life expectancy would be a lot longer if you served a few years for something minor."

"The people I work for are very good at turning addicts into employees. You and your blood sucking kin will soon be their lap dogs," he responded. Liz signed to indicate that he was confident in this prediction.

He knew about vampires and was able to identify the ever so subtle difference in facial features, which humans dismiss as just a given genetic makeup of human. I formulated a whole different set of interrogation questions as I drew in my next breath.

"How many died testing that theory?" I asked.

"A few," he said with a shrug, as though the fact or the number of people was unimportant. Drug cartels thrive on the edges of society where human life is a cheap commodity.

"Is your own life as cheap?" I asked. "Give us some evidence and you may only spend a few months under house arrest in the witness protection program while your bosses do the hard time."

He clammed up at that and got a far away look as he considered his options. The fact that he didn't deny the existence of physical evidence confirmed that there was some.

"We could protect your daughter as well," Liz chimed in. Liz at her best moments read empathic signals so well it seemed like mind reading even though she couldn't actually hear thoughts, I think. This was one of those moments.

"Family protection is a standard part of witness protection," I said rolling with the conversation. "We could even help get your family to this country."

He thought about that, then came to some sort of conclusion.

"The organization I work for is more powerful than your witness protection program," he said. "They have eyes on every street corner. Besides your law enforcement officers will have far too much to keep them occupied when we are controlling your canine cousins as well." Liz nodded her head to confirm this was not a guess.

"And how would a smart man like you do that?" I asked. I could guess at the answer, but wanted to keep him talking.

He clammed up good this time. Liz made a speak-no-evil gesture, which told me he wouldn't be talking any more at this sitting. I left him along with his thoughts. This would give him time to figure out what else he wanted to say to me. That would get him talking the next time instead of hardened against questions.

Back out in the hallway, I whispered to Liz, "Any other observations?"

"He seems pretty confident that there will be a werewolf analogue of the drug," Liz replied.

"It must be coming out soon," I said, more to myself that Liz. I knew that observation would make it back to Mike and the UN, which was the point.

I sent Liz on her way, then went to talk with the other interrogators. Several of us agreed that there was something more here, but that we had little hope of interrogation find it. Of course I didn't mention the werewolf and vampire connections. With no leads to follow and local crime cleaned up, the case would be closed.

After a hasty lunch of cardboard tacos from a mobile cantina truck, the afternoon turned into a big meeting with the higher ups. The same conversation that the interrogators had was rehashed endlessly. It was soon apparent that there would be a lot more useless talking and probably nothing accomplished. I held my tongue as much as possible to hasten the meeting, but it still dragged on two and a half hours. After that, I had enough of work for the day. I took some paperwork to work on at home, knowing full well I probably wouldn't, and left for the day.

I headed over to the Huntsville Art Museum, which was being prepped for a private opening for the Vampire tribunal that evening. I'm not old enough or politically active enough to be part of that, but it's courtesy for local law enforcement to stop by and check on them.

I got a briefing on the evening's events from the museum security manager. They had recently put in security updates, which included bulletproof doors and windows. They had put in cell phone jammers, which was a trend amongst museums to maintain the quiet atmosphere. Only the meeting attendees and some caterers, also young vampires, would be in the building. The tribunal had paid extra to have museum security people posted outside the doors only.

The meeting preparations were looking good. They had a big meeting room with a long table and a number of smaller lounge areas and exhibit rooms near by. The caterers were setting up for piles of food, including freeze-dried blood, a Lithuanian delicacy. The attendees would have plenty to eat and drink as long as the water supply holds out. These meetings had more breaks than formal session. Plenty of private political deals were made on the breaks. I shook hands with a couple of the organizers who had the prescribed praise and respect for local law enforcement. I guess politics looks the same for any sentient species.

I wasn't the only one stopping by for the sake of protocol. Roger and Felicia Harris were there finishing up their pleasantries to establish an agreed upon format of non-interference. They are an elderly werewolf couple. I knew that they were the local pack leaders, but I wasn't sure if was him or her or a joint position. It's hard to figure out the pecking order amongst werewolves, who cooperate so naturally as a pack. There are debates amongst other species as to whether this makes werewolves less evolved for giving away some of their individuality, or if it makes them the most civilized species.

I waited to the side for a few seconds while Roger and Felicia finished their goodbyes. We knew of each other but had never had a conversation.

Excuse me, Mr. and Mrs. Harris," I began. It was appropriate to treat them as elders even if I was a hundred years older. "Could we talk for a few moments?"

"Ah, Detective Mills. How are you this day?" Roger started.

"Well, thank you. However, there is a concerning situation at the moment." I said.

"You mean the drug that causes vampires to fall back to their animal instincts," said Felicia.

"Yes. That seems to be contained at the moment, but that investigation has brought to light a new threat," I said.

They waited patiently for me to continue. They were as still as any meditating Buddhist monk with no more than the slightest rise of an eyebrow to indicate that I should continue.

"We have just learned that the organization that created that vampire drug is working on a werewolf analog," I said.

"You imply that it is not yet on the street," Roger pointed out.

"We think not. The person I interrogated seemed confident it is coming soon, although he didn't know exactly when, unless he had the ability to hide his deceit from an empath."

"Who knows about this?" asked Felicia.

"Just you and Liz," I said. "We finished the interrogation just over an hour ago."

I hadn't given the information about the werewolf drug to any of the vampire delegates because the lack of a local leader or top leader left me temporarily without a proper chain of command. Besides, mentioning it now would have made it part of their politicking and drawn me into the process. Vampire politics can make Washington look like a kindergarten playground squabble. I wasn't anxious to get drawn into the middle of that.

"Thank you, detective Mills. We will inform the werewolf community," said Roger. If my news was regarded with any urgency it wasn't obvious from their slow, deliberate walk as they headed out to their car. Admittedly I may have been a bit overly concerned with this new development in light of the fact that it could be years in the future.

Chapter 9

As I drove home, I turned my thoughts to remodeling my living room, and a new thought occurred to me. There is some truth to the idea of sleeping on something to think it over. You often have new thoughts after not thinking about something for a while. More specifically, your right brain has continued to work on the problem in its non-verbal, creative, symbolic way of thinking. As such, it occurred to me that the best option might be to get my mind off of the situation at hand. It also occurred to me that Huntsville might have a store specializing in Japanese imports to cater to the executives at the Toyota factory.

Once home, I immediately searched the web for Japanese import stores in Huntsville. That found only advertisements for car dealers, restaurants and a national chain of import stores. Undeterred, I called a young woman from Japan who gives private English lessons to Japanese residents. She gave me the name and location of just the type of store I wanted.

The store, named "First Feng Shui Furnishings" had a rather unique layout. Feng Shui has its origins in China, but this store caters to a form popular in Japan today. Apparently Feng Shui practitioners don't like orderly straight isles of inventory. Items in the store were arranged by color scheme rather than function. Thus wood items were lumped together, metal times together, and so forth. Any given type of item might be in multiple places depending upon its color and construction materials.

To the left of the entranceway was a room decorated as a studio apartment, which they used to teach the principles of Feng Shui. I arrived just as an older gentleman was starting one of their introductions to Feng Shui, or perhaps my arrival gave an auspicious size audience indicating that it was a good time to start. There were two young couples and myself sitting around their sample living room. The man who spoke was obviously of Japanese origin, and could have been anywhere between fifty and a hundred and fifty years old. The gentleman named Mr. Fujita talked about giving a room harmony by selecting a variety of materials, wood, fire, earth, metal, and water. Each material had certain colors and shapes associated with it. I took a look back out at the show room and realized that items were chosen to have color, material and shape that were consistent.

The Feng Shui presentation got even more complex as they talked about arrangement of items in the home. I understood the psychological impact of politicians having oversized buildings and desks to make themselves appear more important and powerful to the people that visit there, but I had never considered designing a home for a sense of serenity. While I appreciate the goal, some of the Feng Shui positioning rules seem to stem from a very complex set of logical arguments which seemed like they could have been viewed a different way to come out with a different rule. After listening to the talk, each of us was given a pad of paper to draw out our room and some sticky notes of specific colors, shapes and names of materials printed on them. After a time the customers were so pleased with their room designs and having made good choices of items to furnish them that the rather high price of imported Japanese luxury goods seemed not to upset them. While I didn't feel that my décor would bring me good or bad fortune, I also realized that sticking to the rules will make the décor feel more true to the style in a way that people probably couldn't immediately verbalize but could subconsciously recognize. People have a certain need for consistency which they find comforting, which is also the reason that there are known psychological benefits to watching reruns on TV.

The delivery truck for the store had followed me home, which was the best delivery service I had ever seen. A few hours later, I was lounging on the new futon to catch my breath after arranging my living room in a reasonable interpretation of Feng Shuiness. I had to admit that the environment was very serene and calming. I hadn't done away with the electronics, but had hidden them behind the doors of an entertainment center with hand made lacquer doors depicting a natural scene of mountains, trees, a river, and cranes. Likewise reading materials were hidden in the drawers of an end table. The sparseness of the room made it feel more clean, organized, and less chaotic. This seemed to be part of the serenity formula. This was a room you could come home to without a to do list of things vying for your attention. The living room was no less functional than before. You could still watch TV, take a nap, entertain friends, or flip the futon down flat to have spur of the moment sex.

The calmness in my mind that was spurred by the serenity of the room felt like something that I had been missing. It wouldn't be too many years before I had to move on and take a new identity. For that matter, there was no reason I couldn't leave sooner if the mood struck me. Perhaps next time I would find a life style full of calm and opportunities for meditation and reading. I could live on a self sufficient farm growing food to sell at high dollar as organically grown produce. Or I could be an artist or study martial arts for few decades in some mountain retreat. I could take up some vocation working on the shore of the ocean or great lakes, where I would be surrounded by the sound of waves and get to see the vast variety of moods that the water might display. My eyes gently closed as I let these thoughts roll across one another without giving them any direction. Time lost all meaning.

The phone rang. I answered it calmly on the second ring. It was Gary.

"Christine? Is that you? Are you awake? We have big trouble. That drug that makes vampires go nutso has been dumped into the city water supply." He was excited, like he was ready to jump right through the phone at me.

"Where are you?" I asked.

"Just a couple blocks from your place," he replied.

"OK. Get over to my place, like yesterday," I said.

I looked at my watch. I couldn't have dozed off more than ten minutes. Serenity Christine was gone. Kick your ass Christine was back.

I tried to contact a couple people at the vampire tribunal, but they were already in sequestration mode. The building cell phone jammers were on, and a local company had used it as a showcase for their new state of the art armored glass made to withstand tank cannons. There would be no communication in or out of that building for a number of hours. In some ways, vampire culture is more archaic than the Vatican, which at least uses smoke signals. The vampire tribunal had a four-hour session that included drinks, then a feast. They probably had refreshments with the initial session, so it might already be too late to warn them. That meant we had to be ready for the very worst in about four to five hours. I sent a message out to every vampire in town about not drinking the water. I could only hope that we could contain the coming vampire apocalypse to one area.

I was just finishing getting changed when Gary knocked at the door. I had my battle suit custom made a few years earlier. It consisted of cargo pants with many pockets that were fitted down flat so as not to have baggy protrusions. There was a cargo vest with more pockets. Both the pants and vest were armored with multiple plates of high tech ceramic, which would serve as protection from anything less than an RPG. I had the pockets filled with an array of guns, knives, gas grenades and a number of similar items. Over top of that was a slim jacket. The jacket was black lambskin leather and the rest was made of a jet-black durable blend that clung to my body but didn't restrict movement. I looked every bit the part of a vampire from one of the Underworld movies.

Gary had just eaten, but he wolfed down a soda and a large bag of chips. I checked my emergency emergency blood stash in the hidden compartment of my refrigerator but it was still empty. I would need to be at full strength. I was stuck with an unexciting ice tea made from bottled raspberry flavored water. By the time we finished our snacks we had come up with a plan that was just crazy enough that it might work.

Over the next couple hours, Gary and I called in every favor we had and begged, bought and coerced a few more. If some miracle prevented this disaster, the impact on my reputation would be so great that I would have to leave town, if it wasn't already. Just getting the police commissioner to approve temporarily deputizing a couple hundred extra citizens was a miracle in itself. However, getting the police involved was absolutely necessary to keep the whole operation from being shut down before it started. This one just couldn't be hidden from the population. Hopefully the psychoactive drug story would hold up for lack of any better explanation.

The Huntsville Art Museum sits on one side of Big Spring Park. This building that would normally be a source of civic pride and culture was presently an ominous presence as it prepared to spew forth a vampire apocalypse on the cities residents. Looking at the building in the waning light, I thought I saw movement inside, as though someone had accidentally bumped into a window, only bumping into it at the top of the window in the two story tall foyer. I knew it wouldn't be long before the building doors or windows gave way. A large dump truck had been driven up the steps and parked against the street side doors in an attempt to send most of the chaos into the park where it could be contained more easily, as if dealing with a horde of blood crazed vampires could be called easy.

I turned to survey the troops. In the past, troops drawn from other organizations were called "irregulars". This group brought new meaning to the term. The regular troops consisted of every available police officer, and a second group of security guards borrowed from Redstone Arsenal thanks to Mike Brown's connections with the United Nations. Those professionals weren't near enough for what was about to emerge, so we had recruited every quasi-fighting organization we could find. There was a group from the Rod & Gun Club dressed mostly in camouflage with no small amount of firepower. The second group similarly dressed in camouflage was the local werewolf pack in the guise of a sportsman club. Cindy Rory and her Vampkido group were positioned next to the werewolves as a tacit statement that this battle was not werewolves versus vampires. We had recruited every martial arts club in town, resulting in a number of groups in white or black karate gis and a few more in wrestling uniforms, boxing gear, and even Olympic style fencing uniforms. The most unusual group was the Society for Creative Anachronism (SCA to it's friends) dressed in medieval armor with an array of weaponry right out of a Dungeons and Dragons game.

The combined group of security and martial arts organizations, except the werewolves and vampires, was ninety percent male. I guess a lot of human women only want the benefits of equality but aren't willing to step up when it's time to get their hands dirty. Werewolf groups were always all in for the good of the pack. Vampire groups could vary greatly as each individual determines if they agree with the political views and whether it is worth dying for.

I picked up the mic of the hastily rigged PA system to address the troops. I don't like public speaking, but this has to be done, and I didn't trust anyone else to do it better.

I began my speech, "Welcome, and thank you for responding to our request for help. I know all of you have heard some part of what is going on here, but I will go over it anyway so that we are all on the same page. For reasons currently unknown to us, a drug cartel has been using Huntsville as a testing ground for new drugs. They have been dosing people, often against their will or without their knowledge. There is a problem with the drug formula. It has caused people to become blood crazed, unthinking animals. This is the reason for the massacre at an Alabama A&M fraternity house and two recent police raids. We have learned that the people at a private function at the Art Museum tonight have been drugged without their knowledge. We also know that the drug makes people more suggestible to emulating something violent they see, such as a television show. The group in the Art Museum had a vampire themed party tonight, so they may think they are vampires and try to bite or kill other people."

It's always good to mix enough truth with your lies to make them feel plausible. A few years back, Google did an experiment with a web interface that would flag when the web page you are reading contains information known to be false. The Google experiment wasn't very popular with the focus groups and was discontinued. Apparently, many people would rather live with delusions of their own choosing than know the truth. I was hoping that this meant that most people would choose to believe the explanation of vampires I gave them even if they saw some evidence to the contrary.

I went on, "Some of these people are our friends and neighbors, and many are from out of town. If at all possible, we want to hold them down long enough to tie or cuff them. However, we may not be successful so they might, in their mind-altered state, try to kill you. If it is them or you, do what you must. Each of you knows the people in your organization. The leaders of each organization should split you into teams of five. Three people on each team should be designated to hold someone down. One person is to put on cuffs or tie their hands and feet, and the fifth person is there to injure or kill them only if necessary. I recommend putting someone with military or security training in each group if possible. I would like to ask that groups composed of police officers or active duty military security personnel intersperse yourselves with the groups of temporarily deputized personnel so that you can help the other groups as well if necessary."

As they were getting themselves sorted out, I walked down the line occasionally stopping to answer a question or give a bit of advice. I gave most of the martial arts clubs a few comments on how a fight to maim or kill was different from their mostly safe sport fighting. Most were choosing people they thought would have the stomach for it to be the last resort person. I handed out hundreds of the heavy-duty zip ties that make decent one time use handcuffs.

I was concerned that the Huntsville Fencing Club couldn't kill if they wanted to with those blunt tipped epees. The fencing community had worked for years to make it one of the safer sports in the Olympics. I need not have worried. Their club armorer had rigged hunting arrow tips on the end of the swords. Their coach, a former SEAL commander, was giving the best briefing of any I had heard.

Most of the people looked like they had the right attitude for such a battle, a mixture of determination, confidence, and respect for the dangerousness of the situation. There was one martial arts club that was concerning to me. They were mostly younger and didn't seem to be taking the situation seriously. All of the martial art forms are adapted to be a sport with minimal injuries, but some place a big emphasis on many awards to boost the students self esteem and are so stylized that they are little use in a real fight. This group might have been college age, but their lack of concern made them appear younger in my eyes. In my mind, I had already labeled this group as "the kids".

I pulled aside a few people for a separate briefing. Cindy Rory, Gary, myself, and a few others would act as floaters who could come to the aid of any group that seemed over their heads. Gary and I positioned ourselves on both sides of "the kids". The name has already stuck, so why fight it? I wished again that I hadn't been out of blood.

As I looked over the troops, I kept glancing back at the Art Museum. Now I was seeing activity in the building as the last daylight faded. Most I was guessing was due to bodies being flung against the bulletproof glass. I wasn't near optimistic enough to think that would hold.

About fifteen minutes after the sky had gotten as dark as it was going to, the locks on the museum door locks ripped apart and all hell broke loose.

The vampire horde emerged like a herd of angry cats. There was plenty of anger, but no coordination of activities at all. Some were running, while those with hundreds of years of battle training instinctively took a battle stance. Most had torn clothing and many had a bit of blood dripping around their mouths. Whether that blood was from the buffet table or the other guests was anyone's guess. One was limping along nearly oblivious to the sideways turned foot that screamed of a nasty broken ankle.

There must have been a Civil War exhibit this week because many had muzzle loading rifles or military swords. A couple had even donned Civil War military caps. With this being a meeting of senior leaders of the vampire world it was a good bet that nearly all had been alive in the days of cavalry and black powder rifles. I was hoping there wasn't actually any black powder in the building. The business end of a bayonet could be dangerous enough.

The vampires spread out to run in all directions. The first wave came in at a run. These would be the ones with the biggest adrenaline high, and hopefully the most impaired judgment. The first one to reach our irregular troops was a big man running into a group of SCA knights. Two knights in chain mail went flying over his shoulders then a long sword went through the chest of the assailant. I knew then that my plan of restraining without killing anyone would not go as well as I hoped. I had no more time to think about it as the running first wave hit our lines everywhere.

I positioned myself to take one of them and saw Gary doing the same. I used a chin-high snap kick to slow down my incoming opponent, a wiry man with streaks of gray in his hair. I glanced over at the kids to see that they clotheslined an incoming vampire woman and had a dog pile on top of her as someone restrained her. After that, I had to focus on my own opponent. Gray hair guy obviously had some pretty advanced martial arts training. We went into a flurry of lightning kicks, punches and blocks. At first my game was primarily defensive as I judged his skill. Even at that, we was landing too many. If his judgment hadn't been impaired, I doubt I could have taken him. As is, I started to find the weakness from his impaired judgment. He was launching every attack immediately, not timed to my movements and sloppily placed relative to my position. This meant that he would launch immediately if I gave him an opening without consideration of whether that opening was a trap. I gave him false openings then launched the counter to his attack purely on the assumption that he would make the expected attack. After a few actions following this pattern, I took him down and cuffed him.

I stood up to survey the current status of the battle. Yes, it was a battle not a bunch of people getting arrested. I have seen enough of both to know the difference. My subconscious was giving me warnings that my body was not at full strength and speed. I told my subconscious to shut up and rack in a couple more dilithium crystals. Oh god, I've been in Huntsville too long when I start thinking in Star Trek metaphors.

Seeing the front-runners taken down confused the vampires in the main body a bit. Their brains were still too addled to come up with a decent strategy, but at least they had some measure of recognition that there was danger here. This didn't stop them from moving forward but it caused them to clump tighter into a group. That was bad for our heroes since it meant we had to handle quite a few at once. I had only seconds to come up with a strategy before they got to us.

Trying to grapple and cuff them right off the bat is fine when we have a significantly stronger force. We couldn't make our force any stronger in a few seconds, but we could make them weaker with the right strategy.

I hollered at the top of my lungs, "Beat on them some before trying to cuff them. Pass it on." I heard my words echoing down the line. It would have been safer for our defenders of truth, justice, and nerdy Huntsville citizens if I had given a kill order. I hoped I wouldn't regret that decision.

The majority of the drug-frenzied vampires hit our lines at the same time. Three of them hit the kids, and one more was on Gary. I didn't have one, so I stepped over to help the kids. A tall vampire had a cavalry saber with his hand raised to slice at them. I grabbed the wrist holding the sword, thus taking the sword out of play while the kids used him as a training dummy for some of their best kicks. While I kept holding his sword arm, I took a kick at the adjacent foe. He was just slightly too far away so my kick connected but was no more than a minor distraction. Saber guy was now doubled over, so I cuffed him. The kids had a handle on the second one.

The third was a vampire woman swinging an antique rifle like a club so the kids couldn't get close enough to engage. I slipped behind her while she was looking away. I grabbed her neck in the crook of my elbow and sent her down with a Judo throw. I tried to hold her down a little longer by shoving my thumb into the nerve point next to the vertebrae just above the bottom of the shoulder blades. That didn't seem to be noticed. Note to self, the drug makes them immune to nerve pinch movements. The kids took it from there, so I didn't need to do any more on that one.

Gary was grappling with a vampire man who had six inches and fifty pounds on him. I swiped the knee of the large vampire man and let Gary take it from there. Gary and the kids had martial arts training, but not battle experience. I had used a dangerous but effective battle tactic of letting a few of the stronger fighters slip past the enemy lines to attack the enemy from behind.

I moved back to my spot in the line and surveyed the battle scene. I saw a few drugged vampires and one defender who might have been dead. In spite of my hardened demeanor, I consider every death to be my failure to prevent a problem or handle it better.

One of the more interesting fights I saw was between a lanky vampire man and one of the groups from the Huntsville Fencing Club. The vampire had swords in both hands. In his right hand was a straight bladed sword, probably a noncommissioned officer sword from the 1800s. He had a curved cavalry saber in his left hand, which he was using in broad sweeps to parry attacks from multiple attackers. Tactics for using the NCO sword would be similar to those using a modern sport fencing epee, although the NCO sword would be slightly shorter and noticeably heavier. The vampire was using a series of quick thrusts to attack, and simultaneously minimize the disadvantage the sword weight would give in executing circular motions. In his drug impaired state the vampire still had a beautiful fencing style that reminded me of an old Errol Flynn movie. His form was no doubt from thousands of hours of sword practice possibly with this same style of sword over a century ago. At first the vampire seemed to have the advantage since the modern fencers weren't practiced against this type of two-handed style. However the more experienced fencers soon adapted tactics for facing French grip wielding modern fencers to his style. Once the vampire had sustained a good number of bleeding but not fatal injuries he was weakened and distracted enough for one of them to circle around behind him and bring him to the ground.

I soon had to face another opponent, this time a rather portly man who was more intent on running away than fighting. I was cuffing him when one of the police officers came running over to me. He informed me that the police contingent was being pulled away to deal with an outbreak of crazed individuals elsewhere in town. I had been afraid that would happen since I couldn't be sure I had contacted all of the vampires who weren't in this group. I told him thanks for telling me and I would stay. He didn't say anything, and I didn't ask if I had been ordered away. He probably knew I wouldn't obey such an order anyway in the middle of a battle.

I turned to check on the kids. In retrospect I should have glanced the other direction first to guard my back. My head was yanked back by my hair and both my arms grabbed in a vice like grip. I could tell from the hand positions that there were two people on the two sides of me. I felt the blade of a knife against my neck. My one stroke of luck was that in their compromised mental state they had put the dull spine of the blade against me. I smelled their bleeding wounds and immediately knew that they were female vampires, a couple of tall Amazonians from the position of their hands on me. I immediately thought of them as Frick and Frack.

I smashed my right elbow into Frick's face then twisted my left shoulder forward to take the inevitable stab from Frack on my shoulder instead of my chest. The blade bit deep into my deltoid muscle, just below the shoulder joint. The pain was searing down my arm as she withdrew the blade for a second strike. I grabbed for the knife and caught her wrist. This left me holding the wrist with the knife blade out at arms length with all the strength in my left arm, while I fought a second opponent and the other arm of this one with my remaining hands and feet. I snap kicked at the one on my right a couple times, but couldn't do significant damage. Frick and Frack may have known how to handle a two-on-one fight, but tactics had been replaced by bloodlust, just like a fighter who has lost his temper.

I spun to my left pulling Frick's arm behind her and putting Frick between Frack and myself. I got look at Frack for the first time. She was blond hair and the high cheekbones of a northern European lineage. She also had a long broken wood rod in her right hand, perhaps part of a flagpole. She had forgotten the stake and been hitting me with her fists. Frack drew back and threw another boxing punch with the fist that held the stake. I yanked Frick to the left and the fist broke Frick's nose.

Frack pulled her hand back for another blow to the face. She paused for a second to figure out where to land the punch. Then she noticed the stake in her right hand. I was on my toes dancing left and right to keep Frick's body between us. Frack jabbed low, I shifted to the right expecting the blow to knock the wind out of Frick and miss me, but Frack repositioned her grip on the way in. The stake went clear through Frick's body and deep into my gut. I realized immediately that I had misjudged my opponent by expecting her to have a conscience in her current mental state. I realized that the mistake might be my last.

In my early years I had learned to accept the possibility of my own death. That training came back and gave me a split second of complete clarity. Frack pulled the stake out and came in for a second blow as Frick started to bend double, finally registering the pain. I ripped the knife out of Frick's hand and put all of my strength into a high leap. Both of my feet landed on Frick's bent over back, and I propelled myself into a high mid air summersault. As I was flying up, Frack's momentum pushed both of them towards the ground with Frack on top. My desperate move left me with little choice about how I was going to land. I put my hands out like a high diver cutting into the water with a dagger. Frick and Frack slammed into the ground with my ground-ward dive inches behind them. The knife slid in severing Frack's spine between her shoulder blades. I came down on top of them, impaling my thigh on the stake in the process. Frick was unconscious. Some ironic part of my brain is saying, "I guess you can kill a vampire with a stake."

I rolled over onto my back with the stake still sticking out of my thigh. I felt like I had been hit by a truck. I looked down at my stomach. My heart beat and a little geyser of blood shot up four inches from my stomach. A couple beats later the geyser was three inches high. I knew this was a bad sign. I knew I should put my hand on it, but that seemed like a pathetically inadequate measure.

My eyes drifted shut for just a second then opened to see Gary binding my wounds as the battle raged on. I was fighting to stay conscious. I knew only one thing could save me. I whispered a single word, "blood".

Gary pulled me to a sitting position and pressed my lips against a bloody gash in his arm. I sucked what little was oozing out of the gash then extended my fangs and bit in to find a larger blood vessel. I heard Gary's measured breathing as he steeled himself against the pain of my bite. For a werewolf, my venom only made the bite more painful. He was forcing his arm to stay immobile, but the rest of his body was tensed as he endured the pain.

Vampire bodies have a special adaptation for just such a circumstance, although I can't guess how evolution knew to expect a museum full of drugged vampires with Civil War weapons. I felt the agonizing pain as a couple special muscles ripped open a thin walled section of my esophagus. This allowed the blood to flow straight into a vein leading to my heart.

Another drug-crazed vampire stood over us and raised a muzzle-loading rifle over his head to smash it into us. Gary held his right arm completely still so I could continue drinking while he released all of the adrenaline from the pain into his left arm. His left hand did a powerful uppercut from our seated position. The uppercut connected with the vampire's groin and threw him over top of us to a hard landing. The vampire was temporarily stunned, whether by the strike to the groin or by hitting the ground we may never know.

The adrenaline in Gary's blood stream was now running through me. I rolled over to crouching position, ready to take on any opponent. The vampire that had just attacked us was moaning and starting to get up. I knocked him back unconscious with a sweeping kick to the face. Gary cuffed him as I pivoted to find my next opponent.

Another vampire had already begun his run at me. He was lean and dark complexioned with black hair. He was probably a couple inches shorter than me, and a tad lighter. Only a touch of grey at his temples suggested his age. He went for broke as he came at me with a flying karate kick. The dirty little secret of martial arts is that when all else is equal, strength can be the deciding factor. I had veins full of adrenaline and made the split second decision to overpower him rather than test his skill. Just before his foot hit me, I grabbed his ankle with both hands and threw my entire body hard to the right. The momentum of my body countered his as I spun him a full three hundred and sixty degrees. Having thus exchanged his forward momentum for rotational motion, I let go of him. He sailed in an uncontrolled spin to land flat on his back in the middle of the kids. They all dog piled on top of him. I guess even those kids have developed their signature move.

The battle eventually ran its course. All told, twelve of the drugged vampires were killed. None of the defenders died although there were many injuries, a few of them critical. Doc Bowie offered Frederick Senburg's mansion as a temporary confinement medical facility to hold the drugged vampires until the effects wore off. The police didn't like that suggestion, but there wasn't another viable facility available on short notice. The Doc sold it by suggesting that the unusual behavior could be due to a combination of illegal drugs and a virus and that they should therefore quarantine them. Later, a vampire lawyer took care of some paperwork showing that Senburg's estate had agreed to temporarily lend the property to the Doc as an emergency medical center.

Chapter 10

The true problem was much bigger than a battle with a group of drug crazed vampires. The supernatural community has been working for thousands of years to keep the human population from knowing that we exist. Having a drug cartel not only aware of us, but targeting both vampires and werewolves directly is way too much exposure, and way too many people who know we are here. Humans can't get along with people of different nationalities, races, or religious beliefs. We certainly weren't foolish enough to think that humans were ready to embrace competing species with open arms, particularly one evolved to prey on humans. The whole thing would turn into a witch-hunt with every unsolved disappearance or murder in history being blamed on us. This problem was far from over.

Two men strolled through the airport. Both were in sportswear, but they couldn't seem more different. One man was average height with surprisingly broad shoulders. His cargo pants and kaki shirt gave him the appearance of an outdoorsman who could wrestle a bear. The second man was taller and handsome. He had had on a polo shirt with a college crest on the pocket and an immaculate haircut that came across as the Hollywood version of a handsome medical doctor. The two moved casually, winding their way through the crowds on the concourse. Watching them carefully would reveal that the broad shouldered man was choosing where they go and the tall man was staying with him.

Broad Shoulders stopped in his tracks and looked around almost like a dog sniffing at the wind. Tall watched him patiently. Broad Shoulders headed to their left and they were soon walking on two sides of a tourist who had just arrived from Mexico. A few words of small talk turned into an offer to pay twice as much for what the tourist was carrying. The three went for a private conversation in an employees only area. Later investigation would determine that the doorknob to the service corridor had been turned with such force that the internal mechanism in the lock was destroyed. The tourist was never seen again.

Pedro limped along as he led the burdened mule down the mountain. Pedro understood that keeping a roof over his head and food on the table was the best he could hope for as a mountain farmer with no formal education. He also knew that he would probably drop dead working his fields at an unexcitingly early age as his father and grandfather had. He would be hard pressed even to keep his family fed if he stuck to growing coffee on the steep slopes of their small plot. Pedro understood the potential consequences when he chose to grow a more profitable and much more dangerous crop. His only child, his beautiful daughter, had done very well in the one room school run by missionaries. It was a long walk from their home and she had shown great dedication getting there every day even in the harshest weather. Now his daughter was attending a fancy technical college in Bogota. She had been there a few months and needed to pay for three more semesters in order to get a good job as an assistant nurse. When that happened, she would be the most successful person in their family's history.

Pedro had seen enough of life to understand the men who bought his illegal crop. He knew that they were very dangerous men. He knew that underneath they were very scared men. That was why they reacted so violently in killing anyone who questioned their authority, or anyone they thought might say something to the nearly non-existent law enforcement officers. Pedro knew that he must appear as uninteresting and non-threatening as possible to them. As he approached the compound, he bowed his head even lower and shuffled his feet even more. It made him look even older and broken than he already was.

Pedro shuffled over to the place where crops were bought with his mule following behind him. His thoughts had strayed to the scene of joyful tears as their daughter left on the bus to Bogota. He remembered every detail as the over burdened bus lumbered away on the steep winding road. Those thoughts lingered a bit longer until his subconscious called for his attention. There were not any other farmers with their mules waiting to sell their crops. There was no one standing in front of him to buy his crop. Now that he noticed it, the entire compound was silent.

Pedro cautiously lifted his head to peer out from under his broad straw hat. There was no movement anywhere. No people. No chickens. Even the birds seemed afraid to come near in their absence. There was a small wisp of smoke coming from behind one of the larger motorized carts that rich people called trucks. Pedro shuffled towards the smoke. As Pedro rounded the truck he saw a giant symbol burned into the grassy ground, and a similar burn repeated on the door of the building. The burns were perfectly formed as if made by some fire-wielding god. Pedro considered gasoline and electricity as dangerous witchcrafts to be avoided. The emblem thus burned was the most evil one possible. Pedro understood this evil symbol. This symbol clearly said that the bad men who bought his crop were dead. Pedro turned around and started limping towards home.

Pedro knew of bad men being killed. He knew that it probably meant that other bad men would soon want to buy his crop, and threaten his life if he told anyone about them. After another couple miles, Pedro had a second thought. There was an idea, a rumor, a legend, perhaps all three were the same. This idea said that one day it would happen. The bad men would be killed and no new bad men would come to take their place. When that day came, his crop would be worthless, and even more dangerous to possess. Pedro didn't think this was very likely. However, if the worst happened, it would probably happen to him. Pedro spent the rest of the walk home trying to figure out how to keep his family fed until he could be paid for a coffee crop.

The President entered the Situation Room and took his seat. All of the other meeting attendees were already there. They all knew the president well enough to tell that he had on his down-to-business face.

The President nodded once to the Secretary of the Interior. She dove straight into her briefing, "Ladies and gentleman, it appears that the War on Drugs may be at least temporarily won. There are no drug dealers on the streets. Treatment centers are filling up with addicts who can't buy narcotics at any price. The streets are safer than ever in poor neighborhoods."

"Are you telling me that all of the drug dealers and cartels just decided to go home and plant flower beds?" asked the President.

"No sir," said the Secretary of the Interior "They are all missing."

"And just how did they go missing?" asked the President.

"We don't know sir. There was no fighting, and no bodies have been found," replied the Secretary of the Interior.

"Did one of our organizations do this?" asked the President.

"No sir," said ATF and FBI in unison.

"Usually a decrease in drug organization activity is part of a take over by a rival drug cartel, but this time no one has stepped in to fill the void," said AFT.

"It may not be rival drug organizations," said CIA. "We have reports of opium poppy growers torching their own fields to avoid the mysterious disappearances that have befallen their fellow farmers. No drug organization or their rivals would want to destroy the source of production."

"Who is filling the void?" asked the President.

The Surgeon General spoke up, "The tobacco industry and recently legalized marijuana industry are seeing a record growth with alcohol close behind. While these are not healthy addictions, it is still an improvement in health over illegal narcotics."

The President asked if any of them could shed any more light on the situation. None spoke up.

256

The President said, "I appreciate the good news, but I don't like the idea of not knowing which obviously powerful organization is behind it." He gave stern glances to FBI, ATF, and CIA who sat very still.

The President took the deep breath that they all recognized as the I-have-made-a-decision breath, then went on, "Here is how this is going to play out. The correct crime and drug statistics will come out via the normal channels on the regular schedule. We aren't issuing any big announcements or press releases about it. If someone asks, give some statement about how many small policy, law enforcement, and private reform agency actions add up to a big social trend. Let the media and political analysts come up with their own explanations as to what factors are most important. In the mean time, have each of your organizations start an initiative to find out who is making the illegal drug organizations disappear. Keep your investigations as discrete as practical. Keep the Secretary of the Interior informed of any progress you make, and she will keep me informed."

No one had any questions for The President. People in their position knew that it was their job to find a solution, not ask a superior how to accomplish a task.

Christine unceremoniously dropped the envelope with her apartment key into the mail. She had sold off or donated most of what she owned, thus compacting her entire life into the trunk of the T-Bird. She had only given one regretful sigh at the loss of the new Feng Shui living room. The car would also have to disappear once she reached her destination.

She had said her good byes to Gary and demonstrated her affections. He knew better than to ask her to do differently or allow him to come along. Gary didn't let show how much her departure tore at his heart. Christine would be vacationing and visiting her parents for a while before choosing what her next identity would be. She decided she should rule out a life in outer space, since too many

NASA people in Huntsville know her. She could always come back to that idea another hundred years from now.

About the author

David Young lives in Huntsville, Alabama. He has a Ph.D. in chemistry. He has written books on computational chemistry and drug design, as well as a number of science fiction stories. David is active in the sport of fencing.

www.ingramcontent.com/pod-product-compliance
Lightning Source LLC
Chambersburg PA
CBHW071136170626
46809CB00002B/642